The Beloved Country

by
Sheena Kalayil

Grosvenor House
Publishing Limited

This book is published by
Grosvenor House Publishing Ltd
28-30 High Street, Guildford, Surrey, GU1 3EL.
www.grosvenorhousepublishing.co.uk

A CIP record for this book
is available from the British Library

ISBN 978-1-78148-361-9

Sheena Kalayil was born in 1970, and grew up in India and in Africa. She teaches at the University of Manchester, and lives near Manchester with her husband and two children. The Beloved Country is her first novel.

For my daughters

Part One

1

Before we even knew each other, we shared an ocean. It was a thought that entered my head many times later when we were living by the sea, and in those first few months together we would walk along the promenade, the Marginal, that led from the city up the coast to the Costa do Sol. Sometimes we would stray from the walkway, slide down the sand bank and walk in the shallow waves, our shoes in our hands. While this memory is distinct, I cannot be sure how many times we actually strolled hand-in-hand, the soft white sand pleasantly warm under our feet. Jafar was not given to romantic overtures, and he avoided sentimentality. After the flush of the first months had passed, I am sure that I more often than not walked on this beach with friends; he would either be out of town, or out of contact. But those few times in the early days, I remember the waters of the bay lapped around our ankles like a balm as I felt the sun on my face and his hand holding mine against his hip.

When we scrambled back up the sand bank to the road we did not have far to walk before we reached our street, Avenida Eduardo Mondlane; a main thoroughfare lined with shabby buildings on either side, except for the occasional colonial bungalow with its elegant trellised balcony, sloping tiled roof. Walking away from the sea with the sprawling Hospital Central on our right, our flat was half-way down the length of the road. Some of its offshoots were narrower, roads that went through quieter residential areas on the way down to the Baixa, the pavements often ruined by the rains and by the bursting roots of trees. It was difficult to find a level stretch for more than a few yards so people often walked on the road. There weren't many cars, and the drivers were leisurely and affable, swerving around the occasional pedestrian, zouk music blaring from the car radio.

If you walked away from the Baixa it was quickest to use Avenida Vladimir Lenin, which cut up through the city, to get to the leafier, more exclusive residential areas further from the centre. Busier and noisier, but at least partly-lined with mature, wide-branched trees that cast shadows along its way, offering some respite from the unrelenting midday sun. We often shopped at its mercado, a messy resident, some way northwards up the street. Unlike its more genteel counterpart in the Baixa, the Mercado Central, ours was usually crowded. A visit involved some shoving, elbows and shoulders used indiscriminately to reach the pyramids of aubergines, freshly-wetted stacks of coriander and parsley, and wheelbarrows of pineapples.

Our flat was on the corner of Avenida Eduardo Mondlane and Avenida Karl Marx, in the west of the city, just before Central dissipated into the more run-down Alto Mae. We had found it through Yolanda, a friend of Eduardo, Jafar's oldest friend. The *predio* was seven storeys high. There were three flats per level for the first five storeys, but higher up it was more disorderly.

There, people spilled out into the corridors, whole communities cooking on gas stoves and sleeping in rows on makeshift beds. On clear nights, the children slept on the rooftop. We lived closest to the stairs. The corridor, open-aired with a low wall, looked out towards Maputo Bay in the distance.

The front door, a solid, heavy gate of metal, led to the "porch" where we kept the ironing board. A wooden spring door then led to the living room. There was a lot of furniture, large heavy Portuguese woodwork; tables, side tables, a sideboard filled with Yolanda's best china. It was not chic, but it had character. There was a large family-sized kitchen, but it was always gloomy and lit by a fluorescent tube which flickered. So we used the smaller of the two bedrooms as a dining room. We bought a plastic-topped table, and covered it with a brightly-coloured kapulana: that became our dining table. Our bedroom across the small hall was spacious. Large windows, netted to keep out mosquitoes, a big double bed, a dressing table, a large wardrobe, and a chest of drawers. Both rooms had wooden spring doors that led to the balcony, running along the length of the flat, overlooking the cemetery to the left, the hospital to the right. It was unfortunate that we shared our home with several families of cockroaches.

The flat was our haven: from the bustle, dust, people, sounds, smells of Maputo. The city with its alternating beauty and chaos. Fringed by the ocean on one side, a sprawling metropolis to the other. The buildings changing from the decorative to the functional, from the solid to the more fragile, sprawling on until it reached the thousands of tidy, tiny homes in the bairros. This city, in a country with the most beautiful of names: Mozambique.

Hugging the blue waters of the Indian Ocean, stretching from Tanzania to South Africa, its long languid length eclipsed by the greatness of the continent.

After three o'clock, the balcony was always in shade. We were four floors up and there was always a breeze. It didn't face the sea but we had a panorama of the northern half of the city. Below, the street life continued unheeded. The vendors: mostly women wearing kapulanas, their hair tied up in scarves, offering wheelbarrows of fruits or flat woven bowls of roasted peanuts. The pedestrians, public buses and taxis. And the chapas: the yellow minivans always crammed with people hanging onto leather straps, the conductor coolly hanging onto the door frame, the shouts of *Paragem*! All oblivious to the two of us above, sitting side by side, looking down.

*

I have only gone back in a dream, a dream that mocked with its intermittent truth and lies, that bewitched me with its realness and falseness, a dream with a journey. It came to me last night and has stayed with me. I feel inside me an unravelling, as my mother, with one strong flick of her wrist, would unravel one of her cotton saris. Cream-coloured with a gold border. It rolls and rolls, flutters in the air, stretches out, free again, no longer the small neat square that had stayed quietly waiting in her sari-drawer. And as it billows out a tale is told, dappling the thin material until it reaches the last unhemmed, unfinished, ends. The memories have been unlocked and are vivid, teasing. The scenes are fresh, I can hear his voice, remember my words. I did not expect to recapture them, and I did not ask for these reminders. For I know,

now, the arrogance of my convictions, my ignorance of what was to come.

I read a book when I was teenager, one that I found in my mother's cousin's bookshop in Alleppey, where I received discounts and where I always returned — so frequently that my relative would joke that I alone was keeping him in business. The opening line had mesmerised me with its beauty, the simplicity of its sentiment. *I had a farm in Africa.* Well, I, too, had something in Africa, but I am not sure what. There, under its spell, I lived the life of a different person. There, I was a person of the senses; entranced by its sensuality, the rhythms of life that its people followed. Their enjoyment of love, of physical beauty, of emotion. And there, I was intoxicated, by the pleasure that my body could give Jafar, and that his could give to me.

Every story has a beginning, so where is mine? While my future had been planned long in advance of it becoming my present, cracks began to appear, fault-lines deepened. My relatively unremarkable childhood was followed by an unexpected adulthood. And I slowly discarded, like layers of unwanted clothing, the conventions and expectations that had until then defined me. Perhaps my story begins, if it is not too ridiculous to believe, with that hot afternoon when I was called into the living room of our house in Irinjalakuda. A newly-built house painted a salmon pink with green borders around the windows. Nutmeg and banana trees encircling and shading it. I was called to stand before my mother and father as they had something to tell me. What happened that day echoed through my life.

But I have retraced my steps now, in a full sweeping circle, moving away from my itinerant life of the last few years, back to the beginning: I am back in India and I am on a train. On the Trivandrum Mail that left Chennai at eight in the evening. Opposite me, a middle-aged woman with a thick plait hanging down her right shoulder, wearing a dark blue salwar kameez, golden spectacles on her nose, massages her callused feet with one hand, turns the pages of her book with the other. I caught a few words of its title: "Micro-economics in the ASEAN nations". She must be a lecturer at a college in Chennai, going home for the holidays. Her shoes are laid neatly under her seat. Two older men sitting on the bench beside me are engaged in conversation; they are going to Kottayam to consult on a family problem. No one pays me much attention: after brief hellos, we have not spoken any more. I have been left with my thoughts. Outside it is dark. We have been on the train for more than three hours and I will soon excuse myself politely from my fellow passengers and climb the small ladder that leads to my sleeping bunk.

The train will ride through the night, full to bursting with its cargo of families with small children, college students going home for the holidays, business men with appointments to keep. I am only one of many. Every person, like I am, is going somewhere. I have been summoned home, and my willingness to heed those summons heralds the start of a new chapter to my story. But my thoughts do not move forward; they turn the pages back, as always, back to Jafar. I am unravelling, the darkness is my only companion. The dream I dreamed last night, my tormentor. This is what I saw.

I lie on a bed, the room is stiflingly hot. Every window has been closed to keep out the mosquitoes. I have thrown off the sheet and lie in my vest, my legs bare, my arms outstretched. My hair is pulled back, the fan above is turning slowly, and yet I am still covered in perspiration. In my dream I am back in my grandfather's house, but not as it is now, as it was when I was a child. The house is real; its details, from my childhood, correct.

I see that next to me, in the same room but lying on the floor on a hard straw mat, Thresiamma, one of my five auntie-nuns, is sleeping, snoring gently. She lies flat on her back, her hands folded on her chest. She has taken off her veil, and is wearing a cream-coloured linen headscarf. This is the first untruth, I say to myself, even as I dream: Thresiammachi died two years ago, a peaceful death in her convent in Calicut.

I know that under my bed in the same box as my jewellery, there is a sari, pressed, with a matching blouse, stitched, ready to be worn. In my dream I open the box and run my hands over the light silk. Next to the sari in a small pouch are the miniature bell earrings that I was given on my first birthday by my Francisuncle, all my gold bangles, the anklet I bought in Ernakulam some years ago. This is a truth: we have discussed these, my mother and I, decided on these ornaments. I know that the adornments are waiting for me and I will be wearing them in a few days.

I am no longer lying in the bed, but suspended above looking down on my form. I hear voices from next door, a shriek, laughter. I swoop around the rooms of the house, looking down at the familiar faces. My mother, sharing her bedroom with two other aunts; my uncle in the living room with two other cousins. The house is full; everyone has arrived for an occasion. Suddenly I am even higher, in the sky, looking down at the house. I am higher still, seeing the church at the end of the path, further on the Hindu temple on the other side, opposite the post office. All real, all correct, so familiar to me, my childhood home. I am even higher now and I see the canals, then the soft sand on the beach, the sea. The deep blue-green waves of the Arabian Sea, pouring into the vastness of the Indian Ocean.

Travelling swiftly, flying over the blue waters, then seamlessly, I am in the back of a taxi. The taxi is driving very fast, the streets outside are flashing by quickly. At first I am only aware of heat, the feeling of the plastic seats in the car sticking to the backs of my legs. I am in a light dress, I have a bag by my side on my left. My feet are in open-toed sandals and are covered in a thin film of dust. The dust is coming in through the windows, half-open, and the motes dance in front of my eyes. I am aware in my dream that I have crossed the ocean and, finally, returned.

I look out of the window. The light has bleached the landscape. The colours are muted, nearly monochrome, like I am looking into a faded past. I know that I am in Maputo, driving along the airport road back into town. The driver is making conversation, telling me about the rains they have recently had. Now, it is very hot, "*só calor*". I nod sympathetically, feel a trickle of sweat run down my chest. We are still driving fast even though we are closer to the city. I look for the building of the Ministry of Agriculture. It's still there.

Then I see him. He is coming out of a factory. Was there a factory on that corner? He looks tired, preoccupied, just another worker in a group of men. His eyes are half-closed, like when he is angry. His hands are in his pockets, he drags his feet. He looks up. He sees me, our eyes lock, my heart stops beating. I open my mouth for I have much to tell him. He looks away. The taxi speeds off. I turn around, my words left unsaid, on my knees in the back seat, my palms on the back-view window. I can see him no longer.

The ache is real. His anger: that is real too. If he would look away if he saw me, I don't know. I am not sure, but I fear he would.

2

We are more alike than we think, my mother and I. We both know unhappiness; we both know the solace to be gained from silence. Neither of us has leaned on anyone else or shared our sorrows. Perhaps now it will change, for there has been a reconciliation of sorts, we have drawn closer. If we could speak freely with each other, which I know we will never do, we could learn a lot. For we have one thing in common. We both threw respectability to the wind — in different directions perhaps — but threw it away nevertheless.

When I was seven years old, my mother decided to leave my father, and return to her childhood home in Alleppey. It was, at that time, inconceivable that a marriage be compromised for the sake of happiness. Even now I do not know of anyone in my family circle who has surrendered propriety as my mother was prepared to surrender it. It was decided that the boys would do better with our father. I, it was assumed, would do better with our mother. Standing in front of my parents, I remember wearing my favourite short blue dress. I had been outside with my brothers under the nutmeg trees in the yard, helping Aruna our maid burn the leaves and rubbish in the hole that we used at the back. I had been put in charge of my youngest brother, only three years old then, to make sure he did not go too close to the fire and I had to pass his hand over to my older brother before running indoors. My parents' faces were solemn, pale, neither looked at the other. My mother had been crying, her face was swollen. My father looked down at the floor. My mother spoke:

"Soon we will need to have two houses for our family. You and I will need to go and live in Alleppey with Uppacha. And Papa and the boys will stay here."

I refused to go. I think I cried out. I remember when my parents, both startled by my reaction, moved forward and tried to hold me I swung my arms at them. I smacked my mother in the arm. It can't have hurt much, but she must have been shaken: I was normally a malleable, cooperative little girl.

I can picture the scene. We stand in that room, the three of us, my parents and I. My brothers, as usual, remain outside, peripheral to events. My small body, in its blue cotton frills, takes centre-stage. My mother before me, my father to my side. I imagine them looking at each other, aghast, over my head. Each would set me off on a direction I did not envisage: my father with his ambitions, my mother with her indifference. But I like to capture that moment when I stood between them, a small child, their child. At that moment in time nothing was known.

In the end my parents never separated. Their plans had been thwarted by my unexpected obstinacy. They each occupied a different wing but remained living in the same house, until my father died of a sudden heart-attack, a year into their domestic compromise. My grandfather, racked with guilt that the marriage he had arranged for his daughter had caused her so much unhappiness, never ever forgave himself. He knew that it had been a hasty affair. My father, all agreed, had been extremely fortunate: not only was my mother a beauty, with her golden skin and curly black hair, but she was highly-educated, a lady-doctor no less. Their union, however, had been less fortunate. My grandfather's chance for redemption came with my father's death.

My mother sold the big house in Irinjalakuda, and moved back to her father's house in Alleppey with her three children. We were indulged, and with the resilience of the young, we put behind the trials of the previous years and enjoyed a lively childhood. We lacked for nothing: we had clothes, toys and books. We went to the best schools in the area with other similarly-fortunate Syrian Christian children. My mother's youngest sister and brother still lived at home and they were our companions and confidantes. My grandfather, bespectacled and bald, was a hero of intellect, teaching us poetry and letting us accompany him to the law offices in town where he was a respected barrister. My mother carried on working as a doctor from an office in the house and looked after my grandfather, in his old age. My father's family retreated from our lives, and while I remember that my mother dutifully attended my grandmother's funeral, travelling there and back in a day, she didn't take us. I saw my aunts and uncles from my father's side rarely through my childhood before I left India.

But actions are irretrievable and my refusal to abet my parents' plan, a neat division, as we always divided at the church entrance on Sundays — I would go to the women's section with my mother, the boys with my father — hurt my mother profoundly. I know she felt I had chosen my father over her. A year after my father had died, I chanced upon my mother and aunt, deep in conversation, in the dining-room. My aunt had her back to me, but my mother glanced up and saw me, moving through the room, on my way to my bedroom. "It's not normal," I heard her say to my aunt, before I was out of earshot. "*Ee logathillo?* It's not normal for a daughter to reject her mother." I had turned cold at her words and hurried to my room to digest them. She was right; it was true. Why had I refused? I could not remember how I had felt, just a hot flash, as hot as the fire I had been watching Aruna burn.

I walked on eggshells around my mother for years, my heart lifting when we shared affectionate moments – when she quietly took my comb from my aunt's hands and brushed and plaited my hair herself, always doing it slightly tighter, more expertly, kissing me on my forehead afterwards. When she let me sit in her office with my colouring pencils as she tackled her paperwork, only standing up when she sighed and said, "Come, *mol.* All finished." I had the task of turning out her lights and locking her office door, passing her the key for safekeeping. But, all too often, I remember feeling crushed when I caught her watching me, her eyes sad: she had not forgotten.

By the time she had been a widow for seven years those affectionate moments I shared with my mother had become rare. She had slipped into a chronic condition of disinterest. She continued her motherly duties, overseeing our studies, our health and diet, but she retreated into a solipsism that excluded real interaction. She had been wronged: if my grandfather had chosen another man for her, she could have enjoyed a happy marriage and a happy life, whereas now she had to raise three children alone. And do so in a suffocatingly-respectable environment: her home-town, where the failure of her marriage, albeit now ended, was well-known and a cause for gossip. People loved it when misfortune befell others. Her words always silenced them: my aunt, my uncle, my grandfather. No one could refute her: she became untouchable. She did not walk but floated in beatific isolation.

My brothers forged ahead; it was only I who drooped. I grew from a child into an adolescent and it was my aunt who marked each milestone, advised and consoled. When she married and went to live in Hyderabad, our household changed. Suddenly, the only two females remaining were my mother and I. Dressing one morning, standing in front of the mirror, I had seen her enter the room, then sit on the bed to watch me. It seemed to have come to her attention that, while she had been otherwise preoccupied, I had grown up. I was no longer a child, but a few years shy of being an adult. She looked amused, as she cast her eyes over me. "How unlike we are," she commented.

She had not meant to be hurtful, but I, with a teenager's self-consciousness, felt graceless. I was small-boned, slender, long-limbed. But also aware that, unlike my mother, I lacked the curvy softness that was a measure of beauty in our environs. Her words stung, just as the words, I later learned, of her in-laws had stung her. We are both susceptible to the power of an ill-judged comment. We are, in fact, not so dissimilar.

Books became my escape, the only way I could cope with the conflicting nature of a mother who was prevalent

– with her edicts on what I should wear, eat and study– but wholly detached. I immersed myself in them. Surrounded by the endless beauty of the landscape – coconut trees, the paddy fields, the canals, the lake, the sea – I was oblivious. I read constantly, barely stopping to eat, becoming more and more of a frustration to my grandfather and other members of my family with my withdrawal, my quietness. And yet, still fairly unremarkable. A trying relationship with your mother is not uncommon for an adolescent girl. Sensitivity about your appearance, wondering if anyone really understands you: classic teenage angst, if nothing else. But a few months after I turned sixteen, my mother announced the bombshell that would be, immediately, transformative. My life would alter from the ordinary to the extraordinary. I had done well in my school exams, and so, she said, I would be sent to study at an all-girls Catholic boarding school in the soft countryside not far from the south coast of England. That she wanted me to travel so far away from her supervision, to a country she had never visited, both astonished and appalled me.

On hearing my mother's decision my grandfather begged my mother to reconsider, my aunt wrote immediately on hearing the news, I was still just a child. But my mother was adamant, serene. My father had always insisted before his death that his fortune should be spent on our education, boys and girl alike. And boarding school would mean that entry to one of the older, prestigious universities would be assured. My older brother was already himself in his last year at boarding school, and he had enjoyed it tremendously. She was only giving me the opportunities that my father had desired for us.

I was learning about my parents. My father had had lofty ambitions, far beyond those of most of his siblings. There was no line of Oxford-educated uncles and fathers to inspire him: indeed he had been the first to achieve any education beyond school. His family did not belong to the political elite, nor were they wealthy. Their interests were insular, revolving around the plantation, the misfortunes of neighbours, the health of the elders. And yet my father had wanted his children to stand out. He wanted us to study abroad, while our contemporaries studied closer to home; and he wanted the same for his daughter as for his sons, a nearly unheard-of aspiration.

My mother, well-known in her home-town, had been a trailblazer at college in the sixties, a lady-doctor. Despite her knowledge of medical texts, her clinician's expertise, however, she had an undeniable flaw. She lacked imagination. By sending me away she may have wanted to test my mettle. She did not have doubt, she was unprepared. She assumed that because I was her daughter she would be privy to my every mood, my every thought when, in fact, she had not made enough effort to learn. She was not to know it then, but her decision would lend me the faculties by which I could live, and would live, a life far removed from the confines of her own vision. I would raise my eyes and see the world. We differed essentially: unlike my mother, I did not lack imagination and I did not float.

*

But it did not come at once. I can see the lady-lecturer yawning sleepily below my bunk, still reading her economics book despite the inadequate light. She reminds me of my mother. She must have looked like that when she took the train back to Alleppey from medical school in Trivandrum. My mother would have read her textbooks, revised for exams, unwilling to waste the three-hour journey on day-dreaming. Unlike nowadays, she will have been one of the very small cohort of female students in a male-dominated career. It must have been this quiet, unprecedented self-assurance that allowed my mother to argue with her husband — a good few years her senior — to expect standards from him, and then to turn her back on his inadequacies. I, on the other hand, am not a natural-born rebel. While my mother has an inner strength that allowed her to challenge convention despite having limited exposure to the world outside Alleppey, I acquired mine through circumstance. I did not embrace my freedom; I felt cast aside by my family.

Phone-calls home were brief and infrequent. My grandfather wrote to me regularly, carefully screening his real feelings, giving abbreviated news about my brothers and cousins, my mother adding a brief postscript: eat well, take care of yourself. I went home only in summer holidays, and when I was at university, only once. My older brother, already graduated, was getting married, and my mother had called on my assistance. I had been touched, and hoped — in an oblique, hypothetical way— to broach with her the news of the philosophy student I had met at university. My first prospective boyfriend, and I was troubled by the expectations he had from me, and by my own worrying desires. When I arrived home after nearly a year's absence, however, my mother was distant. I was sent on errands around town, and while my aunts, uncles and grandfather were pleased to see me, commenting on my new hairstyle — my hair now cut to just below my chin — inquiring after my studies, my mother wore her distracted smile.

"You are OK?", she asked, finally, as my uncle drove us to the airport. I was leaving that day.

"Yes, Ma."

"Eating well?"

"Yes, Ma."

"That's good. Plenty of fruit also, remember."

She was looking out of the window, her thoughts appeared elsewhere. Her hand lay on the seat between us, and I was filled with an impulse to hold it. I took it, and she smiled, her eyes not leaving the scene outside.

"Ma..." I faltered. I was not sure she was listening.

She patted my hand, murmured "Yes, you must take care." I felt wholly unsatisfied.

On returning to university in the autumn term of my second year, I resolved to interpret my mother's indifference as a licence to behave freely. There began in me a stirring. Like nearly all children in India I had been brought up with rigorous training in my faith, respect for a higher being. My family were not spiritual; they were pious. Now, on my own, I lapsed. I stopped going to church: a rebellion that was cataclysmic— I had, after all, some five nuns and three priests that I could count as family members — but that went unnoticed, either by my family whom I no longer lived with, or by the people I did live with. I shrugged off that first layer that clothed me and began to engage. I was not in love, but I started sleeping with my philosopher-boyfriend. I was somewhat scandalised by myself: nobody else around me noticed.

Life carried on around me as normal, I was not struck dead.

I thought myself acclimatised: I no longer stuck out with my diffidence and awkwardness, I blended in. Underneath my western clothes, my modified accent, however, I realise I was waiting. These days, surely, were temporary, an episode. Deep down, I expected my mother to open her arms and pull me back, show me the direction my life should take. I still never considered any other conclusion for myself than what I had grown up believing ineluctable: I would return to India, at least until I got married, for was that not the inevitable eventuality for any girl from my background? I would settle down where my husband had settled down, would he be an NRI?, make my own family.

But on graduating, the summons home that I had expected did not come. In the usual two lines that my mother added at the end of a letter penned by my grandfather, she congratulated me on my degree, and as always, told me to take care of myself. By then my boyfriend and I had parted ways. I had found a job of sorts in London, and a friend with whom to share a flat. Again, a letter arrived, this time with a desultory request to look after myself in the big city. I realised, then, that my family, my mother, were not going to offer me up to a suitor. While I had expected a marriage to be arranged — I was after all a decent candidate — my mother seemed to think differently. I began to worry: she must know of my transgressions. My first reaction was fear of her disapproval, and then a resistance: I could not think of a time when she had offered maternal support and advice. Perhaps she was waiting for me to reach out, declare that I needed her. I was waiting for the same.

And so we stared each other out, my mother and I, neither of us willing to break our gaze. My future entered a state of limbo and I have no idea how long it would have lasted. I was living in a country that would soon oblige me to leave: I had no ties, no claim to stay. Close to a year and a half of flitting but never settling, a letter arrived. It was from my uncle, my father's youngest brother Francis, who had also grown up in that simple house in the green hills. He had taken it on himself to invite me to come and stay with him. He was a lecturer in English at the University of Zimbabwe. He was sure that I would like Harare, he would enjoy the company of his niece. My papers could easily be sorted, he was confident I would find a job.

Things can change in a day. My father's youngest brother had spoken up, offered me shelter. Reading his words, feeling, suddenly, that the idea of joining him was unassailable, I made preparations to fly south. I packed a suitcase, said my goodbyes, grateful to an uncle I had not seen since I was a child. He was not to know that within months of receiving his letter I would be living in a flat within walking distance of the same ocean I had paddled in as a child. With a man who had as yet played no part in my life, Jafar. Someone had blinked. Closed their eyes to clear what had passed before, and then opened them to see a different vista. I entered a world which moved to a different rhythm, with different sounds and smells, a warmth, an ache. A new continent will be explored. New characters will drift into view, old ones will fade away. Words will be said, promises exchanged. Bodies will move closer and draw apart, as the plot thickens, the story unfolds.

3

I count my teaching post at the further-education college in Harare as my first proper job, and it has been a talisman ever since. Even in far-flung places any mention has always caught someone's attention, led to a conversation, then the offer of some work. Just a few months ago, when I was handing over the reins of the project I have been involved with for the last two years to my successor, I had the same discussion, and gave the same verdict. Yes, it had been a lovely place to work. Yes, really interesting people. And indeed all that is true. When I worked there the mood was particularly buoyant. It was the mid-nineties, and neighbouring South Africa had just held its first democratic elections. The eyes of the world were trained on the region and its future. The college in Harare was basking in the reflected optimism and was savouring its success.

I stumbled into the job. I was offered it after only a brief look at my papers. I am hoping that I will be similarly lucky in my new environs. While I will, for once, not have to worry about finances, I will also need my own space; I have grown too accustomed to living on my own the last couple of years to relinquish that. Perhaps once again someone will read about the college in Harare and raise their eyebrows. While it looks good on paper, I feel like my description of my duties involves a certain amount of spin. I did not work there very long, not even half a year. And I was younger than nearly all of my students, too enthralled by the complexities of their lives to comment objectively on their academic competencies. They were surgeons who had fled Rwanda and were awaiting papers to live in Canada; engineers from southern Sudan who were oppressed in their own country and were hoping for jobs in South Africa; aid workers from the West who were eyeing positions in the UN after years of experience with non-governmental organisations in neighbouring Zambia, Mozambique and Botswana. I was aware that compared with their life-stories and experiences mine were lightweight, and so the affectionate respect they showed me as their teacher was charming.

I didn't earn much either, but Francisuncle would take no rent. I lived with him in his long, low bungalow in the university grounds, a half-hour drive from the city-centre. I had my own bedroom, my uncle had a bigger bedroom that doubled as a study across the hall. When he had showed me around, Francisuncle had shrugged at the empty shelves, and sparse furniture. He was obviously used to living on his own.

"You can bring a woman's touch, *mol*", he said.

I was shy around him at first. Francisuncle seemed sophisticated, worldly-wise, a university professor, well-established in the faculty, far away from my vague memories of him eating fried plantains, ethakkappam, and making me miniature drums from coconut shells and stretched rubber. And yet he still wore his benien and moonda after his evening bath, spoke to me in

Malayalam. Those first weeks, we talked late into the night about books and films, of people back home. It was, I remember, like watching an old black-and-white film of family memories. He shared anecdotes of my father, whom I barely remembered, and of others who, he gently reminded me, were as much my family as my mother's. He even evoked a different mother. Francisuncle had been nineteen when my parents had married, and he had been impressed by my mother's beauty and elegance. He reminded me that she had once been young, newly-married and enthusiastic about life. He might have felt that he was taking me under his wing; he might, later, have taken charge. We never reached that moment. A few weeks after I started working at the college, Jafar arrived.

I want to give my first impressions but it's been so many years that I wonder if I can, in fact, rely on my untrustworthy memory. I have one photograph of him, if it could be called that. It was taken at the party at Sandra's house. I am in the foreground, talking to Mwaria, whose arm is draped around my shoulders. He is leaning into me, and the image is one of intimacy, collusion. Jafar is in the background talking to one of the other Italian women. Her head is thrown back in laughter, her throat gleaming white in the flash. He is looking down at her, a cigarette in his lips, his eyes crinkled in a half-smile. The impression given is that I was with Mwaria. It is an accurate picture in some ways: there were always other people crowding our life.

He was tall, over six feet, and his skin was ebony-dark. He dressed in jeans and long-sleeved shirts or T-shirts. This set him apart from most of the other Mozambicans, who were slighter, and wore pressed trousers with white or pale suit-shirts, gleaming shoes. He kept his hair short; he had a wide nose, a high forehead and cheekbones, and full lips. He moved with a basketball player's grace and slight bounce, but he was also slightly pigeon-toed, something he was embarrassed about. He had long legs and a way of lazily leaning against the wall, resting on the balls of his feet.

His physical type – his height and broad shoulders – was typical of the Ronga, from the southern half of Mozambique, close to South Africa. But of course when we met I had no knowledge of such intricacies. To me, he stood out less for his stature, more for his demeanour. Whereas the other Mozambicans hung around in break-times on the terraces, chatting animatedly in Portuguese and organising get-togethers, Jafar was more aloof, rarely engaging in conversation. And when he did, he was often monosyllabic. The others did not seem to take offence. I used to wonder whether he was a night-owl, more loquacious after a drink, because they still valued his participation. When he made his occasional interjections it was with a deep voice, a smoker's voice. I always saw him lighting up outside, idly putting the cigarette packet back into his breast pocket. He was thirty-four; I was twenty-four.

We first spoke one afternoon on the terrace. I was walking back to the staff areas after a class, and he was in the middle of a huddle of students on the narrow walkway, his back against the railings, his feet stretched out in front of him. The others with him were speaking in rapid Portuguese but broke off to greet me when they saw me, with their usual disarming combination of respect for my status and indulgence of my age. Jafar remained silent, looking down at me as I tried to squeeze past in the small space. Then with a studied effort he straightened up, moving his feet out of my way, letting his eyes travel slowly up and down my person.

"*Profesora.*" His voice was gently mocking. He gave a small bow and then a slow smile. I mumbled my thanks, feeling flustered, and skidded gracelessly in my confusion. He took hold of my arm and straightened me.

"*Cuidado*," he said, and again I could hear the amusement in his voice.

He had a slight French accent when he spoke English, because he had been living with a Frenchwoman for the past four years. They had worked together for Médecins Sans Frontiers in northern Mozambique, and when their projects had ended, they decided to come together to Zimbabwe to do an English course. Marie was beautiful, with a grave face, ivory skin, a full figure, thick dark hair. They were breaking up, I found out later, and she was returning to France on her own to study medicine; she wanted to become a doctor. He would return alone to Mozambique when his course ended. They were renting a flat in the Avenues, still living together in spite of the imminent separation. I find it hard to think of them together; they were unhappy, and yet, I think she was better for him than I was. She was not afraid to try and change him; I never felt I had anything to offer him.

By the time we met properly he was well-known at the college. It was a breeding ground for light-hearted affairs. The country was, at that time, a regional success story, attracting communities of exiles. Serbians, Russians, Somalis, Sudanese, Ethiopians, Rwandans, Mozambicans – all embracing the opportunity to recover from political and emotional traumas. The classes they were attending, the mellow gentle environment, must have been in stark contrast to their recent experiences. Everyone let go. Flirtations and romances abounded, and Jafar was always a central figure.

While I regarded Marie and her relationship with Jafar with some awe, Sandra, an Italian whose husband worked for the embassy, did not seem to share my feelings. She was very glamorous, pouting, and I think she believed that she had discovered him in some way. She was in many ways similar to Marie; they both had a confident sensuality and I envied them their maturity and worldliness. With hindsight, I can feel more pity for Sandra. I know now that she must have lacked something in her marriage, been lonely with her life in Africa, but then all I felt was amazement at her determination in pursuing Jafar. She did not find Marie, or her husband, reasons for any restraint; and indeed she had a willing accomplice in Jafar.

God knows how Marie felt about it all. By this time Jafar was sleeping on the sofa in the living room and Marie was washing her hands of him. While their final months together must have been painful, they maintained an undeniable bond. He did not move out of the flat, and I still saw them sitting together at the tables outside during breaks. Marie would be talking quietly, seriously; Jafar would be smoking and making occasional comments. They spoke in French together; another sign to me of the commitment they had once had to each other. She would sometimes reach out and take the cigarette from his lips and put it between hers, an act as intimate as any other they had enjoyed in their four-year relationship.

She invited me to their flat once for coffee after an afternoon class. I accepted. She was leaving in a few weeks and I genuinely liked her. I was surprised when Jafar told me later that Marie had confronted him about me. "You like her, I can tell," she had said, and he had told her she was right. She wrote to him once, many months later in Mozambique. By then we were living together in our flat over the dusty street in Maputo. He read the letter wordlessly then asked me if I would like to read it. I refused. Days later, however, I rummaged through his things and found the letter. It was as intimate and accusing as I had expected. She had a special name for him – I had a pain in my chest reading it. She had loved him, he had hurt her, could I expect the same? And more importantly, did he still love her? They had had four years to share, to create, to love; for me this seemed an impossibly long time to compete with.

When Jafar returned, my face was swollen with tears, the letter was still in my hands. He took it, laid it aside, placed his hand briefly under my chin, and then held me in his arms. It was the most tender he had ever been. I cried against his shoulder, hot tears running down my cheeks. He had by then learned how young I was, how unformed. How overwhelmed I was with the intensity of our relationship and how fearful I was of his absences. Later, as we lay whispering together through the night, he stroked my face and my body and told me things that I had been too afraid to ask. I had never lived with anyone before, and his long, involved, and more equal relationship with Marie made our togetherness feel inconsequential. My fears, that he found me lacking in some way, while assuaged that evening, never really went away.

*

I had not expected Marie to really leave, but she did, and in the days and weeks that followed I found myself noticing him more, running into him at college events. I even taught him in a few classes, where he was always polite but said little, completed his tasks, and then leaned back, his chair balanced on two legs, in an attitude of near-boredom. I was aware that I found him attractive, but also intimidating. He was too amused, I felt, at my awkwardness and confusion around him. I felt I had so few feminine wiles to offer that I did not consider myself a contender for his attentions. I was aware that Sandra and others had laid some claim on him; one that I felt I was not in a position to replace. And while he always greeted me with a smile and a sardonic "*Profesora*", we never spoke much beyond pleasantries. He was often with Sandra, and I saw myself as an inexpert rival.

I was only to find out much later what had been in Jafar's mind. He told me that as soon as he had seen me on the terrace, when I had so clumsily stumbled against him, he had thought, "I want her to be mine." But he had held back. The reason for his reticence was that I was Indian. Indian girls just never consorted with African men. They could be looked at, but not touched. He expected any advances he made to be rejected, surely, with derision. He admitted that it was on an impulse that he had approached me that evening at Sandra's house.

On the last day of the academic year, Sandra held a party in her beautiful villa in the Northern Suburbs. She was very generous like that. Her husband was away and she enjoyed company and liked to have an open house. The party was in full swing when I got there; everyone had a glass of beer or wine in their hand. The sofas had been pushed to one side of the large living room, to create a dance area. In the middle of the ad hoc dance floor, I could see Jafar, dancing with Sandra. In a backless, black dress she looked stunning. They made an attractive couple; he had his hand behind her, and she moved her body lazily against his with a sureness that made me look away. The dance floor was crowded, and couples jostled for space. Gabrielo invited me to dance, showing me how to step forwards and backwards, hips swaying, man and woman mirroring each other. I was soon enjoying myself thoroughly. I was then torn from Gabrielo's arms by Mwaria, who was quite drunk and held me too tightly.

And later I danced with Jafar, who found me at the table covered with food, picking at a pizza slice. Sandra was dancing with a tall Angolan doctor, and I had been watching her, wondering if I could wear a dress like hers with such panache. Jafar appeared at my side, and without a word took my hand and pulled me onto the dance floor. Then suddenly:

"Could I have your number phone?"

"You mean my phone number?"

"You are no longer my teacher. I can speak bad English, or I can teach you Portuguese."

I laughed.

"Can I have your phone number?"

"Why?" I asked stupidly.

"Why not? I can invite you to dinner some time?"

"What about Sandra?"

It was a juvenile question, and once I had blurted it out I realised that it had been clumsy.

His face darkened, he said roughly, "Everyone asks me that. What about Sandra. She is married, she has her own life." And from then on it seemed, like he had said, that Sandra and her orchestrations melted away from his concern. His hand was on the small of my back and I was very aware of the closeness of our bodies. We danced in silence. I was mortified that I had annoyed him. He may have been angered by what he saw as my gaucheness, but it did not stop him from swaying my frame expertly to the rhythm.

When the music stopped, I drew away and began to thank him politely.

But he held onto my arm. "You still don't say if I can have your phone number."

I nodded my head, and to my surprise he smiled. It was a guileless smile, and showed off his wide mouth. "Thank you, I wanted to ask you many times. But you were my beautiful teacher. I don't think I learned much in your class."

I smiled back, embarrassed, but my heart was hammering against my chest.

"I think you did quite well in my classes."

"I could do better if I wasn't always dreaming about the teacher."

Despite the inauspicious start, we were bantering with each other and I was relieved. I gave him my phone number, and he wrote it on a cigarette packet, which he then put back in his pocket. For the rest of the party we didn't talk much, but I could see him watching me as I danced with the others. Leaning against the wall with a beer in his hand, his face grave, his eyes intent.

*

I had accepted his invitation but he remained poised for rejection. A few weeks later, when we spent that afternoon in the hotel room, his disbelief resurfaced. We were lying together, whispering softly, my head on his shoulder. He had suddenly pushed me away so that he could see my face. His voice was rough.

"How can you be here, with a black man?"

"Like Mississippi Masala". I giggled, nervously.

He looked at me quizzically, and I had tried to explain, tumbling over my words with the sudden worry of appearing condescending.

"There was this film..."

"Masala? Like curry?"

"In the deep south, I think..."

"Deep south?"

My explanations became complicated, he didn't understand a lot of the words I used and started asking me things in Portuguese. I determined, then, to learn more Portuguese, but at the time I tried and failed to compare ourselves with the protagonists of a film I hadn't enjoyed much. A black man, an Indian girl, in Mississippi. I felt foolish. His lack of knowledge of the film did not make him appear ignorant, but conversely, more cultured, more real. My chattiness, on the other hand, seemed trite, and I grew more quiet, not finding the words, and ashamed of my references to a world of imagery and fakery.

But the overwhelming narrative we presented to the world persisted. Much later, when we were living in our flat above a busy street in Maputo, Jafar would take me one night to the Teatro Avenida. Theatre-going was a very popular past-time for Mozambicans. With no cinema then in the city, and a love of story-telling, Maputenses flocked to the theatres. He had got tickets for a particularly successful Mozambican play that his friends had recommended. I remember being relieved, pleased at the prospect of doing something so conventionally couple-y, after months of feeling misplaced and uncertain. I had worn my favourite top which showed off my neck, which I knew Jafar loved to stroke, and a necklace made of green beads I had bought from the Mercado Central. Jafar had smiled appreciatively when he saw me, crinkling his eyes, and playfully tugging at the necklace. We had walked hand-in-hand down to the Baixa, where crowds had already gathered to buy tickets, and where we received a few curious stares. We were an unusual sight, I admit. There I was – slender, youthful-looking, Indian. And Jafar – tall, broad-shouldered, black. But he squeezed my hand and pushed us through the throngs to find our seats.

Initially I was very impressed by the performance, by the live band that accompanied the story, by the tightly-rehearsed and expertly-delivered dialogue. I didn't understand everything, but the story was not complicated. A young man was bringing his new girlfriend to meet his parents. In the pivotal scene, it was revealed that his girlfriend was Indian. Black man, Indian girl. The actress playing the girlfriend was clearly not Indian herself, but was a light-skinned African girl wearing a wig. The whole theatre erupted into hoots of laughter at the discomfort of the parents, and continued laughing during the sad love-affair, which culminated in an inevitable falling-out. "*Preto!*" she shouted at her boyfriend. "*Monye!*" he replied with disdain. It was not the first time I had heard that hurtful word, and by then I understood its implications. The story upset me, and Jafar was aware of that. He stopped laughing half-way through the play, and then sat with his arm behind me, stroking the back of my neck with his thumb. Some of the audience members sitting nearby stole glances at us. We were seeing ourselves as others saw us: we were a curiosity, a cause for hilarity. We left as soon as the curtain came down, the lovers parted, normality restored.

4

A party, a dance, a tentative courtship. The background: an orderly southern African city of wide streets and avenues, shopping centres, parks, gardens. And trees, which covered the city, flowering at different times of the year so that the tree-scape was almost permanently in colour. Flame, frangipani and, my favourite, the jacaranda. When I think of the first evening that we spent together it is always as a collection of senses: the smell of the jacaranda and the sweet scent of the jasmine bushes that encircled the restaurant. The feel of his gaze on me, my racing pulse. Sitting at that small white table, our knees occasionally touching, Jafar's hand occasionally reaching over into my space. We were a small planet, the candlelight was our star. We were circling each other, in gentle orbit.

He had moved into his friend Natão's flat, sleeping on a mattress in the spare room. His course at the college had ended but he said he needed to stay on a few more weeks to sort some things out, and he also claimed that he was supporting the Mozambican basketball team in the Pan-African Games, being held that year in Harare. Basketball, he told me, was nearly as popular as football back home, and he had been in his high-school team.

We sat across from each other at a table at the restaurant he had chosen to take me to on our first evening out together. I had borrowed Francisuncle's car and had driven back into town to the Avenues, where Natão was renting his flat. Jafar was waiting outside the building, on the pavement as we had arranged, and moved forward when I got out of the car. He was wearing jeans and a light grey shirt, and in his right hand, a small brown paper bag. He came over in long strides, bent down and kissed both my cheeks.

"*Olá*" he said, smiling. His eyes moved over the thin sleeveless cream-coloured top I had chosen after much deliberation, and the barrette in my hair. He briefly fingered the silver earrings I was wearing, then dropped his hand to the bangles on my wrist. "You look beautiful."

"Thank you," I said. "And you."

He tilted his head in acknowledgement and grinned.

"I thought you would wear a dress," he continued, still grinning, making a show of looking down the length of my jeans to my sandals. "You have beautiful legs and you should show them."

His candour silenced me. I was thinking of a retort when he handed me the brown paper bag, then walked to the passenger side and opened the door. "I know a nice place, but we need to drive."

I got back into the car and opened the bag. Inside was a small stone carving, two asymmetric heads leaning into each other. This small symbol of Jafar's rare forays into sentiment, was to take pride of place on my dressing-table in our flat in Maputo. When I left Mozambique it came with me, although I had hesitated before quickly sliding it, unwrapped, into one of my bags. I lost it later, on my travels. It must have fallen out of a box or been forgotten in a frenzy of packing. The loss of my stone sculpture, like the unsatisfying photo that I have of Jafar, was representative of our relationship: it was too difficult to hold onto, and our gazes always pointed in different directions.

"Thank you," I said, my fingers running over the cool smooth green stone. I turned to him. "It's lovely."

He shrugged, and touched my left leg briefly.

"Am I safe?" he asked. "You can drive?"

I laughed and started the engine. We drove along the shadowy streets. The street lights were dim, and there were few shops still open in that area. Most houses were set well back from the road with curtains drawn. Branches of trees bent forwards casting shadows on our faces as we moved along the street. There were only a few cars on the road, and even fewer people on foot. The city retired for the evening early; not many people lived in the centre, most made an exodus to the suburbs after work. The wealthy in their cars to the large houses behind electric gates to the north of the city; the rest in public buses and vans to the sprawling suburbs to the south. As a result, Harare did not have that chaotic lived-in feel that exasperated as well as charmed the residents of Maputo. Sister cities, they were vastly different.

We drove further south to a cluster of shops and restaurants. In the centre of the arc of shops, there was a small Italian restaurant, with tables inside and outside covered with heavy white cloth, each holding a candle in an empty Chianti bottle. The owners were from Italy, via South Africa, and their restaurant had become an institution. I heard, years later, that they moved back to South Africa when Zimbabwe slid into its decline, and the restaurant has now closed down. That evening, however, it was nearly full. Jafar had made a booking and we were shown to our table, outside on the edge of the patio. It was an intimate spot, with only faint lights from the restaurant on one side, but the blackness of the night on the other.

He described the basketball match he had seen earlier in the day. We talked about the Games and how the city seemed to have awoken. He told me how he liked the country, but how he had gone back to Mozambique, to Chimoio, a small town across the border nearly every two or three weeks. The journey could be done in a morning, and he still had some affairs to settle.

"Just to check on things. My flat. If there is a job."

We ordered some food; I ordered wine, he ordered a beer. I was nervous, aware of his eyes, lingering over my face, then my shoulders and neck, without restraint. Once, he reached over and fingered my earring again.

"They are nice," he said.

"Just junk jewellery I got from India," I replied. I took one out and showed it to him. "They are not real silver, but I really like the design and how they look old-fashioned." My voice sounded young, and I suddenly felt embarrassed by the enthusiasm I had shown.

He nodded, amused.

I put the earring back in my ear.

"So why you are not in India?"

I told him about Francisuncle, and his invitation. I told him about my father, how he had died and how I hardly remembered him. How in some ways Francisuncle was helping me learn about my parents before they had become unhappy with each other.

"You were young when you lost your father," he said. He picked up a bread roll and buttered it. "I was older, nearly fifteen. Then, when my brother died I was the oldest boy. I had to become everyone's father."

"It was the opposite with me and my brothers. Everyone looked after us. I suppose we were fortunate," I said.

"And you came here alone?" he said. "You were not in love with anyone?"

His tone was teasing, and I raised my head, tried to look withering. But my eyes quickly fell, and I could feel my cheeks flush.

"I had a boyfriend at university..." I began.

"Mmmm," he nodded his head and then burst out laughing.

"Why is it so funny?" I said, annoyed.

He shook his head, wiping his mouth with the napkin.

"Not funny, no."

Holding his hands up as if in surrender, he let his eyes move over my face again, a smile on his lips. He was enjoying my reaction.

"You are here now, with me," he said. "I must thank that boy for letting you go."

As we talked I began to steal glances at him, at the high cheekbones in his face, at his long arms and broad chest. That I found his presence magnetic was in no doubt. His voice was sonorous, and when he said my name, he assumed complete possession of me. I became oblivious of the couples and groups of diners near us. The waiters came and went and the meal progressed without me taking much notice of what was put on the table, and what was removed. The night became blacker, heavier as I noticed more and more intensely other details: the fullness of his mouth, the vein in the muscle of his forearm, his long right leg, stretched out alongside mine. It was a warm beguiling African night, with a cool underlying breeze that carried on it, I was sure, the sound of the thudding in my chest. Now, a lifetime later, I wonder at the transformation of such an ordinary scenario, nothing more unusual than a dinner-date. Sitting opposite Jafar, fully-clothed, I had been acutely aware of my body beneath the thin cotton top and my jeans. Aware of the shape of my small breasts, of how his hands would completely enclose them. The slimness of my waist, how his mouth would feel against my belly, my golden-brown against the charcoal of his skin. I have lived on my own the last few years, and while I have on some occasions sat across from a man in an evening, enjoying a dinner, I have never slipped into that sensuous reverie that so distracted me that night with Jafar. My body, even then, in the very first gentle manoeuvres towards intimacy, belonged to him.

He did not talk at length that evening, but we made conversation and I began to grow more assured in my ripostes. It was an enjoyable meal. He was chivalrous, enquiring after my food, pouring my wine. He had an easy confidence, displaying no embarrassment when he made mistakes in his English, often reverting to Portuguese, and once, when we were floundering, to French. I took this as an invitation, and answered with alacrity in the same language – I spoke it well – but he was suddenly abrupt.

"No," he said, "I will teach you Portuguese."

It was a memory of Marie, clearly. I looked down at the plate in front of me. I had ordered a pasta dish and the long strands were smothered in a creamy, tarragon sauce. It wasn't particularly tasty but I picked up my fork and stabbed at it. We ate in silence for a little, and I tried to clear the thoughts that were rushing in my head. What was I thinking? After being in a presumably monogamous long-term relationship, Jafar was darting from woman to woman. Sandra, other girls from the college. Now I was sitting in front of him, his date for the night. I suddenly felt foolish. The silence continued for a while. I ventured to look up and was surprised to see him munching with gusto, not sharing my discomfort. He mopped some of his sauce with some bread, caught my eye, and asked me if I had eaten enough. I nodded, and when our plates were cleared away, he smoked a cigarette while I had a coffee. We decided to leave. It was late, and I didn't want to worry Francisuncle.

When we reached Natão's street, I parked the car by the side of the road and turned off the engine. The heavy branches of the acacia tree nearly touched the windscreen. There were only a few lights in the apartment building across from us, and no one in sight. We sat quietly next to each other, and then he reached across and took my hand. Between his thumb and his fingers he held my wrist, then turned my silver bangle round and round. I watched my bangle in its hypnotic rotation, then I turned my head towards him. We kissed. When we drew apart we were both breathing hard. I tried to steady my heartbeat, watched his chest rising and falling, his mouth inches from mine. He took me by the wrist again and pulled me to him. I reached forward again, and let my lips and tongue meet his.

Time fell away, and the only place in the world that existed was the interior of Francisuncle's battered old car. My head fell back and his hand reached forward, his fingers encircled my throat, then fell down to my collar-bones. His thumb slid over my breast and then his hand dropped to my thigh, moving down to my knee and then up. I caught it between mine, tried to speak. He broke away and held his hands up theatrically, then tucked them between his knees. He threw his head back and exhaled loudly. I sat up straighter, adjusted my top. We stayed like that for a few minutes looking out of the front window into the night.

He turned and smiled at me. "Thank you for the kiss," he said finally. He opened his door, then leaned forward again and kissed my cheek.

"I can invite you again?" he asked.

I nodded.

He got out of the car, then reached back inside, his fingers scraping my lips.

I drove back to the university campus and let myself into the bungalow. Francisuncle was already in his room, but called out sleepily.

"*Vannu,*" I called back, then hurried to my room and closed the door. Lying in the bed under the sheets, my eyes wide open, I re-played the whole evening. My heart pounded. I felt alone in the bed, maiden-like. I stretched my limbs out, then curled then up again, my mind awake. Immediately I had a vision of myself, as a school-girl, walking home with Cecily.

We were fast friends through our school years, chattering between classes, sharing confidences. Our mothers had themselves been friends, schoolmates in the same college. Cecily had longer hair, but like mine, kept it oiled and arranged into two tight plaits. She was taller than me, and broader. She was always headstrong and out-spoken. The teachers were always complaining about her to her parents. They said if her parents did not keep a stern eye on her, if they did not try to curb her innate rebelliousness, she would 'go wild'. They even told my mother that she was, with this 'wild' gene, a bad influence on me. When my mother had relayed this information to me I had wondered what "going wild" could entail. I know now my thoughts that night — revisiting the feel of Jafar's hands, the taste of his mouth, his voice in my ear, the way my body was yearning for more — would be a valid prelude.

I was to think of Cecily again, a year later, lying in bed with Jafar in the bedroom of our flat, the sunlight fading outside and a gentle breeze blowing in from the door, open to the balcony. I had learned that after finishing her degree in Physics in Trivandrum, she had married an engineer, a Malayalee based in the Gulf. I tried to tell Jafar of my amusement at what I saw as a great irony. She had always been the one who was expected to shatter expectations.

"And yet," I told him, my head on his shoulder, his hand stroking my back, up to my neck, down to the base of my spine, up, down, " Now, here I am where I am, and Cecily is married to a Malayalee 'with prospects'."

"Is that what you want?"

"Of course I don't. It's just a bit funny."

And I had tried to explain that what I was trying to say was that I had stepped so far away from convention it was almost laughable. Because I am black? he asked. And because we are not married and because you are Muslim and because you have no 'prospects'. Which had been the wrong thing to say. He had pushed me away so that he could see my face. And that means? I had laughed, nervously. Nothing, absolutely nothing. To me, at least. It's the way people talk about a man who wants to get married, how they rate them. It means nothing to me. You have all the prospects I want.

When I spoke those words that evening to Jafar I had truly meant them. I had felt no wish to be anywhere else, with anyone else. His roughness had unsettled me; I had worried that he seemed so prickly, so quick to mistrust. But now I wonder at myself, and I accept his anger. That evening I had told Jafar that he was all I wanted: it was the truth then, it is a lie now.

*

We had exchanged a kiss and it could have ended there. A farewell was imminent as he had plans to leave that he had already delayed. But we continued to see each other. After I had finished work for the day, I would walk down to the entrance of the college. He would be waiting there, and would always greet me with a kiss on both cheeks, carry my books. In the evenings when we parted he would kiss me gently on the lips. I would drive home in a stupor, often one hand on the steering-wheel, the other at my throat. On his last afternoon we went to the café in the city gardens. I had told myself repeatedly that it had been short and sweet, a harmless romance, no hearts broken. But I ached with desire. I longed for his hands on my body, but feared them too: I could not see beyond that moment. Sitting in the café, half-listening to the chatter around us, I spoke little.

"You can come with me," he said, stirring his coffee.

I smiled weakly, and nodded.

"But I mean it," he said again, his hand encircling my upper arm. "Why not?"

"My uncle...", I began.

"He does not know about me. And if you like he does not need to know."

"But my job..."

"We can look together."

I shook my head.

I know now that there was something about me that Jafar just could not resist. While his words were nonchalant, he must have known their potency. After all, he had seen in Mozambique and mirrored all over Africa, how the enclaves of Indians and Pakistanis, mostly traders, had encapsulated themselves from the rest of the population. They did not marry out of their community, they rarely engaged in friendships across racial divides. Jafar, with his Muslim upbringing which he shared with many from those communities, would have had many opportunities to notice these distinctions. He would have been well-versed in the social restrictions and expectations that surrounded an Indian girl. And yet, perhaps because he had overcome that first hurdle and had a sense of my weakening, he was persistent. By then he must have known how helpless I felt when I was near him. He must have known the implications of his invitation, but he could not stop himself.

He had moved his hand to the back of my neck, and we must have made an interesting spectacle. The waiters were hovering around us, exchanging comments in Shona, I was sure, about us. I was annoyed by the attention we were attracting. I turned my back on the waiters, some of whom had supercilious smiles. Jafar noticed my irritation.

"What do you want to do? Stay here?" he asked.

I shook my head.

"I want us to be alone, but where can we go?" I had an idea that we could just sit in Francisuncle's car, which I had parked in the Avenues.

"We can book a hotel room," he said. I hesitated, he took my hand and squeezed it. Smiled, "Just to talk, *filha*". The word in Portuguese set my heart pounding again – I hadn't understood it but the way his voice changed, the melody, was thrilling. He paid the bill and we left.

In the hotel lobby, a soulless businessman's haunt in the centre, booking the room, he winked at my discomfort. We had no luggage and the receptionist had a frozen look on his face. We went upstairs, I glanced back and the receptionist was staring at us goggle-eyed. It was a characterless room, but neat. The curtains were drawn. When I opened them I saw the blank grey wall of the building opposite. I shut them. I lay on the bed, on my stomach, resting on my elbows. Jafar was fiddling with his money-belt, finally got it off. He flung himself on the bed beside me. He was grinning, a wide toothy grin.

"You look very self-satisfied", I said accusingly.

"I can't believe we are here like this. I have you here alone. My beautiful teacher."

His words embarrassed me. I turned my face away so that he could not see. He crept up behind me, laying the full length of his body against mine, his hands ran up and down my arms, then he turned me over to him. We kissed. With his mouth on mine, I felt the pulse on his neck. He traced the line of my eyebrows, my nose, my cheek, the outline of my lips. We lay in each other's arms, not talking. He said he felt warm, so with a lack of self-consciousness that I later became more familiar with, he took off his shirt and threw it onto the chair beside the bed. His chest was hairless. I rubbed my face against the curve of his shoulder, leaned forward and kissed his neck. When I looked up, my eyes met his. "*Pasa para acqui.*" His hand was behind my head, twisting in my hair, guiding me. I could feel his strength and his desire. As our mouths met, his hands slid under my top, over my ribs. He shifted slightly so I felt the weight of his body on mine. His fingers began to pluck at my brassiere. I moved my head away so that I could speak.

"You said we would just talk..."

He let his head fall against my chest and gave a loud groan. "*Estou à morrer*," he said, his voice muffled, his mouth buried in my neck. I laid my hand against his forehead and then, suddenly, we both started laughing. His body was warm against mine, deliciously heavy, and we held each other and shook with silent laughter. It was a lovely moment, one that I would remember and re-play for years after, and I felt joyous. We spent it must have been a few hours like that in the room, our voices low, slipping from English to Portuguese and back, teaching each other words to describe different parts of our bodies. I, giggling at our childish game: Jafar, remaining composed, pushing my top aside so that he could slide his hands over my stomach, his thumb dipping into my belly-button, then to my back, his fingers counting each nob of my backbone, then down my jeans to grip my ankle, my foot. I knew he wanted more, so did I, but what then? We exchanged long, slow, exploratory kisses, lay near each other, enjoying the warmth of our bodies.

It began to grow dark and I said I had to leave. We gathered our things quietly. He had already paid for the room; we handed in the keys and walked out of the hotel. So, it was drawing to a close. A short, sweet alliance. I felt as my feet moved in front of me that I did not know what I was walking towards. We didn't speak as we wended our way back towards the Avenues.

When we reached Francisuncle's car, he sighed and leaned against it. He looked down and smiled at me, reached forward and fingered the earrings I was wearing, then let his thumb trace my lips. I caught my breath, closed my eyes. As I do now, my fingers on my own lips, in this black night, years later. The memory of that moment still takes my breath away, lays me vulnerable to the hot rush of recollections. What Jafar eventually felt for me I doubt I will ever really know. Desire, certainly. Fondness, like that you have for a small furry animal, perhaps. At times, I am sure, disdain. Whether he felt love I never found out. But I know that even then, on that street in the dusk, before all our other more intimate shared moments, I loved him. Later, when we would make love, there were times when we whispered hoarsely to each other. I would tell him of my love, and in my weakness, I would sometimes even ask him to respond. He would reply, "*Adoro*". I adore. But that was not the expression that men and women normally used with each other. The words that I heard on the telenovelas that everyone watched, even by teenagers in clinches on the promenade by the sea. It was something I never had the confidence to clarify. I was just as scared to speak of my feelings later in our relationship as I was early on, fearing that an ill-expressed, inopportune comment could break the delicate thread between us.

"So I leave tomorrow", he said.

I nodded.

"It was nice," he said.

I nodded again, opened the car and got into the driver's seat. He closed the door for me and leaned into the window.

"*Tchau*", he said. I nodded again, and drove off.

*

For the next few weeks, the city held no charm. I taught my classes, but mechanically. Francisuncle and I still kept each other company, but he could sense something was different. He deferred to me unnecessarily, offered to take me out in the evenings to the cinema, for a concert. I always declined. It was too much effort to talk and laugh and pretend I was all right. It was August and Sandra was still at the school, continuing with summer tutorials. I didn't want to see her, or accidentally bump into her. She had tried to get in touch with Jafar a few times; he had told her he was seeing someone else without mentioning my name. I didn't want to see her and think about their practised, intimate relationship. It was better this way; it never would have worked with us, so it was wise not to have got closer.

But every night as I lay in bed, my mind whirred, remembering our exchanges. His face, his voice. I was filled with regret. Regret and shame. I realised that I had indeed been instilled with the conventions that I thought I had shed. Deep down I still believed that a man should be able to provide, declare honourable intentions, shoulder responsibility, commit to wedlock. Jafar had not demonstrated any of those things and I had let him leave. His invitation had seemed lukewarm to me. But had it been? He need not have asked me. The fact that he had was worth more from him than anyone else. I slept badly, ate little. I held my stone carving in the bed with me, rubbed its coolness over my lips and my cheek.

When the phone rang at home one evening I answered it, Francisuncle in the kitchen washing up the dishes.

"Hello," I said.

"Hello."

My hands gripped the phone tightly. I struggled to keep my voice calm.

"Where are you?"

"Here, back at Natăo's flat."

"What are you doing?"

"I couldn't stay away."

"You're crazy..."

"About you, yes."

"What do you want?"

"Like I said before. I want you to come back with me to Mozambique."

"I can't..."

"Of course you can."

And of course I did.

5

A voice speaks in your ear, your heart responds. I had fallen in love and was determined, certain that I belonged with Jafar. I had known him for days, I had known him forever. I marvel at myself, at the sureness of my movements. In all the years that have followed I have never rediscovered that certainty. I was robust, I am no longer so.

It was hard for my uncle. He had been shocked when I told him I was leaving, then sad, deflated. I babbled on about how Mozambique was full of investment and opportunity after the war. About how I could find a good job, better-paid than at the college. My heart went out to him when I saw him looking at me but I also hardened myself against weakening. I thought I was being convincing but my lies must have been transparent. He had asked immediately, "Is there someone I should know about?"

I had gone on the offensive.

"That you should know about, Francisuncle? What does anyone know about me?"

He had started to talk, but I had interrupted.

"I haven't been back home for years. And why is that?"

He lowered his head, and I continued, determined.

"Because they don't want me. My mother doesn't want me ...."

"No, *mol*, you mustn't say these things..." he began, shaking his head, reaching for my hand.

But I pulled my hand away.

"I'm OK. I don't feel bad. I even understand."

He looked down, opened his mouth but he did not know what to say. We stayed like this for a few moments.

"Thank you for having me, Francisuncle," I continued quietly, "But how long could we live together like this, both of us unmarried, before someone started some awful story about us?"

He looked at me sharply. Perhaps he had never understood how fully I appreciated the ways of our world.

"Your father would never forgive me if he knew that I let you go," he said finally. "To live alone, in a country that we do not know." He paused. "With people we don't know."

I had looked down, and then stared directly at him.

"But I have done that before, and no one was worried," I said quietly.

"Yes, but living alone in London is one thing..."

"I've made up my mind," I interrupted.

It hurt me to speak to him like that. I loved my Francisuncle. I was grateful that he had reached out. But he was out of his depth. Fifteen years had passed since I had last seen him in India: he was now in his mid-forties and I was an adult. He may have thought that he could assume the role of a father but he had neither the experience nor, ultimately, the volition. And I could not speak to him of an aching desire. Of a knowledge that I was going to cross a frontier, my life before, my life after.

And now, when this train journey ends, I will cross another frontier. When this train journey ends, my dream begins: I will lie on my bed, back in my childhood home. I will reach under my bed, pull out the sari and the jewellery that my mother and I have discussed. I will run my hands over the light silk as it covers my frame, hang the earrings in my ears, slip the bangles over my wrists. I will walk down the path from the house, see the Hindu temple ahead, turn to the right, to the church at the end. There will be people gathered, and faces smiling. I will attend my wedding.

I am once again going to entrust myself to a man whom I cannot claim to know. But I do know that my future husband has a good job, a home. He is an American. His father knew my father, his uncle knows my mother: he has been vetted. He is of the right faith, the correct background. While I have not met him in person, in our communications I have found him agreeable. We will, I am sure, go out for dinners, go to parties. Our courtship will be in reverse: we will already be married when we sit across from each other, a candle on the table, music in the background. No one will stare if they see us together, we will excite no interest. We are perfectly suited. And so, while my actions may seem foolhardy to some, I feel a composure. Not the near-unbearable aliveness I felt, those years ago, when I told Francisuncle I was leaving.

Of course he wrote a long letter back home. In it he blamed himself; he had been too laid-back. I was a good girl, but I was too trusting. He should have guided me more. I was young, naïve. If he ever voiced his suspicions that I had not travelled on my own, I do not know. By the time my mother wrote to me, in reply to my letter giving my family the address of the flat in Maputo, I was a different person. I had opened the door that I had never seen before, and entered the life that I had never imagined living.

My mother had written in English: I did not read Malayalam proficiently, and it was a language in which she could be caustic and authoritative. But her words were foreign to the person I had become. And her castigations that a daughter living and working alone in such a poor country, a god-forsaken place if there ever was one, was an embarrassment, made me bristle. She had reared up, awake now, after her years of slumber, demanding access to a maternal role. This was the first full-length letter she had ever written to me, the deepest interest she had ever shown me, and she had been driven to do so, not from concern, but from shame. I felt challenged, enraged.

But I was cowardly. I continued to write back regularly, detailing my job and some aspects of my daily life. It was often my grandfather who replied to my letters, my mother reverting to her usual two-line addendum. While I maintained a communication of sorts, I never wrote of Jafar. It was a gauntlet I was unwilling to throw down, fearing irreversible condemnation. I kept a space, nurtured a place that I could return to. Whether I always expected that I would indeed return, I am not sure.

*

I was nervous when we met at the bus station; Jafar had simply stroked my face and smiled, then busied himself with getting our bags stowed away. We got a bus to Mutare, and then flagged a taxi for the fifteen-minute drive to the border. We exchanged few words. At the border we passed through the customs shack, then walked across no-man's land. It was hot, and my bag felt heavy. I stumbled over a stone, his hand caught my elbow, steadied me. Then he slung my bag off my shoulder and onto his. He grinned, I smiled weakly back.

At the desk on the Mozambican side, he was practised, at home. "*Está conmigo*," he said in reply to the officer's queries. The man turned to look at me with curiosity, nodded, smiled. We walked out into the bright sunlight.

Since that day, I have filled endless application forms at immigration desks. My studies have taken me places where I have needed to attend countless interviews, comply with numerous regulations. Where my movements have been documented, stamped with official approval. My passport is filled with small multi-coloured plates, visas for every place I have been to, filling page after page of the small blue booklet. Indeed in the black holdall that has been my main piece of luggage the last week I have a folder bulging with documents: my birth certificate, my degree transcripts, my bank statements, letters, certified testimonials from my employers. I will need to show bundles of paperwork after the wedding, when I present myself at the embassy as a spouse. I've already had a preliminary interview, and a date has been fixed for my second, and hopefully final, interview. I must prove my worth, my intentions, my respectability. While at some point I must have had similar brushes with the authorities in Mozambique, to obtain and then extend my resident's permit, my memory of these is hazy. To my mind it seemed Jafar's words *está conmigo,* she is with me, were enough. I had crossed the border to his land and I was in his hands.

We got a lift with two German aid workers, tall heavy-set men in their late thirties, who had crossed the border with us. As we neared Chimoio, the land became greener. There were more trees, grass, the hills framing the landscape. The Germans stopped the car near the centre and we got out. It was a sleepy town, laid out in the Portuguese style; low buildings, a square with benches, several bakeries — holes in a wall through which frequent batches of fresh *pão* were snatched up by queuing regulars. His flat was above a general store. We stopped to get a tin of olive oil as he had decided that he would cook dinner, before mounting the stairs leading to the upper level. Out of the sunlight, it was cool. I shivered slightly.

His cousin, Naman, lived with him. His was the front bedroom facing the street. The living area was basic; television and small hi-fi, small plastic-topped dining table, fridge and sofa. Jafar's bedroom was large, looking out into the central courtyard. It was a lovely, bright, airy room with large windows at the back, cluttered but not untidy, an eclectic mix of furniture. I learned later that Marie had rarely stayed there. She had been given a more spacious flat, on the other side of town, all paid for, and it was there that they had set up home. While it was simply furnished, it had the luxuries of its own water supply and generator. They had a study there where she did her paperwork, a better-equipped kitchen, a more spacious living -room.

I was happy that I was not staying in their love-nest, and felt reassured that Jafar had kept his own space, even while living with her. I indulged myself with thoughts that maybe it was not all as I had imagined, that they had never really been very close. That they were together only through convenience and circumstance. Only later did I realise, when we lived in our flat in Maputo, that in that city he had no bolt-hole. When he left our home, he did not have his own separate space to return to. By then I envied Marie: at least she would have known where he was, a phone call away, or a quick walk across town. I was never offered that consolation.

I unpacked my bag. I had brought most of my belongings, but they were not many. I could hear Jafar in the living-room, catching up with Naman, and I hesitated to ask him where I could put my things. I opened the wardrobe. It was full, not only with clothes and shoes, but also more books. They were stacked in any fashion on the bottom of the wardrobe, as well as on one shelf. I looked at the titles; they were mostly in Portuguese, and a few in French. I could make out that some were manuals, most were novels. There was space on one shelf and so I put my small pile of clothes there and closed the door. I laid out my toiletries on the dressing-table and started brushing my hair. Jafar walked in and smiled.

"So you are ready? The room is OK?"

I smiled and nodded, turned to the mirror and continued brushing my hair, but with more self-consciousness. He came and sat on the bed behind me. When I finished, I turned around and saw that he had been watching. He reached forward and pulled me down into his lap. I felt small, enclosed by his body. His chest was against my shoulder, his arm circled my back, his other hand on my hip-bone. He moved his hand over my legs, then held my elbow, played with the necklace I was wearing. He was completely relaxed and there was a happy glint in his eye. But I must have looked nervous, because he chucked me under the chin, and his eyes were laughing.

"*Tranquila, filha.*"

I looked at him, and tried to smile back.

"Come," he said, pushing me off his knee, and standing up. "Come and meet Naman."

Chimoio was muggy, a slight drizzle continued well into the evening, all through the simple but delicious dinner that Jafar had made. After we had cleared up, Naman tactfully went out to meet some friends. It started raining, a soft rain, and the temperature dropped. I had brought a sarong, which I put around my shoulders, Jafar closed the windows. We sat on his sofa, side by side, holding hands. We didn't say much, I was tired after the day's events. We listened to the sound of rain. Later, we moved to the bedroom. We made love for the first time. He left the bedside lamp on against my protests. He was at first tender, a little tentative, then rough, demanding, with hands, tongue, limbs. We fell asleep entangled, the sheet thrown off. The rain had stopped and the night was humid. No air stirred except his breath fanning my neck.

*

I loved our simple life in Chimoio, our first days together. Everyday activities — boiling water in the morning for coffee or for having a wash or to clean the dishes, buying a loaf of bread in a long queue — took time, and set the pace for a leisured, patient existence. Naman tended to sleep in late, which made it easier for Jafar and I to get ready, taking turns in the bathroom. On the table in the morning there would be three places laid, three plates, three cups. Some fruit would be cut, and slices of bread would be laid out on a plate covered with a cloth. Carlos, Jafar's empregado, was a slight, very dark boy of about seventeen. His arms were long and lean, muscled because of the work he did every day. He relished his duties, and treated the small flat above the shops and its occupants, us, with deference.

Jafar growled at him when he found fault – not enough water in the large drum that served us all as there was no running water, no bread in the cupboard. "*Desculpe, patrão,*" Carlos would say. "*Desculpe, senhora*", to me. Although I was used to servants in the house, Ammamma had been like a member of the family, joining in discussions on what to cook, what to wear. I felt uncomfortable in Carlos' presence, sorry to be in a feudalistic position, but when I mentioned this to Jafar, he was dismissive.

"The boy has a job, and he does the things that we don't want to do. I don't want to wake up and go to the tap at the Red Cross every morning to get water." And he was right. Neither did I. But in that small flat, when privacy was at a premium, I felt that it was hard to avoid bumping into the quiet, gentle-mannered boy, performing an unenviable task.

We woke up to the sounds of Carlos clattering in the kitchen. I would pull on my kimono. I had bought it years ago from a South-East Asian stall in Notting Hill, and it was my favourite item of clothing. I felt it suited my new life in this exotic country more than the street market where I had bought it in London. It was made from soft cotton, red with a batik pattern of blue and green dragons. It fell to just above my knees, and had wide, flowing long sleeves. When I wore it that first morning in Chimoio, Jafar had murmured his approval. Walking up to me he had traced my body with his hands, and then smiling, had slowly undone the belt, opened the gown and pushed it back over my shoulders. After the first night spent together, he was, at once, completely uninhibited with his actions. Whenever we were alone, his hands went everywhere: he would slide them up and down my back, over my buttocks, up and down the inside of my legs. He would reach forward and stroke my collar-bones, my breasts. He brushed aside any bashfulness I displayed; his self-assurance was overwhelming.

Carlos would walk into the living-room when we were having breakfast, me in my kimono, Jafar, shirtless, in shorts. Jafar would issue a list of instructions for the day, to which Carlos would respond: "*Si, patrao.*" Carlos boiled water for my bath, and then poured it into a bucket in the bath-tub. Carlos took my clothes, although I refused to hand over my underwear, washed them outside, and hung them to dry. He always addressed me with the utmost courtesy.

Naman would emerge from his room later in the morning, smile widely when he saw me, and disappear into the bathroom. He and Jafar had an easy relationship. Both men devoured the newspaper each day at the breakfast table. Years of socialist policies meant that since independence people like Jafar and Naman, from unexceptional, lower-middle class families, had been offered a chance for education. As a result, they were literate and politicised, strong in their views, quick to criticise the politicos and local authorities. Handing over different sections, exchanging commentaries on the articles, and then turning together to the sport pages.

There were still tensions in the country, hanging over from the civil war, between the north and the south. As the north had a significant Muslim population, but held many supporters of RENAMO, the party in opposition, Muslims like Jafar and many in his circle were especially voluble in their castigations. They supported the party in power, FRELIMO, the party of their hero Samora Machel, who had died in a plane crash some years back. For them, the growing tendency to entwine religion with politics, the still nascent rise of Islamic extremists, jarred with the inclusiveness of the socialist dream: Catholics, Muslims, whites, blacks, and mixed-race *mulattos,* all Mozambicans, all working together for the nation.

I loved watching them. The sun streaming onto their bare shoulders and into the room, the table scattered with breakfast plates, coffee cups and the newspaper. They were, to me sitting on the opposite end of the table, two beautiful male specimens. They had a strong family resemblance with their high cheekbones and wide brows, but Naman's nose was aquiline, Jafar's wider. They were both tall, both broad-shouldered, naturally-muscled, both shirtless, both hairless, one dark-skinned (Jafar), the other a pale brown (Naman). When Jafar spoke to Naman his Portuguese was different: faster, more rhotic, more animated. I realised how he moderated his speech with me. Both Muslims, but with cigarettes in their hands, and beers later in the day, it was a languid Islam. They had both attended Koranic school as children, and could recite long stretches of Arabic, but no longer went to mosque. And from what I could gather, Naman shared the same success with women as Jafar.

The second morning after we had arrived, I found an old photo album in Jafar's bedroom, and was curious to look inside. Jafar had resisted at first. "They are so old," he said, taking it away from me. But that had made me insist, and so I lay on the bed in his room, and flicked through. Some photos were taken in his younger days at high school and college. There were shots of a younger, skinnier Jafar playing basketball, at the beach, at family gatherings. And then while some faces recurred, those of Rassul and Eduardo whom I would meet later, there were new faces. In among the commonplace settings – always a beach scene, a basketball court – there were several photos of him in the arms of a different girl on every page. They had their arms around him, they were sitting on his lap, he was dancing with them. I started to ask him who they were, one by one. "I think she was Anastasia. She was a friend of my cousin."

Then, "Jacinta. She and I belonged to the same youth group."

"Clara. That girl knew how to dance."

Then, with growing irritation, "Freda."

"Paula."

And then a small-boned, very dark girl with huge eyes, braided beads in her hair. "Gertrude." He hesitated, then, "She became pregnant, but then had an abortion".

"Oh gosh", I gulped involuntarily.

I peered at the photo. She must have been about twenty years old.

"We were too young", Jafar continued. "And her parents advised her."

"Oh."

"Then I left to study."

"Oh."

I felt hopelessly unworldly. Ridiculously naïve. He took the photo album away and put it back in the wardrobe. "Maybe *I* am too young," I said, and before I could stop myself, to my chagrin, my eyes flooded with tears. He started to laugh.

"No, no. You are not."

His laughter angered me, and I continued. "Or maybe you're too old for me."

That struck a nerve and he stopped laughing. "No, no," he said, lying down next to me and stroking my face. "You need someone like me. More mature, more experience." *Mais maduro, mais experiência.* I was shaken by the photo album, and regretted opening it. Until then, my thoughts had been crowded with Marie and Sandra. I realised that I had met Jafar many years into what was an active social life. The women in the album were all black, Moçambicanas, and I worried about my foreign-ness. Was I simply one of many conquests?

I was learning the ways of a country I had never been to before, and I was learning the ways of a man I hardly knew. Good practice, one would think, for the life awaiting me in a few days. But, at the same time, how utterly different. While, then, my actions were governed by what I was feeling, now they are governed by what I am not feeling. I do not feel displeasure with the man I am to marry, and I do not feel dissatisfied. The love I was feeling, that was making me so defenceless when

I was with Jafar, is absent. It might have added that delicious ache, but I suspect that it colours my perspective of those first days and months. It lends everything an extra glow, an added poignancy. I am more unblemished in these recollections than I really was, I am sure. I am more graceful, Jafar more winning, the tableau we make more touching. My expectations, now, are less airy, more banal. I hope that I will settle in, that I will be pleasing enough. And I hope that I will let myself start anew.

*

Their uncle Nelson and his friend Marcel came to visit a few days later, and with him, Jafar and Naman became even more passionate in their discussions of the country's affairs. Nelson was near forty, small and very black; Marcel of a similar age, a light-yellow colour and tall. They both spoke very good English, having studied in South Africa. While Naman and Jafar threw comments at each other, Nelson and Marcel would turn to me and offer some translations. They treated me with the same deference as Carlos and with the same easy acceptance as Naman. Nelson may have asked his nephew his intentions, but I had no knowledge of such a conversation. He loved practising his English with me; several times he would tease Jafar about his.

"After all that time studying in Zimbabwe, how many months, was it four or five? You still can't speak proper English."

Jafar would smile sheepishly, and then reach out and stroke my face. "When your teacher is this beautiful it is hard to concentrate." The men would laugh and look at me with interest. I would start to protest but they would quickly move on to the next discussion. I felt accepted, un-judged and appreciated but, like a small pet, they did not take me seriously. Too young, perhaps too decorative. I was self-conscious in their presence; I worried whether Naman heard anything of the love-making from our bedroom. If he did, he gave no sign. But the suddenness with which I found myself living in this very male environment unsettled me a little. What was clear was the understanding that Jafar needed a bed-mate, and I was his choice for now. It was inconceivable that the two of us could be in a platonic relationship. Despite being a conservative society, the country simmered with its fascination with heterosexuality: men and women were a recipe for consolation, a throw-back to urgent, war-filled times when people seized the opportunity for comfort before it could disappear.

While they talked the day's newspaper over, I sat with the paper from the day before, and my Portuguese-English dictionary. I was determined to learn and before long I was confident enough to walk downstairs to the small grocery store to buy provisions. The small town square was a gathering place for older men, wearing hats of different sizes and shapes, to sit. They occupied the benches, read the newspapers, chatted. But whenever we walked by, they would break off their conversation, and greet us. "*Bom dia, Tio*", Jafar would say. I would murmur a greeting, to which they would nod their heads, "*Bom dia, Senhora.*"

Often, Jafar would abruptly announce that he had something to do, leaving me with Naman. I would try to ask when he would return, but by then he was walking swiftly away, lighting up a cigarette. Naman was always mild-mannered, courteous, and we would walk chatting in Portuguese. Our conversations were naturally limited by my lack of fluency in the language, but he was an easy companion. Occasionally he would stop and talk with someone. He would introduce me; she is Jafar's woman, *a mulher de Jafar*. The same word could be used for 'wife' and 'woman'; there was an assumption that the woman you were with was your wife, but that it could be a temporary position.

At Nelson's insistence we went one night to his house, a large bungalow on the outskirts of the town. His wife, Jafar's aunt, was plump, light-skinned, with a lively intelligent face. She ushered me into the house, and when I followed her into the kitchen she let me help finish cooking the meal. Their youngest daughter still lived with them; the other daughter was studying in South Africa. Matilda was eleven, with braided hair, and long limbs, wearing t-shirt and shorts. She adored Jafar, and constantly interrupted her father's conversation. "Tio Jafar, Tio Jafar." Jafar was completely at ease with her, pulled her on his knee, helped her fix her tape-player. We ate beans and rice, and had a custard pudding. It was a delightfully relaxed, welcoming evening. I felt reassured to see Jafar in this cosy, domestic environment, happy and engaged. And I liked being there with him: I felt that we were establishing ourselves as a couple and that feeling pleased me. When we left, Jafar said we would walk home. The night was cool and clear. He lit a cigarette and the tip glowed in the dark.

"Nelson said he could give us a lift to Beira in a few days, and we can fly there to Maputo, so I think that should be when we leave." After we had walked a little more, he continued "I will miss this place."

I too was sorry that we had to leave Chimoio, just when we were settling. And not least because Jafar seemed unsure of the move himself.

"I am from there, a *Maputense,* but I like it here," he said, in reply to my questions. "It's a nice city, but it can swallow you up with its people. Its heat, its dirt."

"Do we have to go?"

"It's for a job," he sighed. "I think I will get a job there more probably than here."

A week later, leaving the flat, carrying my holdall, I saw Jafar reluctantly turn back and give the whole place a last look. Carlos stared at the ground as we said our goodbyes. Jafar was gruff, I tried to shake the boy's hand.

"*Obrigada*, Carlos," I said.

"*Adeus*, *Senhora*," he replied.

Naman accompanied us to Nelson's house. Nelson was already waiting for us outside. Naman kissed me goodbye and helped me stow my holdall by my feet. Jafar sat up front, next to Nelson. Driving away, I glanced in the rear-view mirror and saw Naman waving until we were out of sight. I was alone in the backseat, and I was glad of the chance to be alone with my thoughts. In the front Nelson and Jafar were talking. I watched them a while and then looked out of the window.

I felt apprehensive about going to Maputo. Chimoio had not been very far away from my previous life, and the comforts offered by Francisuncle. Travelling hundreds of miles away now to the capital seemed a much bigger step. And what did I know of Jafar? I was still unnerved by the stories in the photo album, still overwhelmed by his physical desire and demands, still getting used to his manners and ways. For him it was a given that I accompany him, but did he really understand the responsibility he was assuming? I realised that I did indeed want him to look after me, but also realised that he was probably unaware of this. He did not turn around more than once on the three-hour drive to Beira, to ask me if I was all right. He was engrossed in conversation with Nelson, and I wondered what on earth they could be discussing at such all-consuming length. By then I was taking everything I saw from my window as a bad omen. The burned-out cars, remnants from the war, the changing landscape, becoming greener and more tropical, but also with an increasing number of poorer mud-houses, and disused churches. All these images accentuated my anxiety that I was leaving my safety-net behind.

We arrived at Beira, and Nelson dropped us at a house in the compound of the World Food Programme. Jafar had phoned ahead, and had arranged that we have lunch with some old friends before heading to the airport for our flight south. I was surprised when the couple greeted Jafar in French: Collette, it turned out, was an old friend of Marie. Their house was pleasantly cool after the hot drive, furnished elegantly with local textiles and prints. They were charming and welcoming. But as I was leaving the living-room to wash up after the journey, I heard Collette turn to Jafar.

"*Mais, qu'est-ce que tu fais avec cette jeune fille?*"

"*Elle parle bien le français...*"

Collette looked at me quickly, embarrassed, but I did not say anything.

When I returned, they had obviously had a potted history of the relationship, because all three turned and watched me as I sat down. Jafar was looking sullen, Collette was flushed red. I remembered Marie, and her statuesque frame, her full mouth, and her strong, intelligent face. I felt, again, how slender I was, how young, how shabbily-dressed. I was miserable, quiet during the meal. Collette's husband, a heavy-set man in his early-forties, was gentle and sweet, topping up my drink, and serving me seconds. By then Collette and Jafar had recovered, and laughed and chatted like the old friends they were.

They drove us to the airport and we kissed our goodbyes. I did not talk while we checked in, walked our way through security and on to the departure gates. In the departure lounge we sat near the windows. The runway was a dust-coloured strip. There was as yet no aeroplane in sight.

"*Estás boa*?" he asked quietly.

I shrugged.

He sighed. "It was a mistake, maybe, to see Collette."

I looked at him. He was watching me.

"I just feel like…" I faltered.

"You are scared?" He fingered the sleeve of my top.

I nodded. "I feel like maybe you don't really need me to be here."

He was quiet.

"It's true," he said finally. "I don't need you to come with me. And I am selfish, bringing you with me when I have no job yet. Everything is new for you."

I watched his fingers on my sleeve. His hands were large, his nails a pale pink, his fingers dark. He slipped his hand inside so that it now closed around my upper arm. His grip was warm.

"But I want you. I know that I want you."

I held his eyes for a long time. The sounds in the airport faded away, and it was just him and me. Facing each other in a dusty, dingy departure lounge. We were holding each other's gaze, our bags around our feet, our voices stilled. On our way down to the city on the white sands of the Indian Ocean, Maputo.

6

My parents' wedding had taken place in a simple white church in the hills. Sweeping views of endless coconut trees before them; behind them the hills leading to the Western Ghats where my grandfather Uppappan, my father's father, owned a rubber estate. By all accounts, Uppappan was a hard man, embittered by what he saw as a constant struggle to make money; shackled, he felt, to a plain and uneducated woman, my grandmother Amma. This bitterness spilled into his treatment of his nine children and my father admitted that he had grown up in an environment that lacked any soft edges, any compromises. The family lived in the most beautiful part of Kerala: hills covered with swaying coconut trees, interspersed with paddy fields, red earth contrasting with the green, green, green. But their lives were hard, not only because they were a simple, rural family; also because Uppappan was a tyrant. Of the five girls in the family, he obliged four to join the convent, through his miserliness, allowing marriage only for the youngest, the chosen dowry-daughter.

My oldest uncle never forgave my father and my youngest uncle, the baby of the family, Francis, for escaping the back-breaking work of the plantation by embracing an education. The sisters all regarded each other with envy: one was in a better convent, one had only gone to a convent at age twenty, and one was married, albeit to an insipid, plaintive husband. My exhausted grandmother could muster no interest in her grandchildren, and spent her days sitting on the verandah chewing paan. Only Francis, and news of Francis, could elicit any animation or feeling from her. Uppappan died before I was born, but he left behind the legacy of a family divided by unequal treatment and uneven fate. This legacy had seeped into my parents' marriage; they could not escape the divisive tentacles of my father's family.

Growing up in my grandfather's house in Alleppey, I had watched as year by year my mother put out more photos of my father. As if each year there was a little more forgiveness and a greater effort to give us insights into our parents. The first photo was their official wedding portrait. They both stare ahead, not to the camera but to a distant point to their right, their future. My mother is large-eyed, feminine, her hair softly curling around her youthful cheeks. My father, beside her, is grave. They could not know as the shutter clicked that they would be embarking on a union which, while producing three healthy children, would cause them much heartache and unhappiness.

More photos emerged the following year of my mother, hair freshly washed, in a lungi and blouse, standing in the sunshine. Obviously my father had been captured by her charms, had wanted to catch the moment. His beautiful young wife. Then photos of my mother in silk saris, a chubby youngster, ordained with kohl and puttu, on her lap. They had found an ease with each other, and had settled into a domestic cosiness. By then my father had become extraordinarily successful, exporting small electrical goods – hair-dryers, radio-alarm clocks – in the beginning to Sri Lanka, and later to Malaysia and Singapore. He had bought my mother a beautiful house in Irinjalakuda and they were enjoying a comfortably wealthy life.

One year my mother unveiled a family portrait, taken a few months after my younger brother was born. My father stands, his hand resting on my mother's shoulder. She is seated on a high stool, the folds of her sari falling in pleasing pleats to the floor, her feet in high-heeled sandals. My older brother is standing next to her, her rock, her right hand. I stand in front of him, in a short frilly dress, my body slightly turned towards her, a small fist on her lap. And also on her lap, swaddled in a white blanket, my baby brother. A happy, beautiful, family. But in fact my parents by then were no longer happy.

What had they fought about? As youngsters we caught only snatches: my mother felt slighted, my grandmother had made hurtful comments about her, my aunts did not like her but found her proud. The fights would then move on to the money that my father was supplying his family: for my errant cousin to study in Bangalore away from the scandals he was causing in the toddy bars, for my uncle to renovate his house after allowing it to half-decay through neglect, for my married aunt's husband to travel to North India for a business deal.

"But we can afford it!" my father would shout. "I am still able to look after my own children and give you a good life!"

My mother had not believed him. The rows continued and their anger grew.

What would have changed if I had obediently accompanied my mother at her request, all those years ago? My parents would have separated, perhaps divorced. Would my father still have died? I imagine the future laid out as a board-game. You roll a die. You take one step, you skip one. Do you still reach the same ending? In some ways, I feel that I *have* reached the same ending. For what awaits me when the train pulls into the station had always been planned. A few different skips and jumps, but the die has been rolled, and a decision has been made.

I am here on the train with my life's worth of belongings: and they are few. Some weeks before setting off I had a cull of my clothes. Most will be inappropriate for Alleppey — too threadbare, too short, too sleeveless. I know my aunt will mutter unhappily if I were to wear my cut-off shorts, my sleeveless vests. I have acquired an ease with exposing my limbs to the world that will remain unknown to my elders. Only one dress remains, my jeans which I have worn nearly every day in the last week, a few tops. I will have to buy new outfits: appropriate for the climate, appropriate for the eyes and sensibilities of my husband-to-be. I can discard clothes fairly easily: it was more heart-wrenching to leave some of my books behind. But most were dog-eared, with broken spines from being passed around friends, read and then re-read. I have a few ornaments, some souvenirs, but I am travelling with only one small suitcase, not even nearly full, and a hold-all. In many ways, I have as many possessions now as I did those years back when I arrived in Maputo with Jafar.

Over the past few days I have moved closer to my new life incrementally. In the last weeks I have dawdled around the country: spending more than a week in Delhi after arriving, then flying to Chennai. I took a bus to Pondicherry, and would have stayed longer had I not been summoned home. In the same way, those years ago, I moved incrementally to our life in Maputo: the bus to the border, the car to Beira, the flight south. Outside tonight it is black, dark, and while I cannot see the landscape I know it well, the shadowy shapes of the villages and towns. Then, I was moving through the unknown to the unknown, my unsettledness tempered by the underlying headiness I felt at being with Jafar.

We had arrived in the middle of the rains, the wet season. For nearly three months of the year torrid heat descends onto the city. By seven in the morning the air is heavy with humidity. Clouds gather in the sky, there is a torrential downpour of warm rain, then the heat continues. The streets remain awash with water for hours after — a drainage system is sadly lacking. The vendors reappear, the heavy sun breaks through. Shops and offices close for a long *sesta,* from midday, when the streets grow quieter, a lull in the day. The hot, humid weather, the pattern of life, was profoundly familiar to me. It had been years since I had lived with the enveloping warmth, the thickness of the air. It was the weather of my childhood and it was disorientating.

I was a child again but living the life of a woman. The fans that we used reminded me of hot Alleppey afternoons after school, but they now cooled our bodies. Not one but two, entwined, perspiring against each other. And I have felt that same disorientation time and time again, on my travels. With a sea breeze, the sound of waves, a heavy night, comes a blurring of time. Even as I lie on my sleeping bunk in this hot train, the sweat gathering on my chest, the night flashing past, I clutch at snapshots. My girlhood games, my girlish body, lying in his arms.

*

We started our life together, living in our flat above Avenida Eduardo Mondlane, settling into the city. Jafar picked up with old friends and showed me the markets, the smaller stores. Carrying my money like the other women tucked into the waistband of my skirt, bargaining in my increasingly confident Portuguese, the bag of purchases swinging against my side, I felt like a citizen of the city. I could pass for a Moçambicana as there was a smallish community of Indian and Pakistani immigrants, who owned most of the shops in the centre, traders who had crossed over half a century ago. They were Mozambican but they were disliked. It was towards them that the term "*monye*", which had been used to great comic effect in the play in the Teatro Avenida, was directed. A disparaging, insulting word. A *monye* was very rich but never invested in the country, people complained. He never went to the bars and restaurants that most locals went to. Most of them were Muslim, but even at the mosque they rarely mixed with others. The judgement was often harsh, sometimes justified, sometimes not. I was treated differently, but only when it became clear that I was a foreigner. The way I lived, using chapas, walking alongside Jafar, shopping at the markets, singled me out as someone who participated rather than directed, and it was appreciated. The irony was that in India I had led a sheltered life that kept me removed from the very poor, kept me aloof from the less salubrious areas.

I found the city captivating but it was at that time still recovering from the war. Not every zone had running water, or even electricity for parts of the day. Without bookshops, a cinema, shopping malls, without many amenities that absorbed your time, the residents of Maputo found their entertainment in other ways. Just before I left, a cinema opened near the Marginal; shopping malls now abound. But in those days, most afternoons, people poured into the sports centres of the colleges to watch the basketball teams practising, a carnival-like event. I met Eduardo for the first time at an evening game. He was tall like Jafar, lean, dark-skinned. He enquired politely after my first impressions of Maputo, complimented me on my efforts with Portuguese. We walked together to the crowded sports centre and found seats. The men put me between them and shouted their comments to each other over my head. Those first months, Eduardo would often call round. He must have missed Jafar's company when he had moved away. It had been many years since they had been high-school friends and shared youthful adventures, but they were close. Jafar often laughed at what he said: I could see that Eduardo made pithy observations that I could not always understand.

As the sun set and the evening breeze started to blow, the tree-lined avenues of the city and the Marginal were filled by people on a *passeio:* the women wearing their hair in their best styles to be admired by groups of young men, smoking cigarettes, a beer in their hands. Taking in the fresh air, chatting to friends and neighbours.

Hours would be whiled away until night-time, when the bars would become crammed, loud zouk music playing, people dancing wherever they could find room. In the early months of living together, Jafar and I spent countless evenings dancing in the bars of the Feira Popular. By then I was more confident and adept with the tempos, and Jafar was amused by how much I enjoyed myself. Whereas, normally, after the first few dances he would want to sit the rest of the evening out, drinking and smoking, leaving me to accept invitations to dance with other men, one evening we barely sat down. He stayed with me on the floor and we danced nearly the whole evening. "It's your day," he said, stroking my cheek, when I had queried his indulgence. I had no idea what he meant, so he had had to explain that we were dancing in this bar, and it was more crowded than normal, because it was International Women's Day. I had not known the date, nor had I ever before thought of its significance. While I had grown up in a country where large numbers of women still suffered from imbalances in equality, and had to succumb to the decisions made by the men in their lives, I had been raised with relatively little exposure to unfairness. That night hearing his words, I had felt, as I often did when I was with Jafar, that his perspective of the world and its machinations, was far fuller than my own trivial concerns. That despite being less schooled than I, he held more knowledge and secrets that he did not always share.

We would spend most afternoons, the two of us alone, on the balcony of the flat. If there was washing hanging from the line we had strung up, it would rise and fall with the wind, throwing shadows, and offering us a screen behind which we sat, unnoticed by the street below. We sat side by side, in our shady hide-out, I on the left, on a huge cushion. Jafar invariably would pull out a cigarette to smoke. I would be in a sarong, or shorts, vest; he would be shirtless. His left hand would lie across my legs and he would slide it up and down as we talked, or rest it curved around my thigh. Those were, I can see now, our most intimate moments. He told me more of his family, a sprawling family not unlike that of my father's. But untidier, more frayed. He had eight siblings, his father and two brothers were dead; one of his sisters had become a born-again Christian; his other sister was prolific in childbirth, eight children by different men, pregnant again; his lazy younger brother; his embittered mother. When I met her the first time, she had chastised him roundly in Ronga for being with a foreign woman again, and even worse, a *monye*. I had met them all over the course of the last few months, and unlike Jafar, they were all pale-skinned, "café com leite". There was an Arab grandparent, possibly a Portuguese in the lineage, which accounted for their appearance. Jafar took after his father, dark-skinned. I had seen a photograph of him: a serious-looking man, same wide forehead and high cheekbones, but slighter, wearing a suit and a tie, a panama hat in his hand.

On those afternoons, in a mixture of Portuguese and English, we shared our histories. He told me how he'd had his first affair in his teens; he was fourteen, she was his neighbour, a bored thirty-seven-year-old housewife. He told me how he had left home at seventeen and gone up north to Chimoio, returning only intermittently to Maputo. How he used to practise dancing with a broomstick before going out to the local barracas, how life had been during the civil war. How he had met a Dutch woman who had loved him, and had wanted to pay for him to study at a university in Holland, but how he had refused, repelled by what he saw as her attempts to own him. How he had started working as a *logistique*, and his four-year relationship with Marie. How he had spent his twenties in and out of relationships and sexual encounters but how he had always been careful because AIDS scared him. How in his thirties all he was sure about was that he wanted me.

When I spoke of my family, my childhood, he would listen. If I were speaking in Portuguese he would correct me patiently, his left hand gently tracing the line of my leg, holding my ankle briefly, stroking my inner thigh. When he turned his face to kiss my ear and then my mouth, I knew it was time. We always made love in the afternoon. It suited my work-hours; I had found a job, teaching most evenings at the university. Sometimes we took a shower together, and Jafar would soap me, meticulously, as if I were a child. The water from the shower head, always cold, would be beating down on my face. I would be gasping for breath, his hands would be running over my body. I felt completely helpless and in his power. He would towel me dry and we would move to the bed. It always started gently, and then pleasure mixed with pain. Later, it would only be pain.

I would change into my work clothes, my hair still damp, my mouth and body bruised. He would lounge on the bed watching me, reading the newspaper absently, then stand up when I was ready and we would leave the flat together. What he did after we parted downstairs for the evening I do not know. When he returned to the flat, usually close to midnight, I would be tired, ready to go to sleep. Sometimes he would have eaten already, sometimes he would be comfortably drunk, sometimes more so. He would want to make love again, and if I were not acquiescent he would sulk while I got into bed. Then as we assumed our sleeping position, my bottom against his groin, he would lock me against his chest. He would always fall asleep before me.

When I think back to those first months it is always with a sense that I am an onlooker, watching the two lovers, their affair. We were, for a moment in time, oblivious to the rest of the world and untouched by it. We had not yet allowed any intrusions, we were still hopeful. Whether I believed then that that was my future, that I would live the rest of my days in that flat, follow the same routine, have Jafar sleeping in my bed next to me, night after night, I cannot honestly remember. I can remember the happiness I felt, the tingling in my body, the sheer excitement. But I remember nothing further.

*

One Friday as we went downstairs, my hair still wet from the shower, he seemed perfunctory in his responses. He had been moody all day and I had an inkling of what he was thinking. Since his return to Maputo he had remained without steady work. He was going to meet someone later in the afternoon from an NGO who had land to work in Chokwe, a verdant part of the country, inland, not very far from Maputo, and who needed someone to help him set up a community centre. He would meet the owner in Matola, a suburb of the city, but he said he would be home before me. He had had many such meetings, and very few had materialised into a job. While in the years since the civil war had ended he had had good contracts working for Médecins Sans Frontières, they were now leaving Mozambique. And with their departure, his resource of contacts was dwindling. Maputo was full of NGOs and UN offices: it was bursting with opportunity. But often a job would be given to someone someone knew, and often the post would be filled as soon as it was advertised.

I, on the other hand, had found my job at the university relatively easily. Now I was meeting new people, establishing myself professionally, my portfolio was growing. I had appointments to keep, meetings to attend, classes to deliver. Jafar must have felt that in some way the city was being kinder to me than it was to him. Whereas I loved Maputo and its care-worn charm, he missed Chimoio, its gentler climate, and his flat, which he owned, unlike the flat we shared. He teased me, did I not see the dirt and chaos? I did, but I also loved the art-deco architecture, reminders that once Maputo was considered more beautiful than Lisbon. I loved the wide, tree-lined avenues, the big hotels on the cliffs, the markets. And then along the sea, the promenade made with white-coloured stone.

When I came home that night, climbing four flights of stairs, as the lift was permanently out-of-order, panting as I opened the door, the flat was still in darkness. Jafar was not back, and even after I had had a shower and something to eat, there was no sign of him. The telephone remained silent. Dead-tired, I put myself to bed, frustrated that he had not called, prepared for the telephone to ring at some ungodly hour to explain his absence.

I woke up the next morning, half-expecting to find him lying next to me, having let himself in at some time in the early hours of the morning. But I was alone in the bed, the clock read eight o'clock. Downstairs there was already banging and clanging from the hardware store on the ground floor of the *predio*. My frustration and irritation had now turned to anxiety. I searched back in my head to our brief conversation. I didn't know whom exactly he was with, how he was travelling. The roads were notoriously pot-holed, land-mined: reminders of the torrential seasonal rain and the war. I had no contact number. By midday, having cleaned the flat and done some grocery shopping, I was nearly frantic. Visions of car wrecks, hijackings, land-mines, left me panicking. With still no word from him, I pulled on a pair of jeans and made my way to Rassul's.

Rassul was the wife of Jafar's cousin Linio. She was beautiful with a sharp tongue and a wicked sense of humour. She and Jafar had known each other since high-school; she was one of his best friends. Despite the vast difference in our lifestyles – she married at nineteen, and had three children in rapid succession – we got on very well. She had seen Jafar through a procession of attachments. I never asked her about them and I never knew if she regarded me as just the latest adornment. They lived in a flat a twenty-minute walk away, homey and cluttered. Always full of people, her daughter Aida constantly running to the bakery to bring back a bag of fresh bread. Rassul made cakes to order and whenever I visited she was either beating, mixing or icing – lemon sponges, rich fruit or marble cakes were her forte. When I got to her flat, she was sitting at the little dining table.

She had guests, a couple I had never seen before. She smiled her welcome, "*Tudo bem?*"

Without warning my eyes filled with tears. "*Rassul, estou tão preocupada...*"

I was ashamed, embarrassed of breaking down in front of an audience. The tears kept flowing, my cheeks were wet, my eyes blinded, I had to stifle my sobs. Rassul led me to the children's room. The three of them slept together, the boys in bunk beds and the girl in her own bed covered with a light-pink blanket. Spluttering, I explained my worries. Could he have been in a car accident? Should I ring the police? If we hadn't arranged to meet back at the flat I wouldn't have expected him to return the same day. I would have assumed he would stay over in Matola, even gone to Chokwe, but why would he not return? The intensity of my feelings, of my fear of his loss scared me. I was shaking as I spoke.

She sat quietly next to me, took my hand, and then said, "You are young, beautiful – find someone else. Jafar is a snake." She chuckled at my expression. She stood up and started folding some of the clothes the boys had left lying around. Three children sharing a small bedroom, running water in the flat for only four hours of the day, and an incessant flow of visitors to be fed and watered, but Rassul seemed the happiest of people. My heart hurt, and I saw myself with my selfish problem in her eyes as being an extraordinarily privileged, spoiled little girl.

"Oh, he is a good friend", she continued. "Good company, but a girl like you is too good for him. He is a typical Mozambican man. They are all the same, blacks, whites, mulattos. To them, love is the bed. *O amor é a cama*. They think it's enough to keep a woman happy."

Then she patted my hand, smiled her wide gorgeous smile and said, "Believe me, he is all right. He probably drank too much, stayed somewhere then forgot to phone. Don't worry."

There was some truth in Rassul's words, I knew, but at the same time I resisted: there's much more to him, I wanted to say. His tenderness, all that he knows. He was not a man who flaunted, like I had seen countless men, old and young, black and white, flaunt the young girls — some infatuated, some paid for — who clung to them. Jafar, in contrast, always behaved with restraint in public. What we did in our own privacy was for us, alone, to know. I was only forming these thoughts in my mind, these defences. I could not express myself and so Rassul continued unheeded.

For the rest of the day she wouldn't let me leave. Linio arrived home, greeted me as always with affection. Rassul relayed the story. I suspect everyone was enjoying this display of young love. The couple who were visiting knew Jafar from long ago. They sighed, shook their heads. By the time Linio finally dropped me home I had been plied with wine and food and I was exhausted. The flat was empty. It was a day later when Jafar came back.

Long after he had left, I would spend hours on the balcony, leaning against the railings. I would scour the street below, hoping to catch a glimpse of him. Eduardo lived further west along the same road and he often gave Jafar a lift on the back seat of his motorbike. I kept the door to the bedroom ajar with a chair so that I could hear the telephone if it rang. Maybe he would call to say that he was coming to see me, maybe he would show up unannounced. For in my mind, it would be on the balcony that I told him what I still have not told him, about that dark knot inside me. My words were rehearsed but were never said. I still have them memorised; whether they would roll off my tongue if I were standing in front of him, I don't know.

But those days in Maputo, I expected an encounter on our private stage: our balcony with its iron railings, unflattering beige-tiled floor. The washing line carrying bed sheets blowing in the wind: our curtain. I would see him below on the streets and he would look up as he passed our *predio*. He would see me, relent, and turn into the entrance. After a few moments I would hear him enter the flat and he would come to stand behind me, his arms pulling me close. I would speak, he would listen; our bodies forgiving, consoling. We would stay on the balcony, the breeze rustling our clothes, until night fell and hid the dirt of the city below us.

Before I left, I gave the huge cushion we used to sit on to my empragada, Hortensia, who came two mornings a week to wash clothes and polish floors. It was lumpy, a colour I didn't like and had gathered a lot of dust being out on the balcony.

7

I will have to get used to seasons again. To leaves turning colour and falling, covering the ground. To bare branches and knee-deep snow. To the promise of spring and then long, light-filled summer days. As a child, it was enough to know that it was the time for the rains or not. My days did not alter much, at least I do not remember them doing so, through the year. And the last few years I have lived as close to the equator as when I was a child. But I have noticed more. The time of the year when there are more mosquitoes, when the nights have less clamminess. The months when the clouds gather but no rain falls. Soon, however, I will be living with distinct chapters in the year: the time for wools, the time for sunglasses. I will enjoy it, I tell myself. I will gather memories, punctuated by the colour of the flowers, the smell of the grass or bonfires.

I gathered memories in Maputo too, defined by its seasons. Not four seasons of equal length, but less tidy; recognisable but less dramatic. The time for the rains, the time before the rains. The month of winds, the month of dust-storms, and the few months in the middle of the year when the weather was perfect: cool and crisp in the mornings and evenings, sunny and warm during the day.

In those months I walked to work. It wasn't a long walk. It took about twenty-five minutes if I took long strides, but it was mostly uphill. I had tried walking a few times in the hotter weather, arriving at work covered in perspiration, panting, dishevelled. But in June and July I enjoyed the walk early in the morning. I would take a chapa back home for lunch and then back to work, and walk home again in the evening.

Once I fell over on the street just outside a bar. There were half a dozen men sitting outside, beers and cigarettes in their hands. I was coming home, and had been shopping, carrying a bag in each hand. I had stepped on an uneven set of pavement stones, and fell forwards in an untidy heap. I had expected shouts of laughter, some comments; I had flashed a good deal of underwear in the process. Instead, two men had left their seats and their drinks and had crossed the road to where I lay, still a bit shell-shocked. They had picked me up, dusted me off, collected all my shopping, picking up errant apples and onions. Then they had asked me if I was all right, wished me a good day. They were the rule, not the exception, in Maputo. Old-fashioned courtesy and chivalry existed alongside the stereotype of the hard-drinking, womanising male. The barracas and bars in the city were full of such men, of all ages and varying marital states, lured by the drink, the music and the putas. These were usually young, lithe, uneducated, alluring and relatively cheap. But a lot of the men were foreigners; these haunts were not for the sole use of locals. The girls themselves preferred a rich expatriate who would pay more and probably visit more frequently.

By the end of July the cooler weather is over, and the Maputo winds pick up in August. Swirls of dust, especially in the early evening, engulf you, filling your mouth with sand if you are not quick enough to turn your back on them. The street vendors cover their heads and wares with scarves until the mini-tornados rush by. The air is dry. Everyone waits for the rains to begin. Before that release, however, there are months of intense humidity and heat. Power cuts. And without fail the water pump in our building would break down.

*

Jafar's absences grew more and more frequent, with no rhythm, no regularity that I could discern. For information on his whereabouts, I relied on a set of contact numbers for those of his friends and family whom I knew. If there was no answer, I had no idea if the telephone was ringing in an empty flat, or if my call was being ignored. In the early days, I went to Eduardo's flat twice, looking for Jafar. The first time, no one seemed to be in. After I had stood outside for some time, contemplating my next move, the upstairs neighbour, her hair in a net, screeched, "*Não está*!", as if she were offended by my uncertainty. The second time, Eduardo answered the door. It was the middle of the afternoon, but I had got him out of bed. I could hear a woman's voice behind him, he was not alone. He looked surprised to see me, replied softly: no, he had not seen him. No, he was not sure where he was, but he would be back soon. There was, by then, a slight smile on Eduardo's lips: my attempts at nonchalance did not fool him. My cheeks were burning when I left.

I would not know if Jafar were alive or dead for days on end, and then late at night he would slip into bed, his hands reaching for me. And I would protest, but never for very long. Inside I ached for more of him, outside I tried to maintain a façade. I wanted to present myself as a worldly adult, not the half-formed girl-woman that I secretly knew I was. I feared that he would find my insecurities trivial, my complaints demanding, needy. For my life in Maputo was not unrelenting hardship. I had made friends, other foreigners who worked for NGOs and aid agencies. Some were exiles, like Pablo, a Cuban nurse at a private clinic, with whom I often went for drives along Maputo Bay. At weekends I went to screenings and plays at the Centro Cultural Franco-Mozambicano. I had a social life that did not involve Jafar, which I had cultivated without him. My friends each had their own opinion about our relationship, a proprietary interest in my welfare. But what did they really know? They lived expatriate lives, with the securities that working for foreign organisations, or living in community groups offered.

When Jafar was not around I craved him. I wanted to do all the things I believed normal couples did. I wanted someone to walk hand-in-hand with, someone to wake up with and plan the day with. I wanted, God forbid, a *boyfriend*: I was not sure what he wanted. As my worries grew, I learned that he was seeing Adelaide, an old flame from the days before Marie. She owned a flat in Alto Mae where she lived with her ten-year-old daughter. Her best friend was Eduardo's current woman. Jafar's father had known her father. She had impeccable credentials: she was a Moçambicana, a Maputensa. I trusted his fidelity, but it hurt to hear of her. As I had always known, I lacked something. I was ethereal to him; I had neither a child nor an ex-husband. I was not a real woman, but a plaything.

I turn thirty in a few months and I am no longer that young twenty-something who feared that her concerns would be misconstrued. I am not that girl any more. I am heading towards my future and I see myself embracing another city, a bigger and bolder city, and another way of life. New conversations, new alliances await me. I see myself joining a family and settling into my sobriquets: wife, aunt, sister, sister-in-law, daughter. Some of these new, some neglected. I see all these things, and, further, the comfort of a routine, a lack of surprises. I hope to look at a clock and think: he will be home soon. I may look at the calendar and think: it is my mother-in-law's birthday on Wednesday. I will be content with normality, calm.

I did not have calm those days in Maputo. My mind was in torment, at not knowing where he went and what he did. I yearned for him, for the tenderness of our first months. One night, when the news of Adelaide was still fermenting inside me, the phone rang twice. Each time I hoped it would be Jafar. Instead, both calls were from Jules, a Frenchman who worked for an NGO operating from Maputo. I had met him a couple of times and I suspected that he liked me. He flushed red in my presence and was generous with his compliments. He had travelled to India before university and he liked to talk to me about his experiences. At times, he was brusque with Jafar, who brushed me off when I wondered if Jules was being rude. "These things happen when men are jealous of you." He would chuck me under the chin, and grin widely. I would pretend to be annoyed, but secretly my heart would soar with pleasure.

On the phone that night Jules asked me how I was and we exchanged a few words. Then he talked of a job, a short contract for three months, something I knew would be of interest to Jafar: an appointment would be made in the next few days. It was with some annoyance that I replied that I didn't know where Jafar was, and I didn't know when he would be back. Jules stayed on the phone longer than he needed to and I was tempted to invite him round: I was lonely and I would have liked the company. Perhaps I had visions of Jafar returning, to find us chatting and laughing, a bottle of wine on the table. He had Adelaide; I had Jules. When Jules called again two hours later, Jafar had still not made an appearance.

When I heard the key in the door, and Jafar came in, I was lying on the sofa, a book in my hand. He came through, kissed me, "*'Tas boa... não dormes?*", moved my legs so that he could sit next to me, started to stroke my thigh. For a moment I did not respond, and then the question came out before I could stop it, and hung between us.

"Where have you been?"

It was beginning and in fact from then it never stopped. The pretence fell away, he could see then, and from then on, the real me. Scared and overwhelmed.

His eyes clouded over.

"Out."

"Out where?"

I could feel rage welling up, and I gripped the book in my hands to stop them from shaking.

"Out *where*?" he repeated. His hand moved up towards his breast pocket, reaching for his cigarettes. I knocked it away furiously.

"Tell me!"

He looked at my hand and raised his eyebrows, reached again for a cigarette.

"Don't smoke, you know I don't like the smell of smoke in the house."

My voice sounded shrill, even to my ears. I didn't want to sound like that, I wanted to stay calm. He made a disgusted sound and started to get up off the sofa.

I held onto his arm.

"No", I said, and I forced my voice to keep steady. "No. Stay. Please."

And so I asked questions and he answered them. Yes, he was seeing Adelaide. Yes, she knew about me. No, he had not re-ignited their old relationship. She had a television in her flat; he could watch the football at her house. The Olympics were on and Nigeria was doing well. He was showing solidarity with an African team. I shook my head, appalled. He was being disingenuous: I refused to believe that the reason for those days and nights when I never saw him could be so mundane, so derisory. I wanted to challenge him, to show my scorn: "Is that what you want? Should I buy you a television?"

But those words would have revealed what, in thinking them, I had only just realised and what, for Jafar, was already patent: it was I who had the financial means to buy a television, not he. It was not I who had time, with my busy schedule and stimulating career, to watch football matches, but Jafar, who had had no consistent work for a year, longer even if you counted his sojourn in Harare. He was not the kind to wait at home, to have dinner prepared, to ask me after my long day at work. If he whiled away his time meeting friends, drinking, smoking, watching football, what better alternative could I suggest?

I remained silent and he said, What is this about. I said, I'm lonely, I feel alone here in Maputo. I do so many things without you when all I want is to be with you. I miss you when you are not here, you walk out the door and disappear. Where do you go, why do you hide, why will you not let me enter your life?

He did not answer. Then, "Guess who turned up at Eduardo's house today."

I shook my head, still trying to collect my thoughts, and he continued. "Sandra".

I stared at him. He nodded. "Sandra", he repeated. "She is visiting Mozambique with her husband. She found out where my mother lives, went there, found out where we were living, also where Eduardo lives. Came to find me."

I continued staring. My heart pounding.

"And?"

"And we talked. Then we went for a coffee, then I took her back to her hotel."

"And?"

"She found me. If you really want, you can find me any time. This is a small town in a city."

My voice was trembling when I spoke next. "Do you want me to feel ashamed? Is that what you want? You want someone who runs after you, following a trail, like a...private detective?"

My last words had been in English. I was not sure whether he had understood.

I pushed his hand from my leg, switching back to Portuguese. "You *let* her find you. You *let* people tell her where you were."

His face was inscrutable. He turned his head away.

"What about me?" I continued. "Do you know how *I* spent my day? Can you be so sure that *I* have been alone? Or if I have been with someone they are 'just friends'?"

He looked at me sharply.

"So, what do you mean?"

I shook my head.

"Pablo? That Cuban always inviting you?"

I glared at him.

"You see? You see what I feel?"

I had scored an easy victory, one I would later regret. I had seen my avenue to Jafar's weakness, one that I would pursue again, but I also broke something with my careless jibe. A layer as thin as an eggshell was shattered and we started hurting each other.

*

A few weeks later the head of the department at our university invited me to a dinner with some visitors who were interested in setting up a scholarship fund. Simon was an attractive man in his late-forties, an American who had started working for the Peace Corps in the Congo before returning to Yale to complete his doctorate. He had lived in Maputo for fifteen years, spoke Portuguese fluently and had only recently divorced his Mozambican wife. He had been influential in the university for all that time. As Jafar referred to him, *o branco poderoso*. Simon had asked me along, he said, for support, but there were others, more senior than I, whom he could have asked. I hesitated, but not for long. I did not know when Jafar would return that night. I had seen him the previous evening but not since, and the thought of dressing for dinner and being picked up was, I admitted, appealing.

I was getting dressed in our bedroom, when I heard Jafar arrive, the metal gate that preceded our wooden front door slamming with a colossal bang. He appeared at the bedroom door, walked up and kissed my cheek, "*Tudo bem?*"

"I'm going out," I said, not turning round, "I have to accompany Simon to a dinner with some visitors. I don't know if we have anything to eat in the fridge?"

He did not answer. I looked up, he was no longer there. There was an unusually strong breeze in the flat. I stepped out of the room.

"Jafar?" I called. He was not in the dining room, the curtains were billowing outwards, and when I looked into our living room I saw the front door wide open, the gate unlocked. The wind from the bay-side was picking up and blowing through the room. When we had first moved into the flat I had thought the metal gate and the metal slats that were nailed down above it were an extra security system. Maputo was a city known for burglaries, even in a *predio* as delapidated as ours. With more than a million inhabitants and an inadequate police force, the residents themselves adopted their own measures: we all contributed towards a stipend for our guard downstairs. I later learned that Yolanda had been less concerned with security. She had chosen solid metal slats to keep out the wind. The corridor faced Maputo Bay and the metal gates were one more barrier against the gales and storms that blew in from the east. That evening my hair blew around me while I struggled to shut the gate and the door. I went into the kitchen. He was not there either. What on earth?

I went back to the bedroom and pulled on the short, slim green dress that was by far the most exceptional item of clothing I possessed, put long green-glass earrings in my ears, my bangle. I wore this ensemble much too often, as I did all my clothes, but I knew I looked well in it. I twisted my hair into a bun and clamped it in place. The evening winds always succeeded in reducing any untethered hairstyle to disarray in minutes. Jafar must have gone downstairs to pick up some cigarettes, I told myself. But I knew he had an unopened pack: it lay on the dressing table in front of me.

I had arranged to be picked up downstairs on the street; I did not want my superior to climb up the dark, smelly stairwell and ring for me. Before I left the flat, I left a note on the kitchen table for Jafar. It was a work dinner and he was welcome to join us, I was sure. We would be eating at Clube Navale, and then Simon had mentioned taking the visitors to Tchova, so I could meet him there later if he wished. It was a popular hangout, set in the garden of a house in Polana. Live music, not always good, but always loud. Tables with thatched umbrellas scattered around the lawn, a bar on the far end. Jafar knew it well: he was friends with one of the musicians who had a regular slot.

I ran down the stairs. There was a smell of urine to complement the stairwell's other charms and I was glad I had arranged to be met on the street. When I stepped onto the pavement he moved out of the shadows. He reached out and grabbed my elbow, swinging me round to face him. We stared at each other.

"Where did you go?" I asked. He dropped his hand to his side, and I brushed a strand of hair from my face. Some had already come loose in the evening breeze.

He was not smiling and his eyes were angry. They flickered over my dress, my earrings.

"Going for dinner?" he said.

I said nothing.

"And then?" he continued. I was suddenly miserable. I opened my mouth to speak, but no words came. He reached out and gripped my upper arm, repeated.

"And then?"

I pulled my arm away. He dropped his hand. I looked down at my feet.

Against the grey cement, covered in its film of dust, my feet looked clean and bright in my sandals. I looked up.

"Why don't you come", I said quietly. "I left you a note upstairs."

One of the third-floor residents crossed the road towards us and skipped towards the entrance. We murmured our greetings and moved aside to let him pass. I heard him mount the stairs, his footsteps growing fainter as he climbed beyond the first floor.

Jafar took my elbow again, but this time his hand was gentle. He held it briefly, his thumb massaging the bone. "Did I scare you?" he asked. He had almost whispered, but his voice, with its deep notes, as it always did, seemed as if it was in my ear, speaking directly to my heart.

I shook my head, but then whispered back, "A little." I reached forward and laid my other hand on his chest. "Please come."

He shook his head, and pulled out a cigarette from his breast pocket.

"*Ja chegou*," He motioned with his head, "Your lift is here," and then walked away, lighting up, cupping his hand around his cigarette against the wind.

At Clube Navale, in the open-aired restaurant by the small marina, the ocean lapped against the sides of the cliff and the lamps that encircled the eating area swung in the breeze. I was distracted. Simon had introduced me to the two Americans who wanted to set up the fund: two very intelligent, interested, informed, curious women in their fifties who were impressed, moved, excited and determined. I listened to them with one ear but I knew Simon was annoyed by my disengagement. My mind was filled with questions: why had I worn this dress? In truth, I had considered Simon's invitation a date, a chance to glance a childish blow at Jafar: I did not lack for admirers. Why had I spoken so carelessly to him, and my casual reference to Simon? I did not need permission, but I had been near-dismissive. I knew then that I had wanted to hurt him. I had wanted to show him that I had a position of some status. I did not like myself. Perhaps, as I had always wanted, I *had* grown over the last years, developed a few more artifices, become more adept at the games and manoeuvres that I had so admired in others, but which I now found petty and mean-spirited.

I had looked out to the ocean, the moon flitting in and out of the clouds. It was not an extortionately expensive restaurant but it was still too pricey for Jafar and I to consider it a regular haunt. We ate the grilled fish and drank the wine. When Simon suggested Tchova I was relieved. After an hour or so I would be able to excuse myself, and leave him with his visitors. It would be too loud for conversation anyway.

When we arrived at Tchova I saw Jafar, standing at the bar with Eduardo. Excusing myself I walked towards them. I felt like I was walking over a meadow, long prairie grass brushing at my bare legs, my stride long. I had learned, by then, of my gracefulness, of the shape of my body. As I moved towards them, the noises about me became distorted as if someone had flicked a switch and the world was in slow motion. Jafar was watching me approach; I wanted to feel his hands on me, to hear him say my name. I was walking away from the others who, like me, were only visitors to this land: we did not own it. And I was moving towards Jafar, who had extended an invitation. I remembered his words when we had first crossed the border together: *está conmigo*. He was the reason I was where I was. Not for my evenings at cultural events with friends, not for my growing significance at the university, not for my enjoyment of living in a sensuous African city. I was only where I was for him.

I was trembling by the time I reached them. Eduardo moved aside so that I could stand between them, and I moved into the small space, pressed my body against Jafar and pulled his head to me. I kissed his mouth. I kissed him as if we were alone, in our bed, our tongues exploring, our hands quietly removing our bits of clothing. When I drew away, I saw that his eyes were laughing. He turned to Eduardo and shrugged his shoulders, half-apologetically.

He could see, I thought with a pang. He could see that I longed to be a woman for him — like Marie and Sandra, and all the others had been — a seductress, a huntress. I flushed, embarrassed now by my gauche execution. I had wanted it to be an apology for how I had behaved and a reminder of what I had to offer, but it had been undignified. I was an inexpert femme fatale I concluded. Jafar saw my discomfort and took my hand.

"Thank you for the kiss," he whispered. He was still smiling, but not unkindly.

In the end, we all sat down together at a table some way from the music. It was a success. The American women were delighted with Jafar and Eduardo, charming Mozambicans, the real thing. But barely half an hour later, the two men got up. They were going to meet some other friends, they said. I saw Simon watching as Jafar kissed me on the lips, *Até logo, filha*. I did not talk much after that. I felt it had been an evening I would have liked to live again, so that I could do better. It was near midnight when we left the bar. After dropping the two Americans off at their hotel Simon drove me back to the *predio* and stayed downstairs, the engine running, until he saw me wave to him from the balcony, as he had asked. I did not see Jafar again until the following evening.

*

I swung my legs down off the sofa, closed my book, got up and went into the bedroom. I had made my point. If he had been complacent before he would be no longer. I could hear him lighting up a cigarette, whether in defiance or in desperation I no longer cared. It was too late now for him to call Jules: if he missed out on that opportunity he had only himself to blame.

I stood in front of the dressing-table mirror and looked at my reflection. I looked tired, thin, my hair was messy, my face was shiny. I had dark circles under my eyes. I took home a good salary but food was expensive in Maputo. The supermarkets selling cheeses and nice yoghurts, tinned tuna, cookies, were extortionate.

I bought simple food; when I was eating on my own so much I was disinclined to cook. I knew that I was not taking care of myself, but my energies were consumed in finding emotional strength. I wondered, suddenly, whether I had told Jafar that I was trying to save money to study more. I had not yet let him in on these plans, and this thought depressed me.

I leaned forward, my palms flat on the dressing table, leaned forward until my forehead rested against the coolness of the mirror. I looked at my eyes. My irises were dark brown, but had flecks of a lighter brown, almost orange. My eyelashes were long, black, the lower lashes slightly curled. My eyebrows were thick and dark, but arched naturally, they were neat. My cheek bones were high, my mouth was small. This was my face: I knew it well, but I was no longer sure I knew the person behind it.

I examined my tongue. I did that every night, it had become a ritual. The previous year, in the rainy season, I had got a kidney infection. My tongue was white; I was completely dehydrated. Pablo had taken me to the Clinica Especial, a branch of the Hospital Central that catered for middle-class Mozambicans and foreigners who could pay in US dollars, and they had admitted me immediately. I had been on a drip for two days. When I was discharged I had returned to the flat to find that Jafar had still not come back. When he did, the following day, he had been contrite. He had made me an omelette, and had fed it to me in forkfuls while I lay in bed, forcing me to eat it all. Then he had taken off his clothes and had joined me under the sheets, holding me tight and warming me with his body. "*Desculpe, desculpe filha*", he had murmured over and over. He had ministered me for the next three days, cooking a hot meal every afternoon and forcing me to eat it, reading the newspaper on the balcony while I dozed on the bed. As always, I could think of an event which confirmed that he had feelings for me; just as easily, I could think of an event which proclaimed his disinterest.

I heard him move next door, taking off his shoes, and putting his feet up. I undressed, and reached for my towel, hanging on the door. As I moved to the bathroom, I saw him out of the corner of my eye. He was stretched out on the sofa, quietly smoking, staring up at the ceiling. I turned on the shower and stepped into the tub. Jafar opened the door of the bathroom. He stood in the doorway for a few seconds, then came in and leaned against the sink.

"Go away", I said, without looking at him.

I turned away from him; I didn't want him to see my face. My anger had subsided, replaced now by a numbness. Many years later, I still remember how I felt that night, standing under the shower, letting the water soothe and cleanse me. While I had been, at that moment, utterly lonely, I had never ever contemplated calling anyone, pouring my heart out to a confidante. It was inconceivable that I would allow anyone into our world, no matter how painful that world was becoming: we would have become, like that night in the Teatro, players in a story that an audience would relish for its pathos.

I don't know how long Jafar stood there watching me but when I turned off the shower he was gone. I walked into the bedroom and saw that he was lying in bed, his hands clasped behind his head. Because of the heat we used only a sheet to cover us, and he had pushed this down to his waist. There was a faint smell of tobacco in the air, with fresher, minty undertones. He must have collected his toothbrush when he had come into the bathroom, and washed up in the kitchen sink. I slipped off the towel, pulled on my night-dress. I turned back to the mirror and dotted my face with face cream. As I rubbed it in I caught his eye in the mirror. He was looking at me, his face serious. I climbed under the sheet.

I lay on my side facing him. He had thrown open all the windows and the breeze was cool. The bedside lamp on his side was on, and he hadn't drawn the curtains so there were lights shining through from the street. These would go off near midnight. He reached one hand out from under his head, and laid it against my face.

"*Tens uma cara muito bonita.*"

I could say nothing. Inside my heart was aching, and I remembered, suddenly, that day in the hotel, it was so long ago, when we had lain like this.

"What did Sandra want?" I said finally.

"To see me."

"Did she want you?"

"I think no. I don't know."

We lay in silence.

"Jules rang, about a job."

"I'll phone him tomorrow."

"I'm tired."

"*Dorme.*"

I closed my eyes, turned away onto my left side. He lay beside me, I think he was awake. He kept the bedside lamp on for some time. Outside, I could hear the last cries for the bus to Chamanculo, the last roars of chapas leaving the city. I think I fell asleep, but I woke again when I felt his hands on me. He was lifting my night-dress off me. I muttered sleepily, but he moved his hands up my side, around my belly, cupped my breasts. His mouth was against my ear.

"*Dorme*", he said.

8

I have travelled far and wide since that night. I have studied, grown up. It is thousands of miles away, a lifetime ago. I put my hands to my throat, then my breasts, my thighs and think, are they the same as before or when your soul changes, does everything else change too? Do I still have the same eyes, the same limbs? Do I have the same body that he touched? I have lived a quiet, contemplative life the last few years: I have slept alone, woken up alone. I have grown to enjoy my own company. I will be starting afresh, as one half of a couple in a new country. But for now, I am back in India. The beginning and the end. The beginning of the end. The words become my chant, the tempo dictated by the rhythm of the train.

Two years after leaving Francisuncle's home, I came back and spent an evening on the verandah of the house in Alleppey with my mother and grandfather. Then, as now, I had been summoned back. Years before I had stood in front of my parents in the house in Irinjalakuda, the three of us an unhappy triangle. Words were said, actions would echo. And again, that evening on the verandah in Alleppey, another triangle. By then my father had been replaced by my grandfather. My body was no longer a small form in blue cotton frills, but the body that I have now. Again, a proposition would be made, but with more hesitation: again, it would be turned down, but with more humility. For we had all grown by then. My mother would speak, a small white envelope would change hands, be tucked away, forgotten until it was opened again and told its story. The beginning of the end.

*

I had been fast asleep when the telephone rang at two in the morning. When it rang persistently, I roused myself, stumbled in the dark to the living room where the telephone sat on a little stool, cursing Jafar, assuming that he was phoning me drunkenly from the barracas, "I am coming in a taxi, wait for me downstairs because I have no money on me."

It was not Jafar, but the disembodied voice of my uncle, my mother's brother, telling me that Francisuncle had died, that the funeral would take place in Vazhakulam in a few days' time. Francisuncle had met a widow on a trip back home, they had mutual friends. She was a nurse who had worked in Dubai for fifteen years, and had returned five years previously to Kerala after her husband died. They had got married in Kottayam, where she was from, and made plans to emigrate to New Zealand. They had been travelling by bus to Changanassery for the confirmation of her grandson when the bus overturned into a ditch. Of the forty passengers aboard only five survived. Francisuncle and his new wife, her name was Rani, were killed instantly.

It was the first phone call I had received from my family, from India, since my arrival in Mozambique. My body went completely cold, I started shaking, but I held onto the receiver, listening to my uncle give me more details through the buzzing sound in my ears, my eyes closed. The next morning, strangely awake, I managed to arrange a flight to Madras through Johannesburg for the day after. I would be arriving in Kerala the day after the funeral, there was nothing I could do. I packed my bags, and left notes at various houses for Jafar. I didn't see him before I left.

The flight was uneventful, disrespectfully routine. I sat slouched in my seat, my arms crossed over my chest, my hands tucked into my armpits, the headphones on, listening to the music channels, one by one. I didn't look at the passengers next to me. I ate the food off the plastic trays, drank the insipid tea. I even managed to sleep, guiltily, wearing the eye patches from my on-board pack. I hadn't seen Francisuncle since the day I left his bungalow in the university campus. I had been quick in saying goodbye, Jafar had been waiting for me in town. I had been so completely absorbed in my love affair I hadn't appreciated the way he had kissed me on the forehead, the sad look in his eyes. I had written him from Mozambique, but the letters had mostly talked about superficial things. I skirted around real news as I did with my mother, and I had no idea what he knew or what he could surmise about my life in Maputo.

During the long flight I had a lot of time to think. Other than weekend shopping trips to Nelspruit, a small town over the border in South Africa, I had not left Mozambique in the last two years. I had not seen any member of my family in all that time, I barely knew how they were doing in their lives. My brothers had settled in Houston, my mother and grandfather were pottering around, my mother in retirement and my grandfather in his dotage in Kerala. I had removed myself from my family, and Jafar had become my family. He had consumed me; I had become part of him.

I arrived in India, organised a connecting flight to Kochi, and took the bus to Ernakulam district. The landscape, the scenery, the language – all were immensely recognisable to me. And rather than being unforgiving, they seemed to welcome me back. I felt a consolation which I had not expected. In the small hamlet where my father and Francisuncle had grown up I became one in the groups of people from both families, joined in sorrow. The funerals had taken place without any hitches other than the absence of many family members who hadn't managed to make the journey. Francisuncle and Rani were buried at St Stephen's church in Moovattupuzha. The graveyard is beautiful, set high, at the top of the hill, coconut trees surrounding it, a lush view of the valley below.

Back in Alleppey, at my grandfather's house, having survived an awkward few days with my father's side of the family, many of whom I had not seen since I was a little girl, I sat on a rocking chair on the verandah with my mother and grandfather. My mother, to my surprise, had held me in a long embrace, her chest heaving slightly, not speaking, when she had seen me. The warmth of her welcome had brought a lump to my throat, but I could not think of anything to say. When she broke away, she had rallied somewhat. She had busied herself with showing me my bedroom, telling me where to put my things, asking after the funeral — she had not wanted to leave my grandfather unattended. I was to sleep in my brothers' old bedroom, the one that they had shared through our childhood. The rooms were all configured differently now, my mother explained, especially as my grandfather now needed more assistance and a live-in helper. The bedrooms were a bit dusty and either too cluttered or too bare. The house needed a lick of paint, had become a bit shabby and care-worn. But there were still the lovely latticed window shutters that I have always adored and there were still the ceiling fans that I used to imagine swinging on. The heavy high wooden beds that as a child I had a penchant for rolling off in my sleep. We brought a tray of tea to the verandah and commented on the surprising coolness of the evening before. The plants in large pots in front of the house were beautiful; the anthuriums a triumph with their voluptuous red flowers. I have always envied my mother's green fingers. The tall slim coconut tree which stood near the gate swayed gracefully, having watched a few generations of cousins grow up, get married and move away.

Despite the sadness I had in my heart for Francisuncle I felt a contentment. The years had dropped away, and I was sitting barefoot in a salwar kameez of light cotton, making desultory comments in English and Malayalam with my elders. I had had little time to talk properly with them the last three days, and I realised that the companionable silence that was developing between us was slowly growing heavier with potency.

"Francis wrote about how you left his house," my mother began. I cupped my hands around my mug of sweet tea and nodded.

"He told us you had strong reasons to leave and that you could not be dissuaded."

There was a pause and I realised that I was expected to respond.

"I have a good job in Mozambique, Ma", I said.

She snorted. "Ha!"

There was a long silence and my grandfather and I exchanged looks. He had long retired, but in his heyday he had been a name in the town, walking to court every day with his briefcase, well-known, and well-respected. But unlike the rest of my mother's family my grandfather had always been less enthralled by the status that being a member of one of the oldest Syrian Christian families in town, and one of the most educated, brought. He had tried to complement my mother's indifference, but not, I used to think accusingly, try to amend her behaviour. Now, seeing them sitting side-by-side, companions now in later life, I understood more. My grandfather was still devastated that his daughter had suffered an unhappy marriage, and then premature widowhood. And he had only endeavoured to ease her pain, provide comfort.

My mother sighed, and I steeled myself.

"I will not ask you questions as I do not expect honest answers," and she swatted a weak protest from me with an impatient swipe of her hand. "I will tell you some news. I do not want an immediate reaction. I want you to listen and think." She glared at me, willing me to defy her. I had no such inclination.

"You remember V.S George who lived opposite? The family name was Velliamparambil. Anyway, they moved to Chicago many years ago. Maybe you don't remember. Their youngest son, Sebastian, is now about thirty. Unmarried still. Like you. A worry to them. Like you."

My tea had grown cold and I put it down on the verandah. My fingers trembled. Was this not what I had waited for? Had I not for years wondered at her silence, despised her lack of interest?

"I don't want to know why you are staying so long in that place," she said, "But you must remember your father and who he was."

The mention of my father was unexpected and I cleared my throat to reply. But my mother carried on, her voice now low and without its abrasive edge.

"I know my faults as a mother. I know that you are where you are because of me. I must accept at least part of the blame. But now I am offering you a chance. The chance is there."

I raised my head slowly to look at her, and to my amazement saw that she was staring at me, tears gathered like small pools in her eyes. "You are so beautiful, and so lost," she said, her voice quavering. My grandfather reached out and took her hand. She patted my grandfather's hand and regained some composure.

"Your father always said you would be beautiful. And, like in so many other ways, he was right." A tear flowed down my mother's cheek and I had to turn my face away because I couldn't bear to watch. She had never spoken like that before: when I was younger I had always been too sunburned and insubstantial for her liking. I was never considered by anyone to be a beauty like my mother.

She stood up and walked through the door to her bedroom that opened onto the verandah. Through the light cotton curtain I could see her collecting something from her dressing table. She came back outside with an envelope in her hand. Wordlessly, she slipped out a photo and passed it to me. Thick black hair brushed back from his forehead, a flash of white teeth. I closed my eyes.

"Like I said, no immediate reaction please," my mother said.

My heart was beating, my throat was dry and constricted. A chance, she had said. A chance for what? On this verandah, here in this house I played in as a child, where I read my piles of books, Jafar was unreal. I had seen him in a film, met him in a dream. He did not belong to this life, this world. A chance to belong. Somewhere, somehow, a breeze had tossed the pages in the air and the script had changed hands. I was playing someone else's life; not the life that had been assigned to me.

After that conversation there was a huge silence between my mother and me. I stayed on for two weeks. A tense and fraught two weeks. I cooked, cleaned the house on the days that Ambiga didn't come, held my grandfather's hand as he talked of his memories of life before my grandmother died, accompanied my mother when she went shopping and visiting friends. I wore saris on those occasions, and everyone pinched my cheeks, said I had grown even thinner, that I spent too much time in the sun in Africa, that I needed to fill out and become more womanly if I were to get married.

I was being a dutiful daughter, and I had learned that my mother did indeed love me. This discovery should have been momentous, but it had arrived a little late. It was an appendix, an anti-climax. While growing up, I had always expected a conversation like the one that had taken place on the verandah — of course I would study, possibly abroad, but of course I would return and accept an alliance with a suitable man — it was, now, an inconvenience. I was not that same girl any more. My mother had opened the door and I had walked through to another life.

I didn't refer to her words again before I left and I think she began to despair. By the end of my stay she no longer wanted me. It was embarrassing for her. She couldn't tell the rest of the family and their friends about the life I was leading; in fact, she must have realised how little she knew of it. I could see the hurt I caused her, and that hurt me. We never again discussed my plans. She didn't want to know. It was too much for her to know. By the time I left, I could sense some relief. It had been exhausting emotionally; it was easier when I was not around. She came with me to the airport in Kochi, where my connecting flight to Madras was leaving from. At the airport, just before I went to the departure gates, she kissed me awkwardly, then pressed an envelope into my hands. I put it into my bag. We didn't say much.

*

I got back to Maputo after dark. On the way back from Johannesburg I met an old student. Julião worked for the Ministry of Defence, he had been in South Africa for a conference. We sat next to each other on the plane and he told me that his driver would be waiting for him at the airport. He offered to give me a lift back to the city and I accepted. But as we walked through the arrivals lounge towards the exit I saw Jafar standing outside with the other families and friends of the passengers. He raised his hand in salute when he saw me. I told my old student that I would not be needing the lift and walked towards Jafar. He bent down to kiss me but I turned my face and his lips brushed my cheek. He had borrowed a car from Jules' NGO and he ushered me into it, taking my hold-all off my shoulder and slinging it into the back seat. I said nothing, and apart from his customary "*'Tas boa?*", he said nothing either. We drove back into Maputo. I stared out of the window. He put his hand on my knee but when I didn't respond he took it away.

Back at the flat I went straight into the bathroom. I wanted to wash the long journey off my body, wash off the feel and smell of India. He went into the kitchen and started rummaging through the fridge. I came out, wearing the soft red kimono with the spray of dragons, my hair hung wet down my back. His eyes rested on me. "I missed you," he said.

I just nodded. If I spoke I would start crying.

"*Eu se que estás zangada*," he said.

I shook my head, "*Estou cansada.*"

And it was true. I didn't feel the rage I had expected. As always when I saw him, I felt that ache, that yearning, that longing to lie quietly with him. To smell his skin, and caress his face, to lay my hands flat against his chest, and move my legs against his.

What had he been through? We had both lost our fathers, but I had still had a childhood of privilege and comfort. When his father had died from cancer, Jafar had been fifteen. He was not the eldest son, but his elder brother had moved to South Africa to work on the mines and had not returned for years. The responsibility of looking after his mother and sisters and younger brothers fell to him. In any case, his elder brother Amade was killed two years later in a mining accident. The family had not seen him since he had left. If that was not enough heartache, the youngest brother died from malaria before Jafar had finished his schooling. A civil war that lasted seventeen years and that left the country with a legacy of landmines meant that he had witnessed terrible scenes. He had told me once of an airlift that MSF organised of women and children who had been blown apart by landmines. The stench was awful he said, the people looked half-human, the moans and gurgles were unbearable to hear. The war had made life urgent, intensifying feelings, fear and love and anger. The peace had been a huge release, people could live again, but there were other enemies – AIDS, landmines, poverty.

He had lived through all of that; I had not shared in any of it. My life appeared pristine to him. I faced societal problems, pressure from my culture, exclusion from my family. For him, these worries must have seemed trivial. You don't want to do that, so don't do it. You think you'll hurt them? Maybe you will, but they won't die from it. They think you are a bad person, so fuck them. In his eyes, I had never suffered because his benchmarks were higher than mine. We both came from "Third World" countries, but my upbringing had been, I could see now, in a gentle, middle-class environment. He had survived great hardship through his intelligence and no small measure of luck. He had done well for himself, but now he was struggling again, working on and off, beset by plaintive family members. He was angry with life, and maybe he blamed me in some way.

We went out onto the balcony and leaned against the railings. That simple act was so familiar, so natural, we had done it countless times before and we were doing it again. Resting our forearms on the black metal, pushing our legs through the grilles, looking up at the sky, then down onto the street. It was almost as if the last two weeks hadn't happened. The streetlights lit our faces with an orange glow. There was a blacked out section of the city to the north. A power cut. The night winds had started up. The streets and avenues acted like wind channels, and when night-time fell you could hear the howling. Often storms would come in from the Indian Ocean, but Madagascar usually bore the brunt. They were much weaker by the time they hit Maputo.

Jafar was smoking a cigarette, flicking the ash into the air. He asked me about the funeral, I told him about the whole fortnight. He said that he had been with Eduardo, out of the city, when I had left, but that Rassul had rung him at Eduardo's house the next day to tell him that I had gone.

"I thought you weren't going to come back," he grinned widely but his eyes were searching.

"This is where I live," I said, "Of course I would come back."

"You didn't want to stay?"

I shook my head.

"Did they want you to stay?"

I nodded. "They couldn't make me."

He fingered the sleeve of my kimono, then slipped his hand into it and curved his hand around my upper arm.

"*Filha,*" he said.

The tears rolled down my cheeks and he wiped them away. He lifted his fingers to his lips and tasted them, then spoke.

"I have never felt that you were mine."

His words astounded me. His eyes, when I looked up, were grave. I was seeing him differently. I had complained that I had little access to his life, but how much did he have to mine? I had been to India and back, and I had not once said his name. He was an unknown, never-mentioned, and I had not spoken of any plans to reveal him, to introduce him as the man I loved to my family. Perhaps he had been expecting that: he had never said, but I had never asked. Now, all these years after, and much too late, lying on my bunk in the darkness of this hot night, where there is only space for honesty and lucidity, I know what he knew: we had never belonged to each other and we never would.

We stayed on the balcony for an hour it must have been, then we went to bed. Jafar held me in his arms, I held him back and I thought "So this is it." The words had formed easily. I like to believe that I had made my choice, my mother's request forgotten. I like to believe that I was finally courageous enough to leave the planet we inhabited and join the rest of the world, be honest and brave. I never found that out.

The next few weeks we stayed close to each other. He came to pick me up from work in the evenings. We walked home hand in hand. Sometimes we took a chapa to the Feira Popular and had a drink before heading back to the flat. One weekend we took a ferry, a scary, overcrowded, rolling tugboat, across the bay to Catembe Island and had the picnic I had prepared. We munched sandwiches sitting on the sand, and then we fell asleep on a grassy mound, under a tree. We went to a gig at the Club Desportivo downtown. Jafar knew the two guitarists, they had grown up in the same area, and we got free tickets to the concert. They sang in Shangaan.

The crowd knew all the lyrics of the songs, Jafar translated for me, his arm encircling my waist, his mouth against my ear. We woke up together and we went to sleep together. We made love with tender, soft, movements the one day, clawing and scratching each other the next. We lay naked for hours on hot afternoons staring up at the ceiling until we felt hungry and then we ate quickly and went back to bed.

*

The Maputo winds started to rise and sweep the street of their dust. Dust clouds circled the air, and then descended gently hundreds of metres away. It was a way to remind everyone that we lived in the same city, shared its dust. Dust that began its life in your back garden could easily be transported to the manicured green lawn of a house off the tree-lined Avenida de Kenneth Kaunda. It was the great leveller.

One afternoon a few months later, Rassul and I were in her flat, in the children's bedroom again. I was lying on Aida's bed, and she was folding clothes, sitting on the bed opposite, her mouth stretched wide, her white straight teeth and golden skin shining with amusement. "You didn't suspect?" she asked.

I shook my head. I was aware that my hands were shaking, and then I looked at her and smiled. "Aaah", Rassul sighed. "I love that feeling. Even after three of my own, and God help me no more, I love that feeling." By now I had stopped listening to her. The tiredness I had been feeling was not because of the heat. My lack of appetite was not a precursor to everyone's first fear, malaria. The fullness of my breasts was not because my period was due, and I realised that I could not remember when had been my last. When I understood, my heart stopped for a few seconds, before beating faster than ever.

It was too early in the week to expect Jafar back. He had recently started working with an NGO some way outside of Maputo, and so during the week I did not see him. He stayed there in the compound, and returned to Maputo on Friday afternoons. He would meet me after my last classes of the week, and we would go home together, catching up our news as we either walked back or took a chapa. While I missed him when he was away, there was also a sense of relief. I knew why he was absent, and I could fool myself that if not for the job he would be near to home. In reality, little had changed after the first weeks since my return from India: after the reunion on the Friday evening, I could not tell for how long or when I would see him for the rest of the weekend. I could only be sure that at some time at night he would crawl into our bed, his arms encircling me, pulling me close to him. By the time Jafar got the job in Chokwe, the sweet, honeymoon days had ended, and my demons had returned.

That Friday evening he was not there to meet me downstairs in the hallway. I worried that he would come back so late that I would already be asleep, and would have to wait one more day before telling him. I took a chapa back to the flat. It was empty, but I started getting a light supper together, thinking that he must have had to finish a project and had been forced to get the later bus back to Maputo.

He didn't come back that night. Or the next. I phoned Eduardo but there was no answer. Rassul and her family were visiting relatives in Beira. I walked over to his mother's house but couldn't make myself go inside. I stood outside, under a window, but I didn't hear his voice. He had left his clothes and things in the flat, and I searched through them, trying to find some clue of where he could be. I found none. Looking through my own things in desperation, I found that a small white envelope which months ago I had tucked under the messy pile of socks in the drawer of my dresser had been opened. The photograph it had held lay half-in, half-out.

9

I am awake now and I will not be able to fall asleep again. The sun outside is beginning to rise, rose-pink. People have stirred and splashed their faces with water from their bottles, trying to wash away at least some of the dust that blows in through the windows. The lady-lecturer is tidying her braid, smoothing her salwar with her hands, slipping her feet back into her shoes. Suitcases are being pulled down, opened, closed. I am still lying on my bunk, not ready yet to climb down the ladder and join my companions below. I will miss my hard, blue-plastic-covered bed. It has been my little island, a place to gather myself. The activity below me has jolted me out of my reveries, back to the real world, this train, this last journey.

The train will arrive in Ernakulam in the next hour and tomorrow I will meet the man I am to marry. In the compartment there are smells from the evening meal, the steward now moving up and down the carriages shouting "*Kaapi, kaapi, choode kaapi...*" My throat is dry, so I will have the coffee but I will not eat. I will be bedraggled when the train pulls into the station, but there will be no chance to freshen up. My uncle will put me in his car and we will set off down the highway.

*

Five months after I last saw Jafar, I left Mozambique. In that time I had tried all means to find him, but had failed: he did not want me to find him. I knew he was alive, because Rassul, although she wouldn't say specifically, had been in contact with him. I heard later that he had stayed on in Maputo only for a short time after, in a flat in the Torres Vermelhas. These were twin blocks, near the Hotel Cardoso. Some of the flats on the higher floors had stunning views over Maputo Bay. They were twins only from the outside. One tower consisted of upmarket flats with a dollar rent, surrounded by a metal fence, a security guard in a box at the gate. I had actually been there once: a young Canadian woman who worked for a Christian NGO had invited me for dinner one night. Jafar might have been in the opposite tower at that time, but I can't be sure if he hadn't left already. The other tower consisted of similar flats, but all were Mozambican-owned, meticais-bought. The water pump didn't always work, neither did the lifts. You often saw groups of children crowding around the tap on the ground floor, filling up buckets, balancing them on their heads, and then beginning the slow trek upstairs. The towers were both fifteen stories high. From what I gathered later, it was Naman's sister Amina who found it for Jafar. I had not thought to call her – we had not met for a year or so – but even if I had she may not have told me. He stayed there for a month or thereabouts and then went back up to Chimoio on the bus. Up the coast road, then inland to the hills, re-tracing our steps from just over two years ago. A journey of at least a day and a half, not for the faint-hearted, the bus slowly making its way on roads that were damaged by the war and which still, in places, harboured landmines.

Those first days after he left were days of intense anguish: he did not know what we had made together. My heart quickened at that thought. A nugget of joy tucked itself into one corner, uncertainty seeped into the others. He will have felt betrayed I was sure, and I feared his anger. When I went to see Rassul after she returned from Beira, she had had a closed look on her face. She had heard from Jafar, that was clear, and I dreaded to think what she had deduced from his behaviour. When I had asked her to tell me where he was, she had shrugged her shoulders, shaken her head. "*Não vale a pena...*" She still had her same easy manner, but whatever she had been told, it had relegated me to the ranks of the privileged, those who were far from her concerns. We could look after ourselves.

One night, returning from work where everyone wore sympathetic smiles, and offered reassurances that what had happened was entirely expected, I walked up the stairs in the building, feeling my way with my hand on the wall. The light-bulbs in the communal areas had blown weeks back and had not been replaced. A warm gush spread between my legs, and then another. In the darkness, I put my hand under my skirt, and it came back sticky and wet. My hand, when I peered at it, was black. Hours later, in the clinic where my Cuban friend worked, I lay on a clean white sheet, on a clean hard bed. Pablo hovered, averting his eyes while the tears streamed silently down my face. A little life, a tiny heartbeat, lost.

I felt that I had lost everything, including myself. I blamed Jafar, but he had not even known, and so, in horror, I realised that I was to blame. I had thought that I could choose, but instead I was chosen, and had failed.

I searched back through my life and I rested on a chance for solace. I prayed. I prayed that heaven was as beautiful and gentle as I had always been told it would be. As I pray now, my little soul, alone on my bunk in the shadows, at least no one can see me. My tears run freely, my throat is dry. I hope you are not alone. I hope that you are not scared. I hope you know that you were loved. That you were like a small bird in my hands; fragile and elusive.

My life dissolved and I dissolved. On being discharged from the clinic, I took a short leave of absence from work on the grounds of ill health. I didn't want to see anyone; I didn't want to speak to anyone. I only wanted to see Jafar and to talk to Jafar. I believed that, eventually, he would come back. He would, of course, worry about me and want to see me. He would be angry, but I would be able to explain. And then, I would be able to share. To share the grief, it seemed too much for one person alone.

I heard nothing. The phone stayed silent, he did not appear one night, slipping into our bed, his hands reaching for me. His clothes hung in wardrobe, untouched, until the day I gave them to my empragada Hortensia, a week before I left. I never heard his voice again, I never saw him again. He was indeed, I realised, part of a dream. Had it really happened? Had I really thought that I would live here with him, raise children with him, grow old with him? I spent hours on the balcony of the flat, hoping for a glimpse of him on the streets below. Even, on my very bad days, hoping for a glimpse of a small child, holding his hand. While I believed I would die, I didn't. At some point, although I have no concrete memory of it, I made a decision to survive. I knew that I could not stay and so I made arrangements to leave. My plans to study further, in London, fell into place. I would start my studies in the new academic year.

I called Rassul, a few weeks before leaving, to give her this news. It was good, she said, unsurprised, then enquired after my health. She knew I had been 'unwell', that I had been in the clinic and she hoped I was better. Her voice was calm, gentle even. But, to me, the message was clear: I could afford to have the best treatment available, unlike others, Rassul included. What happened was unfortunate but, well, the country was full of tragedies. I had the freedom to leave, all ties now severed. On the phone with her, I felt the chasm between us. Yes, I was better, I replied, both of us tip-toeing around each other, our words formal, polite. We neither of us mentioned Jafar.

I saw Eduardo before I left, while I was working out my notice. I had, by then, arranged where I would live in London, found out where my department was based. I even had my lecture schedule, starting only six weeks away, in October. I was looking ahead, perhaps I was getting better. I had gone to Tchova with a group of friends. I had long since stopped scouring the crowds in case I saw his face, chanced upon his profile. He would catch my eye and would raise his hand in a salute. I had stopped looking for him.

I was sitting facing the stage, someone tapped me on the shoulder. Eduardo's face loomed, he kissed me on the cheek. It was a shock; I hadn't seen him for months. Jafar's oldest friend and confidante; I had never managed to find out what he really thought of me. But that evening he was kindly. He sat down, and before I even asked, he told me that Jafar was in Chimoio, and that he,

Eduardo, had been up to visit a few weeks back. Was he all right? Oh, he was fine, doing odd jobs at the moment but he would find something better soon. Was he coming back to Maputo? Not likely, he didn't like the city, he was glad to be in his own house again.

I hesitated before continuing. But Eduardo must have read my thoughts, because he got up to leave. I started to speak, but he shook his head. He bent down and kissed me again, laid his hand on my shoulder, and then walked away. I could have followed him, pulled him aside and demanded some answers. I could have slapped him, screamed at him. But I couldn't get up out of my chair. All colour had left my face, all feeling had left my body. I don't remember how the evening ended. I think I drank more than I had ever done, and more than I have ever done.

I twisted away from the country I had grown to love. Its charming, beguiling adornments fell away, and a harshness, a lack of sympathy was revealed. I was insignificant in its story; I would not be missed. Rassul, Eduardo — I was angry with everyone, covering up for him, staying loyal to him, closing ranks, shutting me out. I saw myself as they saw me: a *monye*, a passing fancy, an inconsequential visitor. It was how it had always been but I had fooled myself to think things had been otherwise.

There was never a painful, touching goodbye. We never exchanged addresses, tried to stay friends, promised to stay in touch. I'll let you know how things are going, let me know if you are ever in the area. When the plane took off from Maputo airport, banked over the palm trees, the bay a blue crescent in the distance, I laid my palm against the small oval window. That was my farewell.

Part Two

1

I live in a cream-coloured house, with a green lawn at the front that slopes gently to the road. The house has large windows, and a green door. There is a beautiful wisteria that hangs over the porch, producing gorgeous purple flowers in the spring. We have a bench below the front-room window, where we often sit on summer evenings, watching the sun set. I've planted an apple tree a few metres from the road, and a few bushes along the driveway, but we are still waiting for them to mature. Our road is lined with trees; our neighbours are hard-working couples with young children. Our backyard is dominated by a swing-set, a small slide and a sand-pit. We dote on our daughter, Shayla.

The garden of the house is my domain. Sebe would help if I asked, but I rarely do. I tend the borders, cut back the bushes and feed the roses. I mow the lawn, rake up the grass, add to the compost heap I have started at the side. Our patio is cluttered with pots: my herbs, Shayla's runner beans and tomatoes, and our flowers. We have a table and chairs, and in the hot summer months, we have all three meals outside. I love my garden, and my first cup of coffee in the day is taken by the back window, looking out.

I am still slender, but more toned; I take more care of myself. And my hair is longer now, scraping my shoulder-blades. My skin looks fresher, brighter, even though I am older, as I have a better diet now of lean meat, fresh fish, lots of fruit and vegetables, wild rice, couscous, and even dark chocolate – luxuries that were unheard of on my travels. I no longer eat on the hoof, but cook proper meals in our bright, lavender-scented kitchen. I drink milk every morning, mineral water with meals, and wine only at weekends.

I have a wardrobe full of clothes, for all seasons. In rich colours, soft cottons, wools, linens. I take care when I dress and I enjoy it – I realise that I am lucky enough to carry clothes well. For years in my twenties I had very few possessions. I travelled around with my worldly belongings in one suitcase, and lived in countries where the weather dictated that you wore light clothes and open sandals on your feet. I had approximately three outfits that I swapped around, alternated, wore in different ways. When I stopped moving around, I started gathering, collecting. I still feel that I live light, but I have ten times as many possessions as five years earlier, something I sometimes marvel at.

Sebe and I have been married now for just over five years, and have been living in this suburb on the outskirts of Chicago for nearly as long. He had a flat in the city which he sold quite easily while I was waiting for my papers to be sorted to join him. He had explained that we were more likely to afford a place in the suburbs that had space to grow in. I left the decisions to him, as wherever we moved was a new start for me. But I had been pleased with his choice. We drove up towards the house that day when we moved from his flat, and he pointed it out as we turned into our street. It has a pretty aspect, with the wisteria over the front door, and its gentle colours, and I love the space.

We left the car in the driveway, bursting with our boxes and bags, and as we walked through the rooms, the wooden floorboards glinting pleasingly in the sunlight that suddenly poured through the open front door and windows, as if heralding our arrival, I had felt a thrill. It looked familiar — laid out in a style that I had seen in films and on television shows — very American, but it was also completely empty. It did not have one piece of furniture, no curtains, not even lampshades. It could have looked stark and inviting, but in the golden light it felt, even though by then it was nearing evening, as if we were stepping into a new day. I had turned to Sebe, and he had smiled with relief at my expression. "Like it?" he had asked, and I had nodded. We were still, then, deferent, polite, still used a certain formality with each other, but I think we both felt a drawing together, a stronger sense of being newly-weds. It was fitting that we should start our brand-new marriage in brand-new environs. We would furnish our house and fill it together, just as we would furnish the empty spaces and fill in the gaps in our relationship.

I have my own office downstairs, the walls covered with pictures from my travels, and he has his across the hall. Shayla doesn't have a playroom, but she has free rein over the rest of the house. She has even set up a small zoo in our bedroom. I love seeing signs of her on the stairs, in the living room: little clues to her adventures, insights into her psyche.

*

Five years is not a long time for a marriage, but it is a world away from the first meeting Sebe and I had in the house in Alleppey. He had been more appealing than I had expected, more keen to find out about me. That had not been easy, as chances to spend time alone together were rare. He was more personable than on the phone, when his tone of voice and total confidence, at times, had grated. He seemed a little shy, a bit more nervous, and I liked that.

He came round to the house the day after I arrived, unceremoniously summoned at the last minute from Pondicherry. I had flown into Delhi, having left Indonesia where my field work had taken me, packed up my life from the last two years. The intention had been to catch a flight down to Kerala the following day. But in the airport the seeds of another idea began to flourish. I had not had a holiday for a long time and now I had more than two weeks at my disposal. I began to feel that I needed a bit more time, a bit more of a transition period from the life I had just left and the start of my new life. Two days previously, I had been emptying out the office and room in the small bungalow that I had used as my base for the last two years. I had been invited to several dinners and drinks parties to say good bye to my colleagues and friends. They had all been affectionate, curious about what I had told them. While my departure had been imminent anyway — my contract was expiring — they were, I knew, intrigued by my impending nuptials, announced without preamble, out of the blue.

I didn't feel, driving in a taxi from Delhi airport into the centre, the city with its imposing hotels, fountains and apartment blocks flashing past, that I was ready to immerse myself in my family, and the flurry of pre-wedding preparations in Alleppey. Once I got there, I would have to engage, chat, impress. Over the years my visits back to India had always been rushed affairs: depending on where I flew into, there always followed a series of connecting flights and train rides that needed to be endured, hours to while away on various forms of transport, before I arrived back at my grandfather's house in Alleppey, ready to attend someone's wedding, engagement or funeral. I wanted to feel that this time was different. I decided to spend some time on my own first, to gather my thoughts before heading south.

My mother, when I called her the following morning to tell her of my plans, had been exasperated. But there was an element of understanding, I could tell. Huge changes were afoot, all decided in the space of a few months. It had all happened quickly, for everyone: the date of our wedding had been fixed just over two weeks away to fit in with Sebe's availability, a window of opportunity. My mother must have sensed I needed a breathing space. She made me promise to phone her every day or every other day. Sebe had not yet arrived himself and I could assure her that I would, of course, arrive in good time.

While I had seen myself using the days I had acquired as a chance to meander down to the wedding, simply to catch my breath, they began to grow in import. My mind, until so recently filled with thoughts of my thesis and a no-more-than-mild curiosity of Sebe, became crowded with other thoughts. It was as if after a long hibernation I was waking up, shedding my old life, each day bringing me closer to the real world. I found a room in a cheap guesthouse near the train station, spent the days walking around in Delhi's winter sunshine; the evenings, back in my room, a blanket around my shoulders, recording my impressions in a notebook. Every day I decided where I would go and what I would see only when I woke up, taking autorickshaws and buses at whim, living in the moment, letting small decisions direct my wanderings.

I had not been back to Delhi since my grandfather had taken us all up north for a cultural tour. It was the year after my father died. My grandfather must have felt it would serve two purposes: distract us from sadness, show us the grandeur of our capital. It had been an enjoyable family trip. My mother had seemed less aloof, more inclined to smile. She had ordered two new sundresses for me from a tailor in Alleppey for our holiday: I had worn those symbols of her attention with pride. As we traipsed through the old Mughal monuments and negotiated meals and transport, my older brother and I spent most of our time doubled up in paroxysms of silent laughter over my grandfather's atrocious Hindi. He had insisted that he take charge, despite my mother's better command of the language. Memories of that happy week, a capsule of joy from long ago, flooded back, as, twenty years later, I walked the streets of Delhi again. I felt an urge to reconnect with my past, with my childhood, as if I wanted to rewind time, so that I could begin again, as new.

The fractured Hindi that I spoke, as well as my Indian looks but lack of a travelling companion and dusty clothes, meant that I drew a lot of attention and elicited a lot of questions. Where are you from? I am Indian. Yes, but you're from outside, aren't you. And why are you in

India? To which I answered, time and again, I'm getting married. Questions that emphasised how young I had been when I had left India, my responses accentuating how my life was going to change in the next few days. And there were couples everywhere you looked: in the parks, in the gardens of the monuments and tombs that I visited, in the fast-food stalls, in the shops of Connaught Place. Delhi was a city of lovers. Everywhere, a man and a woman, of similar age, either both dressed in jeans and sunglasses, or the woman wearing a salwar kameez, the man in jeans, or both dressed in traditional clothes, holding hands. Married, fully-licensed for public displays of affection. People who looked like me, and gave me an insight of what we would look like, Sebe and I, walking together. And how different we had appeared, Jafar and I.

I went to see Cecily, my old school mate, who now lives in Delhi. And after nearly a week in Delhi, I ended up flying down south and taking a bus to Pondicherry, somewhere as a child I had always wanted to visit. That it had been a French colony had always fascinated me. When I must have been nine years old, we had visited my great-uncle who was a lecturer at the university in Madras. I remember that he had told me about this small, neatly-laid-out town, a few hours from where we sat, on the verandah of his large two-storied house not far from the centre of the city. Where you could buy croissants and the restaurants served French onion soup.

I walked along the promenade every evening, enjoying the warm breeze from the Bay of Bengal, listening to the voices speaking in French, Dutch, American English, Irish English, German and Hebrew. The ashram a few kilometres out of the centre attracted visitors and residents from all over the world, and I felt comforted, as I always seem to, to be one of many. My second night there, the centre buzzing with people, the air thick with the smell of jasmine and hair-oil and cooking, scooters and cars jostling for right of way, I phoned my mother from a kiosk.

She had answered after just one ring.

"Thank God it's you," She sounded frazzled.

"What's wrong, Ma?"

"Sebe is here!" Her voice was a piercing whistle and ended on a high note. I had rarely heard her so agitated.

"He's early, Ma."

"I know! But he says that he wanted more time to see you before. You see, such a good man, and I was so ashamed to say that you were not here."

I was quiet. Hearing that Sebe was in Alleppey, in my grandfather's house, hearing that he had by now met my mother, my uncle, was disconcerting. I tried to pull myself together.

"I can go to Madras and get a train," I said, finally, "I'll be home day after tomorrow."

"Good. You must come quickly, this looks very bad. I didn't think he would just turn up. And I look very bad, letting my daughter roam around. I hope he will understand."

"Is he there now?"

"He is having a rest. He is very jet-lagged..."

Somehow, the thought of Sebe sleeping – overcome with jet-lag, grubby, probably finding the heat unbearable, helplessly swiping at mosquitoes – made me let out a chortle. In the photos I had back at the guesthouse I was staying, somewhere in my hold-all, he was spruced up, clean-shaven, hair recently washed, gentle sunshine on his face, showing a nice set of American teeth.

My mother was annoyed. "This is a time to laugh, *edi* ?"

I felt hysterical, weak, and I forced myself to control my laughter.

"Ma, sorry, I'm just nervous, that's all. Tell him I'll be there day after tomorrow."

This had calmed my mother, and she sighed.

"He is so nice, *mol*. You see how he wants to see you as much as he can? He wants to show us that he is just like us. And your uncle lets him come here, because he wants this to be good for you, *mol*. We are doing all of this for you."

I nodded my head. Clearly, I was meant to feel grateful to my family and to Sebe but I felt piqued: Sebe was rescuing me, apparently, from my floundering efforts of the last years. There was some truth to that, but I did not appreciate the reminder. I had ended the phone call soon after. The next day I left Pondicherry and took the bus to Chennai. That evening I boarded the Trivandrum Mail for the endlessly long train journey back to Kerala, in a hot compartment, with only the dark and my thoughts as company.

By the time Sebe came with his uncle to our house in Alleppey, I was feeling slightly resentful towards him. They had brought over the sari that I would wear for the reception, the manthrakodi, the sari that he would put over my shoulders during the mass as a sign that he would clothe me and shelter me during our marriage. I found that presumptuous: he could have waited until after our first meeting, to see if it went well. Grudgingly, though, I had to admit that I liked his thick curly black hair, his very white teeth. He has dark brown skin and a dimple on his chin, bushy eyebrows. He is good-looking, I suppose, although I'm still not sure I would have picked him out in a crowd.

It was about nine in the morning, before the heat of the day set in. Everyone chatted and tried to pretend that it was all very casual and normal and we are very civilized and sophisticated, not like people in villages. Our kutty has studied abroad and is marrying a foreign man, a Malayalee from America, and our families are very open to new ways and we will not follow all the old traditions like some of our simpler neighbours. We will not stare at her and question her family about her rather than speaking to her directly, and we will not even ask for a dowry as she is an educated girl and will no doubt find a job in America. We are not even worried that she is quite thin (that is the fashion these days) and that she is not wearing gold (will she at least put on a nice necklace and earrings and bangles for the wedding?) and that she doesn't speak much and hardly smiles (for a kutty from outside she seems quite shy and not brash like we had expected).

I had joined everyone on the verandah carrying a tray of cups filled with coffee, hot and strong and sweet, and a plate of ethakkappams that my aunt had just fried up in the kitchen. My mother had decided that was the best way for me to make my entrance. I was wearing a churidar that my mother had bought me in Cochin. I was surprised at her choice because I would have bought it myself. It was light-green and cut simply, it flowed lightly over my figure. The chunni was a darker russet colour, and of a very light cotton. I wore my hair loose around my shoulders; I had washed it that morning and so it shone comfortingly. I was nervous, a bit irritable because I knew that I was on show and was irked by the mythology that had been created around Sebe. And I was very very hungry, as I had had no time to have a proper breakfast.

When I stepped out of the house onto the verandah everyone had stopped talking for a brief instant, and then had tried to resume their conversation quickly, talking over each other. I laid the tray on the table, and while straightening up I saw Sebe looking directly at me. He was staring, a terrified expression flashed briefly over his features and I felt a stab of indecision. But when I turned around and found my seat next to my mother, I saw her smug smile, and I looked back at him and saw him blushing furiously, staring at his shoes. I felt a surge of relief, and then, I must admit, not a little self-satisfaction.

I was relieved that he was not disappointed by me, in the flesh. I leaned back in the chair and let all the words wash over me. I sneaked a few good looks at him, but mostly I just contemplated when I could have my first ethakkappam. He didn't speak to me directly that time, but I heard him talk to the others, with a little surprise at his accent, stronger in real life, pure Chicago. He didn't speak in Malayalam, so everyone spoke in a mixture. His uncle was jovial, playfully slapping him on the knee. He was enjoying himself tremendously.

We had spoken already, so were not complete strangers, but we were both a bit over-awed by the gathering on the verandah. I think it dawned on us, at the same time, and I drew from this a surprising sense of comfort, that our marriage would be a union, not just of ourselves, but of our families. The elders were involved, and were paving the way. So that morning, I barely uttered a word. I would slip into a daydream, often at crucial moments, like when his uncle had politely asked me something. Then my mother or my aunt or whichever member of my family was sitting next to me would give me a push, apologise for me, tell them I was still tired after my train journey, point out that I was too thin, and then make a joke that Sebe would have to fatten me up. I remember being surprised at how readily everyone made jokes, even quite bawdy ones, and at how the atmosphere was much less solemn than I had expected. My mother at times burst out laughing, pinching my cheek affectionately. It was all I could do not to gawp at her.

When Sebe and his uncle left, my family breathed a sigh of relief and then immediately began analysing every nuance, every comment, and berating me on my silence. "You must show your spirit," my uncle said. And grinned delightedly. "*Aavene pidichu, mol.*" I have never seen him smile so mischievously.

2

I work part-time at a nearby college, teaching some classes and also supervising students' work. I've started a research project that the college is excited about and they have been very supportive. As ever, I feel that I landed the job by sheer luck; my post in Harare played a small part, my everlasting talisman. But they seem happy with me and Shayla has settled into the kindergarten for staff at the college. Sebe leaves for work early, and then Mondays and Fridays, Shayla and I have some time to ourselves. Sometimes, to indulge her, we lie on our bed and she makes me into a silly shape. Feeling her little hands move my arms and legs into position, smelling her head when she climbs over me, all seriousness, to adjust a stray hair or limb, my heart soars. My daughter is the most beautiful thing I have ever known. Her dimples, her perfect soft skin, her silky hair. I stare at her in wonder of her complete perfection.

She's great company, a chatter-box, and babbles away happily while I am strapping her little body into her car-seat, holding her hand as we walk along the road, when I am giving her a bath on the days that papa comes home late. In public, however, my little girl is shy. She gets a lot of compliments on account of being adorable, but she views each stranger with wide-eyed suspicion, her little hand resting on my leg for security. In groups of children, she does not take the lead, but is quietly pliant, trotting behind obediently. My daughter breaks my heart with her little ways and with her anxious looks.

And five years on Sebe and I are a happy couple. Ours was never a romance in the conventional sense. You meet someone and get to know them. You fall in love. You agonise over whether they are right for you. After various feints and passes, you commit to each other. We did everything in reverse. I had agreed to marry him even before we met in person. I had called my mother not long after I arrived back in London those years back. I told her that I had left Mozambique, about my postgraduate studies, about what my research would focus on.

She had been quiet on the other end of the phone. For once, I did not assume that her silence was condemnatory. Somehow I knew that my voice was different and she could discern that change. My words had been prosaic, but she could sense something, I knew. I longed, at that moment, to confide in her but I held back. It was too raw: I would not find the right phrases, I would upset her. She spoke in a soft, low voice. It was a good idea to study more, I had always been bright, academic. I would do well. I explained that I would spend a year, maybe more, in London and then apply for funding to do fieldwork. She asked for a few more details, told me of relatives who lived at least fairly near where I would be travelling to. Her cousin worked in Papua New Guinea, my godfather now lived in Australia, I had a clutch of second cousins dotted around Malaysia. I gave her my number in London and was surprised when she rang me a few days later to 'see how the meeting with my supervisor had gone'. When I offered to call her back — I assumed it would have been very expensive for her — she told me of the new satellite technology found everywhere now in India. It cost her pennies she said.

So we took to phoning each other at least once a month, even after I left London. Given that we had barely communicated since I had left home aged sixteen this was a huge change. The men in our lives – my father, my grandfather, Francisuncle – had all passed on, and it was like it was just the two of us. We have never, either of us, counted my brothers. They both manage to sail along through life, unscathed, unfettered either by social rules or personal worries, unaware of the small tornado at the centre of our family, my mother and I. We had sparred, undeniably, but now, there is a quietness, a remorse for missed opportunities, an understanding.

But I decided, as I have done time and again, against telling her of my last days in Maputo. I swaddled my sadness, the small dark knot. I kept it inside me, for me alone and no one else. When I arrived in London I had felt like I had been thrown into a bucket of cold water, my whole body immersed in a chill, my hands gripping the sides. I felt that I could not hold an ordinary conversation with anyone. I did not want to talk about myself but I was of great interest to everyone. Mozambique? What's that like?

How could I explain? It was a world away from the dingy classrooms, lecture theatres, student flats and houses that I found myself in. The layers of clothing I had to wrap around my frame, like bandages over my wounded body. The intellectual, informed conversations. The dismay at political manoeuvrings, the derision of popular television shows. I retreated into myself, spent hours in the library, made a few friends but shunned large parties and gatherings. I was angry: at myself for imagining I could live a life consumed by sensuality, at Jafar for laying me bare. I had only had one lover before him and no one had touched me in the way he had. I felt so betrayed, so incensed by his disappearance, his lack of knowing our secret sadness. His faulty conclusions and of being denied a chance to explain, to shout at him, berate him, hit him. Of being denied the consolation of the warmth of his body, his arms tight around me, his voice in my ear: *não tens culpa, filha.* A consolation that I ached for. I wanted to punish him.

I had a clumsy, ill-advised affair with one of my lecturers. He was not much older than me, bespectacled, nice-looking, a head of well-cut, brown hair. After several conversations in his office, where he made it clear — subtly, but nonetheless clear — that he wanted to sleep with me, he invited me to a concert of his friend's band. We went for a drink after. As we sat opposite each other I knew that I would spend the night with him, at his flat. Later, over coffee, sitting at his breakfast bar the next morning, I felt immeasurably unsatisfied, filled with bitter regret. I had punished myself, no one else. I realised that I did not want to speak: I found it exhausting. I would have been happy to take vows of silence for the rest of my life. I left hastily, leaving the lecturer's feelings hurt and his pride dented. He tried to see me again, but I refused and our dalliance became a source of concern and some amusement in the department. We met for a coffee a few months later to smooth things over, but parted acrimoniously. Soon after, I went to Indonesia for the start of my fieldwork. I knew then that I was done with physicality. My body had been another's but was no longer so. I felt no physical desire and did not find it difficult to live accordingly. I had a new passion, my old passion: my books. I read, I wrote. I watched, I listened. I was not prepared to engage.

I think I would have carried on, I believed myself happy, were it not for my mother. I had called her to tell her that I would be leaving East Timor in a few months, my permit was expiring, and hoped to stop by and see her on my way back to London where I had the option to complete my thesis. I was in the bedroom of the small bungalow I was sharing with another research assistant. I had pulled the telephone into my room, and I watched its black cord snake across the room and out of the door. There was a slight delay on the line; I was thousands of miles away from the house in Alleppey.

"So much moving around, *mol*," she said. And she sighed. In the background I could hear a voice calling out. As I often did when I spoke to her I shut my eyes and imagined her sitting in the living room, the latticed windows, the ceiling fan swooping around up above. When she spoke again it was to tell me that Sebe's uncle had approached her again a while back and had asked after me. Your *mol* is still single and our nephew is a very good boy and is still looking for a wife. Maybe if we let them contact each other, now is the time and something will happen.

"He is highly-qualified," my mother said. "A lawyer."

I was alone in the bungalow, and knew that my flatmate would not be returning for some hours. So

I could speak freely, without worry of being overheard. And yet, at the same time, I knew I couldn't speak freely.

"OK," I said, because it seemed that she was waiting for a response.

"And you've seen the photo. He's handsome, isn't he?"

"Mmm."

As always I felt a small annoyance. My old bitter self looked up. A good job and good looks. The distillation of person's worth into these two factors had always appeared despicably shallow. But, whereas before I would have shown my annoyance, now it was a momentary flash, and then passed.

"Most importantly," my mother continued, "He is still available. I thought we would miss our chance when you gave me no reply that last time."

"Yes."

"Maybe he has been waiting for you?"

She knew she had gone too far because she did not reprimand me when I chuckled in disbelief.

When I sighed into the phone, she sighed, in echo.

"Let me know," she said. "When you decide. Then you can contact him directly."

She had not used 'if'; it was 'when'. She knew our conversation spelled some kind of change, a turning of the tide.

I pressed the phone to my ear. We were silent for some time, I could hear her breathing and further in the background, the swooshing, the ceiling fan in the living room where the phone sat on its own dark wood stool. I was tired, drained. The last few months had been busy, especially as I could see my imminent departure looming.

But I knew I was tired for a different reason. And my mother knew too.

"*Mol*," she came back on the line. Her voice was low. I remembered sitting on the verandah in Alleppey with her, more than three years ago, my grandfather still alive. She had spoken just as softly then. "Are you there?"

I nodded. Then managed to murmur into the handset.

"*Mol*," she repeated. "I cannot say that I know him well, but I'm sure he will look after you."

She had spoken the words that, until they were said, I had not known I wanted to hear. My eyes filled with sudden tears and I swallowed the lump in my throat. The relief I felt was palpable. My body sagged, physically, as if immediately I expected a hand to reach out and support me, steady me. I lay on my side on the bed, my hand on my throat, my eyes closed. I had spent the last three years as an itinerant, in guise of fieldwork for my research, but really, I realised suddenly, because I did not know where else to go.

*

When everything was in place I admit that I worried about the physical side. In the old days it was taken for granted that a marriage was consummated on the wedding night. I remember a confusing conversation I overheard when I was about six. It was between my mother and her younger sister. My aunt was getting married the next day. My mother was telling her how she had also been scared and how it had hurt and how she hadn't liked it. But that my aunt had to be strong, and stay relaxed and that later on it became easier. They had giggled, then wept a little, spoken in whispers, used words I didn't understand, covered their mouths with their hands as they rocked with convulsive laughter. They thought I was asleep. I tried to tell them I was awake, I wanted to ask them exactly what they were talking about, but my thumb was in my mouth, I was sleepy and what I thought were words were probably just gurgles.

What Sebe and I had never initiated in our emails was any mention of previous lovers. We were blank sheets of paper, waiting to be written on. This was, of course, unrealistic, but neither of us was bold enough to start that conversation. It had been liberating to write to Sebe in English. I spoke no Indonesian, but in East Timor where I spent most of my time some people still spoke Portuguese, a legacy from its years as a colony. I had become conversant in Portuguese from my years in Mozambique, but had never reached the level where I could express my thoughts with complexity. I had to limit myself to simple declaratives and interrogatives, and now in my longer and longer emails to Sebe I revelled in metaphor. While these virtual communications were pleasant, when the wedding took shape and form I began to fully appreciate that I was to be a wife. At some stage, I had to accept, I would have to re-join the physical world: we were going to share a bed, after all, as well as a home. When I had watched the other couples on my wanderings in Delhi, this had been one of the many thoughts in my head. They would have mostly, like me and Sebe, only spent time alone together after their wedding had taken place. Now they held hands, and whispered to each other, smiled into each other's eyes. At some stage, I was fairly certain, this would be true for the two of us, but I had no idea of how it would transpire.

In the days before our wedding, after our first meeting produced the seal of approval from both sides, Sebe and I were chaperoned on various outings. He had not been to Kerala many times, and so under the guise of sight-seeing the families organised trips to showcase the booming Kerala tourism industry. Always a chance, then, for me to be invited along and for the two of us to get to know each other a little bit, surrounded by clucking, chattering elders.

My uncle had a friend from school who owned a resort on one of the islands on Lake Vembanad. He arranged for an afternoon visit, and even managed to get us all a houseboat to take us there. When we arrived at the resort, Joshi was waiting to receive us. My uncle introduced us, Joshi ruffled my hair, gave me a strong side-on hug, and told me I had grown a lot since he had last seen me. The grass below our feet on the island was lawn-like, well-trimmed and a perfect complement to the dark brown wood of the bungalows, which were arranged around a swimming pool. A tourist was sunbathing, lying on her stomach in a bright blue one-piece swimming costume. My aunt, picking up her sari with one hand while climbing off the boat, averted her eyes, muttering something about people forgetting to put on their clothes. The men looked at their shoes and talked loudly as we moved past.

Sebe was staring out at the lake, his hands in his pockets, lagging behind. He caught me looking at him and smiled suddenly. I liked the way the dimple on his chin became more pronounced. He came up beside me.

"I'm bushed", he said, "Can't seem to get rid of the jet-lag."

I made sympathetic noises, and we turned to join the others who were going into one of the bungalows. Joshi was giving us the full tour.

"It's pretty, isn't it," he said.

I nodded.

"Do you want to stay here a few nights after the wedding?"

I looked up surprised. He was looking down at me, his eyes a little uncertain. He was jiggling his hands in his pockets.

"I suppose we could", I stammered, "It might be expensive..."

"I just think it'd be nice to spend a bit of time alone together some place nice before I head out back home. Your papers may take a while. And, I mean, we could get to know each other a little more without hundreds of eyes staring at us."

"Watching our every move."

He put on a very convincing Malayalee accent, "Are they talking? Are they suiting?"

I laughed out loud, he smiled back.

"Let's see what the rooms are like, and then you can decide."

We stepped through the doorway. The room was exquisite. Simply furnished — double bed with white, cotton linen, mosquito net, wardrobe — with walls of heavy logs, a thatched ceiling. The shower room had modern, gleaming fittings, brass taps and towel rails, but was open to the sky. The thought of power-showering under the stars filled me with glee. It must have shown on my face because Sebe said "great" and then went to speak with my uncle. They huddled together for a bit and then the two of them approached Joshi. He leaned forward to hear Sebe whose face was beginning to flush slightly. Then Joshi guffawed loudly, whacked him a few times on the back, waggled his head delightedly. Everyone was grinning. Except me, and Sebe, who had a rigor mortis smile on his lips.

Joshi came up to me, pinched my arm and gave me a disapproving look. It was a familiar complaint: I had no womanly curves, an essential quality in a spouse. But his eyes were filled with such affection I had to smile back. Then he hugged me tightly, picked me up, swung me around as if in demonstration: "*Edi, ichiroode vannum vekkanum!*"

While everyone had their own idea of how our wedding night would be spent, Sebe and I both agreed that what we needed most of all was a good sleep. Arriving late at night at the bungalow in a taxi from the wedding party, he had taken the bag out of my hand and said, "You go ahead and use the bathroom first." I was grateful. The day had been long with more of everything than was normal. More clothes, more make-up, more church, more food, more talking, more smiling. The wedding ceremony already seemed liked a distant memory. There had been no hitches, and to my surprise I had not been that nervous. But it had been lengthy, and the day had been an endless series of activities. I had barely looked at Sebe.

I took my night clothes into the bathroom with me, and closed the door. Showering under the stars was as wonderful as I had imagined, and that was the first time that day that I felt something close to happiness. When I went into the bedroom, wearing the long, white cotton night-dress I had bought for that night, my hair still wet and hanging down on my shoulders, I had no idea how I would find Sebe. He was sitting on the bed, changed into a t-shirt and shorts. I caught a glimpse of his legs which were long and hairy and strong-looking. The bed-side lamp was on. He looked at me and smiled. "You look nice. Feel better?"

"Yes, it's lovely. You go ahead now." My voice sounded uncertain. I am talking to my husband! I thought.

He nodded, grabbed a towel, went inside and closed the door.

I combed my hair and looked around. The bedroom was so beautiful, with its wooden beams, and bronze ceiling fan, the white cotton sheets. There were heavy old lamps, and even a bookshelf with books. Hard to believe that, outside, the backwaters lapped the island, and a cloud of mosquitoes hovered in wait for an open door.

Sebe came back in the room, still wearing the t-shirt and shorts and drying his hair with a towel.

"You must be really tired," he said.

"You too."

He walked up to me, and took my hand, and kissed my cheek. Our first kiss.

"It was a nice day."

I nodded.

"Listen," he hesitated. "We can take our time. Let's get some sleep. Have a nice breakfast tomorrow."

I nodded. And we lay down side by side, man and wife, not touching, on the bed. I thought I would lie awake for hours, but I must have slept instantly.

*

Joshi had no idea that our night together in his resort would go so differently from how he was imagining, spinning me around like a child. My aunt rescued me, took me by the hand and we stepped out into the full glare of the sun and walked to Joshi's office. It was comfortingly shabby, paint peeling off the walls, cluttered with chairs and tables, ceiling fan wobbling as it turned weakly. Joshi cleared some space for us, took out two stand-alone fans, and turned them onto full speed. Then he shouted for Bimal, who appeared sweating under the weight of a tray laden with a coffee pot, cups, and little steel bowls filled with idli and saambar. We sat, drank and ate. My uncle and Joshi talked loudly in Malayalam with Sebe's uncle about life in America, occasionally breaking into English to quiz Sebe. He answered equably but looked uncomfortable as he sat, perched on the edge of his chair, trying to eat off his lap. He spilled some coffee. Loud calls for Bimal again. Sebe was wiped down, served with a fresh cup. I sat in the background, licking my fingers and slurping my coffee.

After we ate we headed back to the boat. As the elders walked on ahead, Sebe hung back with me, took my elbow and said, "Shall we go to Ernakulam tomorrow? Just the two of us? Do some sightseeing?" It was hot, I squinted against the sun. He smelled slightly of sweat, and his hand on my elbow was warm. He had nice hands and I was surprised to enjoy his touch. I looked up at his face and felt a pleasure in that action, of raising my face to his. His eyes had the same uncertain look as before, but momentarily travelled over my features, from my eyes to my mouth, back to my eyes. Again I felt a sensation, an enjoyment of being looked at, and looked at with appreciation. I nodded, and he nodded and then he helped me back into the boat.

3

I have started swimming again, after a long hiatus. I belong to a gym a short drive away which has a rectangular pool with crystal-clear water. I cleave through the water, up and down the lanes, up and down, feeling the muscles in my legs and arms stretch and ache. Sometimes I take Shayla with me, and put her in the crèche while I do my lengths. Other times, I take her in the water with me, with her yellow rubber ring. She loves the water, but has to bring her ducks for comfort. I have managed to limit the ducks to three. She likes the number three, being three years old and knowing that there are three people in her family. Shayla wears a turquoise blue one-piece that shows off her silky brown skin. Her hair, when wet, lies in wavy tendrils around her brow. She likes my black two-piece, but doesn't like the white swim-hat I wear when I'm doing my lengths. When we are in the baby pool together, she insists I let my hair down. Then she cups her hands to fill them with water, and pours it over my head. Before any swimming practice can commence, I need to be as wet as her.

Sebe works in a law firm, and we sometimes go for dinners with his colleagues. Those days Sebe's mother comes round to baby-sit Shayla. She is a widow, a sprightly seventy-five-year-old, from Thekkaddy originally, but an American for more than thirty years. We speak in Malayalam, but she always talks to Sebe in English. He is her youngest, and her baby. She is considerate to me, and completely without curiosity. We got married when she thought herself old, and now her main concern is her health and well-being, and, thankfully, not the quality of her daughter-in-law. She wears black tracksuit bottoms, crocheted jumpers and woolly hats in the cold. She has never commented on how I look and what I wear – a novelty for me from an elder – except for the day Shayla was born. I lay in the hospital bed, feeling like I had been through a war, but my mother-in-law pronounced me 'radiant'.

My mother when she came to stay with us two years ago, also took to wearing trousers and tracksuit bottoms. I smiled seeing my mother's legs, still long and slim, usually swathed in the pleats of a sari or lungi, encased in polyester hues of red and navy. She topped these unflatteringly ordinary trousers with mismatched layers of cardigans and various t-shirts. I have always been amused by my mother's complete lack of vanity. I am not the only one to have noticed this: her siblings and cousins despaired of her dress-sense. When we stayed in my great-uncle's big, rambling house in Madras my mother's cousin, Liza, who was eighteen at that time, would come and sit in the bedroom in the mornings and watch as my mother put on her sari. My mother was taller than the other women, slim but voluptuous, with long arms, fingers, toes, and legs. Her belly was lightly rounded and a golden colour. She would pleat her sari thoughtfully, holding the palloo between her teeth, then tuck in the pleats, and arrange the rest of the sari over her blouse. She always wore her blouses fairly longish; she was quite prudish unlike her sisters. Liza would berate her: the style now was very short and very tight, with a deep-cut neck, why did Chechi wear such old-fashioned blouses? The other cousins, Joseph and Benny were both a bit older than Liza. They were good-looking, with deep voices, big and strong, and they lifted me onto their shoulders with such ease that I felt they would throw me right off. They teased my mother endlessly, even though she was renowned for her beauty. About her old-fashioned shoes, about her hair, curly and completely untameable, about her coquettish mannerisms. I marvel, now, at how the family has dispersed, and how many seem to have arrived in America. Liza is now married and a lecturer in Iowa; Joseph and Benny live in New Jersey with their families.

My mother, when she came to Chicago on her visit, loved our house, took over the kitchen and began producing hot curries and delicacies that Sebe and I both devoured. She used the food-processor that I had bought but had until then left unused, darted from the microwave to the hob. Bemoaned the quality of my pressure cooker: did I not know that you could get better ones at the outlet store? She was so completely at ease away from Alleppey and her house that I had to comment on it.

"But I've been coming to the US for years," she countered. And she was right. While I had been flitting around the world, semi-incommunicado, my mother had been keeping tabs on her other children, my brothers, both of whom lived a few states south of me. I caught a glimpse of the lives that the rest of my family had been having over the last few years. They lived in houses, like mine now, and they met the kind of people that I was meeting now, and they talked about things that I talked about now. I was catching up. My marriage had indeed been less of a pact between Sebe and me: rather an invitation for us to join in with the lives of the other members of our family. Even Sebe, when I question him about it, admits that he sees more of his relatives — uncles, aunts, cousins—after marriage than before.

My mother oozes contentment now. She is less abrasive, warmer, more mellowed. She looks older, too. I was a little taken aback when I saw her, looking frailer, more lined, more weathered, but still incisive in her comments and opinions. She treats Sebe with affection, and not a little gratitude for accepting her errant, flighty daughter. I still get annoyed and even confessed to Sebe that, before we were married, I had gritted my teeth at the way he was painted as a knight in shining armour to my damsel in disgrace. He always laughs, assumes a world-weary expression and agrees, yes, he has been a martyr. But then always kisses me softly after.

*

It is hard now to remember what I was feeling during our first tentative communications; they were so hurried, at times so clinical. There was no mystery, no suspense: if we liked each other enough, we would marry. When I gave my mother a mumbled go-ahead over the telephone from my bungalow in Indonesia, she slipped into action. Commandeered one of my young cousins to drive her to the nearest internet cafe in Alleppey town, where she then commandeered the young man working there to help her. She sent me Sebe's email address. We began to write to each other, careful, informative emails, detailing our interests and daily lives. Favourite colours, favourite films, the best book we had read, the ideal holiday. My days were filled with writing reports and discussing theory: I enjoyed seeing an email in my inbox that was not connected with my studies. I relished their chasteness. I revelled in their intangibility. I sent him a photograph of myself, taken some years before at a do in London – I was in a crowd holding a glass of wine in my hand, grinning inanely. I had not enjoyed that evening and my smiles had become wider in inverse proportion to my discomfort. I had almost hoped that the photo would put him off – she looks so westernised, she's drinking – but he had written back saying that he had liked it.

Sometimes we broached more personal subjects, but not often. I began to look forward to his messages; he was articulate and at times surprised me with his humour. He phoned me a month into our exchanges. It was awkward, because I didn't know what to say, and I was vaguely put out by how American he sounded. And then I sent him more photos, of myself, standing grimy and sweaty with my colleagues and others in the village where we were carrying out most of our fieldwork. He phoned me again.

"I like the photo you sent," he said.

"Thank you."

"You're very photogenic."

"Thank you," I repeated. Then, "I've always thought that when people say that they mean you look rubbish in person."

He had laughed, and I could detect a sense of relief, a melting.

"I really don't think you'll have that problem," he said. He had said it with such ease, it was almost flirtatious.

And then we were both silent. We had momentarily forgotten ourselves, and were we sitting over a dinner together this would have been the moment we both took a sip from our glasses, studied the menu and gathered ourselves somewhat.

"So," he continued, "My mom told me that my dad lived in the house opposite your family home in Alleppey."

"Yes, that's right. I don't remember your father, he must have left before I was born, but I do remember your uncle."

"Thomaschayan? Really?"

"Yes, he used to ride a motorbike to college, and my brothers and I thought he was very...cool."

"Really?" He was laughing again. "You must have low standards."

I started laughing myself.

"Oh yeah, you should see him now. He doesn't have a motorbike any more. He exchanged it for a lawnmower."

We both laughed, and then he said hurriedly, "I'm very fond of him, don't get me wrong. He's always been more like a big brother to me, rather than an uncle."

"I know."

And so we carried on. Our emails became longer, more connected. He began to ask after my day and whether a meeting had gone well. I asked whether that secretary who was dithering had finally typed up his reports. I began, vaguely but slowly, to piece together a picture in my mind of what life would be like, living with Sebe, in Chicago.

He called again one night, at the time we had pre-arranged. The time difference meant spontaneity was impossible. We had by now been in touch for nearly three months. He spoke slowly, as if he had prepared a speech.

"I've really enjoyed emailing you and talking to you. I think we have a lot in common."

"Yes."

I realised I sounded a bit abrupt and added hastily. "Yes, I have too."

"I have some leave to take", he continued. And there was a long pause.

When I didn't say anything, he came back on the line.

"I heard you are going home when you finish up in Indonesia. Should we, uh, should we meet then?"

"That would be nice," my answer came readily, too quickly for my liking. What did he mean, anyway? Meet where? For what? I opened my mouth, to backpedal, but he had already started talking. As if he had read my thoughts, he spoke slowly so that there would be no misunderstanding.

"So, if you're...satisfied ...I'll call my uncle. To tell him that we will go ahead with everything?"

I was quiet.

"And arrangements can be made for when we are in India?"

"Yes," I said. "I'll call my mother and she can take care of things on our side."

I heard him clear his throat.

"I think," he began, and he stopped as if searching for the right phrase, "I think that it's been ...exciting talking to you."

His choice of words was unexpected.

"Mmm."

"And I'm very much looking forward to meeting you properly," he continued. "I'd like that very much."

We parried back and forth, yes it will be nice to meet, yes really looking forward to it.

He called his uncle and I called my mother. 'Marriage' had not been mentioned, but after all, we were only speaking and writing to each other with that in mind. When I told my mother that I was happy enough with him, my family did the rest. All I had to do was book a ticket to India. It was probably similarly fast-moving for him. I never wondered whether he ever got cold feet.

*

My mother has only seen Shayla as a baby and we are due for another visit soon, so that she can see how her grand-daughter has grown. I'm hoping next year, to take Shayla to India. Shayla could acquaint herself with the house her mama grew up in. While my mother is still a fairly unknown quantity to Shayla, Sebe's mother is well-established. Shayla adores her and loves it when Ammachi comes to stay the night to baby-sit. I find it so heart-warming to see them together. As a small child I had been terrified of my grandmother, my father's mother. As was the custom in the old days, Amma had worn heavy gold ear-rings that stretched the holes in her ears to fist-sized open caves. Her paan-stained teeth, her very long grey hair, and above all her ear-lobes flapping against her shoulders filled me with dread. As the only daughter of my father I was always the one to serve Amma with her morning coffee or sweetmeats, a task I fulfilled with hammering heart. She would look at me distractedly, before turning away and re-plaiting her hair. Shayla and her grandmother are, in contrast, co-conspirators. When Sebe and I leave the house the two of them are already whispering about what bedtime game will be played.

When we were first invited to a dinner to meet Sebe's colleagues Harvey and Theo, and their wives, we hadn't needed a baby-sitter. We had only been married two months, and I was still new to Chicago. We all met at a seafood restaurant in the city. I wore a red halter-neck dress that I had never worn before, but which I hoped I looked good in. Long silver ear-rings, and silver bangles. I had been apprehensive about meeting Sebe's friends and joining his established American life. Harvey and Theo greeted Sebe with fist-bumps and slaps on the back. He kissed their wives, Dee and Beth on their cheeks. They all seemed like old friends, and I hung back nervously.

Harvey broke away from the group and approached me, kissed me on the cheek.

"So you are Sebastian's new wife."

"I am."

"You're just as beautiful as he's been saying. I'm glad he wasn't lying."

The others crowded round. We must have been the same age, all of us, or in the same range, but I suddenly felt ridiculously young, the blushing bride, and the wives flapped around me.

"We must meet up for coffee."

"If you need to know about anything, just call."

"Is this your first time in the States?"

"She's new to the States," Sebe broke in, "But she's been around more than any of us."

I was surprised when, with pride, he told them how I had lived and worked and studied in three continents.

"I don't even make it to the South Side much", Theo joked.

They were impressed, drew back, and we sat down and ordered. It must have been strange to them, I could see. One minute, Sebe had been one of the guys; the next, he was on a plane to India to bring back a wife. They were too discreet then to ask about the details. That night we all talked about their work, Beth's new project at the ad agency she worked at, my papers and first impressions of Chicago, Harvey's upcoming promotion. The men arranged to meet later that week for a soccer game; their law firm was taking on a rival firm in a charity fund-raiser. They were nice people, and I enjoyed the evening. On the way home that night, Sebe, his arm around my shoulder, said with the same pride in his voice, "You knocked them out."

I have been so touched by his generosity. He showed this capacity very early on. A few days before the wedding we had got a lift into Ernakulam. We had managed to organise a day to ourselves, and the elders had given their blessing. We had thought to wander around, go somewhere for lunch, and then get a lift back in time for dinner. Everyone thought it was a good suggestion. ("You see how considerate he is?", "You must take full opportunity to ask any questions.") I was looking forward to it; it would be good to get out of the house, look at shops. But I was also dreading it.

I had become intensely aware that while I had led a life that had been somewhat unconventional, Sebe was just as unconventional. He was born and grew up in the States. From what I had heard, his parents were both educated and must have been fairly progressive. They chose to leave India and never returned. His father had died a few years back but his mother continued to live on her own, she hadn't moved into one of his brothers' homes. I assumed she was a feisty, independent older lady. Sebe was thirty-two years old, an American.

I was as certain as I could be that his relationship with me would not be his first. After all, he was a man, and men's lives have never undergone the scrutiny that a woman's would. I knew that many men in his position, with Indian heritage but a foreign nationality, asked for an arranged marriage after youthful adventures. My own cousin, Marthammachi's son, who studied in California and who secretly harboured an American girlfriend, asked for his parents' advice when the love affair fell through. He ended up marrying a pharmacist from Palai. They now live in Fresno and have two young sons. I knew of many more — my mother had been spending the previous weeks happily recounting these assurances that, yes, we have moved on, yes, there is a new clique of western-born Indians, but yes, sometimes the old ways still suit the younger generation.

But even given all that, I still maintain that Sebe is untypical. With his credentials — an American passport, a profession, nice looks — he was a catch for any family with an unmarried daughter to offer. He was over thirty, but it would not have been frowned upon had he requested a much younger bride, in her early-twenties, freshly-graduated from a college in Kerala. A bride who would look up to him as the wiser, older man, who would be excited at the prospect of travel and setting up home in a western environment. Instead, he had chosen me: I was nearly thirty, I had spent nearly half of my life outside of India, and I had lived away from my family for all that time. He was worldly enough, surely, to suspect that I had not lacked in opportunities for a love affair in all that time. That was something I hoped for but could not assume. In the old days, your spouse was your first partner of the opposite sex. Much had changed since then, but for many couples, even in a modern India and for modern Indians, this was still true. I was concerned. Meeting Sebe in the flesh had been very different to exchanging letters and emails with him. He had become real. He had an openness that was unexpected, and a happiness about the impending nuptials that made me ashamed of my relative indifference. I realised that I wanted things to work out between us. And if he asked, where could I begin and where could I end?

My uncle dropped us in town, and we arranged to be picked up later in the afternoon. Sebe was wearing a cream-coloured kurta, jeans, and sunglasses. I had opted for jeans and a white cotton top. We were already beginning to resemble the couples I had observed in Delhi. Ernakulam was busier than I remembered. As children we always used to go to the park for picnics. The hedges were trimmed into animal shapes, an elephant, a giraffe, a hippo. I had no idea where that park was in relation to where my uncle had dropped us and wondered why I had not thought to ask. After walking around in the heat and traffic fumes, we decided to go into a shopping mall and spend an hour traipsing in and out of shops. But neither of us seemed to be in the right mood. When he suggested a coffee, I concurred.

We went back onto the street and crossed the road to India Coffee House. He gallantly opened the door for me, pulled out my chair. Not very common behaviour in Ernakulam, and the waiters were agog. We sat at a table near the window. He took off his sunglasses and smiled at me.

"Good to get you alone for a change."

"Yeah."

A waiter arrived and Sebe ordered.

"*Runde kaapi.*"

"Will sir be wanting with sugar or without?" the waiter asked in English. Sebe was put out, but hid it well, turned to me. I shook my head.

"Without."

The waiter glided off, Sebe sighed.

"Asshole," he said with a grin. "God, they know how to make you feel a complete outsider."

I paused.

"Aren't you?"

"An outsider?"

I nodded my head.

"I suppose. I'm American, but I'd like to think of myself as a Malayalee as well. If that's possible."

A silence descended for a while.

"You're very pretty", he said finally. "And you've got this fragile thing going. But I think you're also pretty tough."

"Maybe."

"I wouldn't have thought you would have gone for all this."

"Arranged?"

He nodded.

"I wouldn't have thought you would either," I said.

What did we mean? Maybe different things, but I wasn't sure. We both knew gorgeous, intelligent and happy people who had had arranged marriages like ours, and who now had gorgeous children, intelligent relationships and happy lives. We were neither more interesting nor more desperate, but I thought I understood what he said. I had taken a circuitous route to this coffee-shop in Kerala, and perhaps he had too.

I realised that if I didn't speak then, I would lose my nerve.

"Sebe". It was the first time I had said his name. "Can I ask you something?"

He nodded, leaned forward. I almost thought he was going to take my hand.

"Have you been in a relationship before?" It sounded awkward, I felt my cheeks redden, but he nodded again, approving of my question. I felt a sting of irritation.

"I did have a girlfriend. She was a Greek-American. We met at work and we were together for a few years, it didn't work out."

"Why not?"

"Well, I guess I was aiming to make a name for myself at work at that time, I wasn't really interested in a relationship. I wasn't very involved."

"And you're interested now?"

He nodded, our coffees arrived, and we waited for the waiter to go before continuing.

"My uncle suggested an arranged marriage. Things are different nowadays. He's not that much older than me and he went for one. And I think he did great, my aunt's great fun. I suppose I realised that you could actually be happy, have a nice life with.... I mean, we talked a lot before deciding, didn't we? And I knew about you, your family. And I liked that you were independent, a bit of a rebel. Do you mind me saying that?"

I shook my head.

"And when we spoke. I liked your voice, you know, soft, musical."

I looked down. It was as I had expected, and I was not surprised. While, when I had been younger I would have been consumed with curiosity — was she prettier than me, how much had he loved her — now I felt a detachment. I could sense how it all had passed before. He had come a long way to be where he was now, the present.

I waited for him to ask me back, but he didn't.

"I was in a relationship", I said, finally.

He did not respond and when I looked up, I saw that his eyes were on me.

"I'd have been surprised if you hadn't been", he said at last. "But if you're worried about how I feel about that, don't be."

He took a sip from his coffee cup, grimaced.

"There's an awful lot of hypocrisy that goes on," he continued. "I like to think that I am a bit above all that. I mean, *you* could be unhappy about my old girlfriend, couldn't you? I'm hoping you will understand that that is all in the past."

I didn't tell him that when I had asked him of his past affairs I had not expected him to respond in any other way. I was building courage to say what I thought I needed to say.

"It was very intense," I said carefully.

There was silence.

"What are you trying to say?" he said after some time.

I said nothing. I knew then that I would not tell him everything. How could I tell him about the small dark sadness when I had not told Jafar? It was our little tragedy, our tiny lost soul. That loss was ours alone and did not belong to this conversation, to the man sitting opposite me. Every married couple must have secrets from each other, I thought to myself. He had not revealed his all to me; I did not care and I would not ask him.

I let the silence grow.

"I take it you're talking about sex", he said at last.

I said nothing looking down at my cup.

We drank our coffees in silence. A fly was buzzing around the table and settled on my saucer. I waved it away.

"And what did you do?"

"What do you mean?"

"I mean, what did you do, how intense was it?"

He regretted the question as soon as he had asked it. He pushed his cup away angrily and looked out of the window.

We stayed like this for some time, in silence, but eventually got to our feet. Sebe paid for our coffees and we went outside. We walked along Marine Drive and attracted a lot of attention from the young boys selling their wares, and from others who giggled at us and did somersaults.

"I can't say that I am happy," he said eventually. "And I'm surprised at myself I suppose, that I am so bothered. But I'm glad you told me. I'm sorry if I was rude."

We didn't touch or take hands. I walked, distracted, my thoughts on the sea. It was a beautiful blue and green, the Indian Ocean. The same sea that over thousands of miles away laps against the east coast of Africa, washes the coast of Mozambique. We walked along the promenade, his hands were in his pockets, his sunglasses were back on his nose. We spoke later. We agreed that we had enjoyed the day, and that it had been good to be alone for a change.

4

Shayla doesn't want me to leave. It will be the first time that I have spent any time away from her, and I am surprised at myself for agreeing to go. Rather than spending my first night away from my baby in a nearby hotel, or even a nearby state, I will be boarding a plane and flying thousands of miles away. Sebe's mother will come and stay while I am away, help him with the cooking and ferrying Shayla to kindergarten. She has done more for her older children; they had their kids before Sebe's father died, and so the two of them had been active grandparents, at the beck and call of their children in opposite sides of Chicago. There is a huge Malayalee community here in Chicago, something that surprised me when I went to our first gathering. Hundreds of families, booked into a large hotel ballroom, to celebrate Onam.

The September festival was my favourite as a child. We ate up to fifteen small curries, a mere tablespoon of each, all arranged on a fresh, green banana leaf, like an artist's palette. In Chicago that day, someone had procured hundreds of banana leaves. From the Caribbean, I wondered? Everyone was wearing their best kurta, best sari, prettiest dresses. Some teenagers had stuck to jeans, and one fifteen-year-old girl had arrived head to toe in black: over-sized t-shirt, scuffed jeans and Doc Martens. She made me smile. I had not worn the traditional cream-coloured cotton sari with its wide gold border, but a silk sari with alternate shades of green and fuschia. A sleeveless, very short blouse. It was daring for back home, revealing a lot of back and midriff, but being a married woman now, I am allowed more leeway. Sebe's eyebrows rose when he saw me, but he made no comment. The atmosphere at the gathering was carnival, the music loud, the voices a mixture of American and Malayalee.

After being introduced to nearly everyone that Sebe's family knows, I finally made excuses about using the bathroom, and left Sebe haplessly talking to the town bore, Bennykuttan, a fifty-year-old engineer who, from his anecdotes, must have solved most technological problems of the last century. I left the ballroom and moved down the hallway in search of a quiet spot.

"...and fucking casing the joint, man".

"More than you'll ever know."

The voices broke off as I rounded the bend. Four boys had had the same idea as I. They were in various postures of cool disdain, their faded t-shirts and scruffy shoes proclaiming their protest at attending this very long and dull cultural frenzy.

"Sorry," one boy hastily stood up straighter. "Didn't see you."

I was amused. Being a married woman lends status like nothing else.

"Do I know you?" I asked him. He did look familiar with his very long tousled hair and square jaw, but I had met so many people that I could not keep up with matching names and faces.

"I'm Bimal Nayar's son, Renji," he replied, extending his hand. "Sebechetan's brother and my dad were at school together."

I nodded, and the three other boys introduced themselves, shaking my hand with impeccable manners. I leaned against the wall, and they produced a beer for me from a crate they had secreted from the ballroom. They were all, I guessed, not more than twenty years old. I sipped my beer, and enjoyed listening to them explain why they were outside in the hallway, not mingling with the others. Renji was often press-ganged into providing live music for the dances some of the girls were going to perform. This time he had left his guitar at home.

"I just get sick of being dragged out, the performing monkey," he said while his friends chuckled.

I felt sympathy for him. They were, all three, so American. The lack of cool that these huge, chaotic events held must have been deplorable. They were beginning to ask me what I thought of Chicago when Sebe appeared.

"Thanks for abandoning me," he said putting his arm around my waist.

I grinned. "Sorry."

"Yeah, right." He looked at the boys and then at the beer in my hand. "Hey guys. So you've met my wife."

I watched him tease them with a familiarity that reminded me that he knew them better than he knew me. And I watched them tease him back, but with restraint, deference to their elder. We had been married a mere six months, but had gained old-married status among the youth. And now, a few years on and having produced a child, we are card-carrying members of the respectables. We haven't attended every single event that the association organises, but last year Shayla so enjoyed dressing up in silk skirts and blouse, bangles and a puttu, that I have resolved to attend at least the Onam celebration each year.

As my trip is imminent, I have been spending some time looking at my wardrobe and wondering what to take. I would like to travel with as few clothes as possible so that I can take my books and also bring back some trinkets and souvenirs for Shayla and for the house. I wonder at my 'no-more-than-three-outfits' philosophy of days gone by; now I am thinking about matching shoes and accessories. I have, finally, settled on three outfits. The difference being that this time they are three separate entities, rather than interchangeable.

I am reminded of a conversation I had some years ago with Beth, Theo's wife. She had come visiting on a Friday afternoon, when I was frantically finishing off a research report. The deadline was the next day, but I still welcomed the chance for a break. I made coffee for us, and we settled at the breakfast bar of the kitchen.

"It looks nice", she said, gesturing at the shiny new worktops, the pictures on the wall, the plants on the window-sill. "You have a real flair."

I murmured my thanks, while her attention moved to me, my clothes and hair and face. "And I love the way you dress. You always look sensational. I'd never get away with those colours you wear."

I was used to compliments from a Western perspective; I knew that back home my look — floating textures, no make-up, jangly but inexpensive jewellery, invariably coupled with jeans — would bring sighs of exasperation and despair.

"We were all surprised when Seb told us he was getting married", she said suddenly.

I nodded. "I can imagine."

"You know about Angie?"

The Greek-American girlfriend. I nodded.

"Well, I hope you don't mind me saying, but she was crazy about him. We thought it was mutual. But obviously not."

Outside in my back garden, which as yet had not been tended to much, a small bird landed on a bush. I watched it peck away at the leaves. Collecting something for a nest?

"I guess it's hard for me to imagine marrying someone you don't know." She laughed.

I smiled. "It happens even when you've been together for a while. You learn new things about each other."

"Yeah, that's true." She laughed again. "But with you guys you don't know each other one day and then you're sleeping together the next!"

I couldn't blame her for her curiosity, as I had worried over the same thing the first weeks of our marriage. Sebe had left four days after the wedding. Our wedding night and the next we had spent at Joshi's resort. I had seen him looking at me when he thought I was unconscious of his eyes, but we had slept side by side, not touching, both those nights. And both nights I had slept really well, while I had expected to be unsettled, unable to relax.

In the mornings we woke up at the same time, early, when the room started getting over-warm. We used the bathroom one by one, spoke to each other politely over breakfast. We didn't mention our conversation from a few days earlier in the India Coffee House in Ernakulam. We talked about the wedding and recalled amusing incidents with our family members. One of Sebe's uncles had got terribly drunk, my aunt had got terribly weepy. Sebe's cousin, a shorter rounder female version of him, had arrived at the last minute without her family and turned out to be a hoot. In her strong American accent she happily berated fastidious aunties, flirted with all the men present, and ate copiously. We didn't have a full count of family members from both sides as the wedding had been arranged so quickly that not everyone could make the long journey on time. Sebe's family had promised another celebration in Chicago, when I joined him. With so much to rehash, there was much to distract us from the huge, unassailable fact that we were now married.

After breakfast, we took books to the side of the pool. I swam and then he did. We had lunch later, and then retreated back into the cottage for the hottest part of the afternoon. We lay on the bed, side by side, the ceiling fan at its highest speed. He fell asleep while I stayed awake, stealing glances at his slowly rising and falling chest. We had showers again before dinner because of the heat, then some more polite conversation. He talked about his work in Chicago; I talked about my studies and the thesis I was finishing. At bedtime, he kissed me on the cheek again, before we lay down. After those two restful days, we went back to his uncle's house close to Kottayam. A flurry of visits and shopping and then we were driving him to the airport to fly back to Chicago. At the airport, he kissed me on the cheek again to say goodbye, and everyone smiled and laughed happily. I made the same journey three weeks later, after my papers had come through.

When I landed in Chicago, things were different. He was more relaxed, more at ease and happier. He was pleased to see me again, which I found touching. We had been invited to his mother's house so that I could meet his brothers, none of whom had made it to our wedding. But Sebe assured me that it would be a flying visit, and we would have a chance for proper introductions after I had settled in. On the drive into the city, he pointed out landmarks, told me about places we would visit. He had taken some time off work and was able to help me acclimatise to my new home. We went back to his flat, which was already half-packed-up. We would be moving into the house in five days' time.

It was a one-bedroom bachelor pad, and without any pictures or books out that he might normally have had, with packing boxes everywhere, it looked forlorn. He apologised, showed me where everything was and asked if I wanted to go for a walk. I was grateful for the chance to stretch my legs, and we walked around a few blocks before heading back. We did the same every evening those first days. Those nights, again, we lay side by side on the bed, like two innocents.

Later in the week, we moved into the house a few miles out of the city. It was a hectic day, but with not many possessions, we ferried most things ourselves in the day. That night he suggested a take-out. We had Chinese food out of cardboard boxes, and a bottle of wine between us. Our rings, bought at a jeweller's in Kottayam, glinted on our fingers. Husband and wife. Mr and Mrs Velliamparambil! I got a bit tipsy, and laughed when I tried out my new name.

"You don't have to change your name if you don't want to," he said, when I had giggled for too long.

"It can be yet another decision we can make later," I raised my eyebrows theatrically.

"What's the other decision?" he asked.

I was emboldened by the wine.

"When you are going to take me as your wife." And I giggled again.

He didn't laugh, but got to his feet and walked over to my side of the room. He took the wine glass out of my hand and put it on a packing box. Then he kissed me on the mouth. I remember the taste of wine, his hand behind my neck, and the noises in the street below. I remember feeling a pleasure in parting my lips, in letting his tongue gently seek out mine. We didn't make love that night, nor the next. While we both had had partners in our past, and perhaps because of that, we began our marriage chastely, tentatively. The days after that first kiss, we started holding hands when we walked around the city. He started brushing hairs out of my face, putting his hand against the small of my back when we crossed the street. We started cooking dinners together. He took the lead, and I was happy to wash and cut vegetables. He was a passable cook. I knew that I was better, but he seemed eager to please me, and I appreciated it. The night before he went back to work, he undressed me and then undressed himself. The house was quiet, still. The sounds we made echoed in the emptiness; there was no furniture and we lay on a sleeping-mat on the floor. I closed my eyes and allowed him to explore my body, which he did slowly, attentively, as if I would disappear from under him if he did not take care. Rather than feeling exposed, I was moved by his gentleness. And when

I curved my legs through his, ran my fingers through his hair, he became more assured, as if he had been waiting for a sign, for my consent.

After, we lay together, slightly awkward, his arm across my waist, my hand on his chest. The lights from the street shone in through the thin blinds of the bedroom. My mind was a blank, but I could feel his heart pounding under my hand. I didn't feel love, but I didn't feel nothing either. Rather than being driven by an emotional attachment that needed a physical release, we were enacting the physical expectations of married life, and it felt good to be on that road. He took my hand and kissed it. I smiled, he smiled back.

*

It was difficult to explain all this to Beth, and I didn't try to that Friday afternoon. I let her blush, and then laugh again, embarrassed. "I'm sorry," she said. "That must have seemed terribly rude."

"Not rude. It's just a different situation."

"Yes, absolutely." She was contrite, and tried to back-pedal.

"Anyway, we're just thrilled to know you, and Seb is so happy."

"I'm happy too."

"Yes, I can see. You two are really cute together."

"So are you and Theo."

"Yes...you're right."

She knew that she had offended me and to her credit, she did not hold that against me. With time, the novelty of our relationship wore off, and Sebe and I became just another couple in the bunch.

We have settled into a routine now after the first couple of years' commotion of moving house, being pregnant and adjusting to married life. He loves playing soccer, and does so once a week with his friends from work. After the game they all go out for a beer, and he will get home late that night. Sometimes, he will have a shower downstairs and sleep on the couch so as not to wake me. Sebe tries to come home by lunchtime on every third Friday, and then we start our weekend as a family a bit earlier. Often we take Shayla back into the city, to Grant Park. It's become one of my favourite places; I love it when we chance upon an outdoor art or music performance. I love the feeling of space that you can find, the endless varieties of people you can see, the snatches of different languages that you can overhear. I love trying to identify them; I am not always able to, but I have heard such a spectrum, from Farsi to French.

Once a month we meet up with all his family members at someone's house. Both his brothers are married, both to American Malayalee girls. Shayla loves seeing her big cousins, all teenagers now, and they adore her. Sebe's family is a loving, supportive unit who all get on with each other and who have no further interest in each other's lives. It's perfect. I had worried about the strings and tentacles that marrying into a close-knit family would involve. But everyone is so caught up with their own dramas they do not bother with ours. I know that Ammachi is quietly very satisfied with the way her family has turned out. In spite of being widowed somewhat earlier than she had expected, her three sons are all professionals with fairly stellar careers. With everyone being so busy, we see each other once a month, and that's enough. Even when I told them about my upcoming trip, there were no admonitions and no concern.

My mother, on the phone from Alleppey, had more to say.

"What on earth are you doing?"

I sighed.

"Setting up a partnership project with the Pedagogical University..."

"No, I mean really. What on earth. What about Shayla?"

My Achilles' heel. My heart contracted with a stab of pain.

"Of course it will be difficult, Ma. But Sebe is supportive, and Ammachi..."

"I fear for you. You are starting again."

I could only guess at what she meant.

"Ma. I will be gone for ten days. It's something I've set up from start to finish. I think Shayla will be proud of me when she can understand it a bit more."

There was a loud harrumph at the other end of the phone. She has learned, she is no longer unprepared. My mother can see things that others cannot.

5

The early part of the afternoon has always been my favourite time of the day. When I was living in the tropics it was a time for a nap or a lie-down. As a child, it was a time to lose myself in the book I was reading. My brothers often chivvied me to join them in an unwisely active game: I always refused. Later, as an adult, it was a parentheses in the working day. It was impossible to work in the heat of the day, and people often went home, returning to work when the sun was less punishing. While I never fell asleep in those periods, I always spent those muted hours lying on my bed, preparing notes and sorting out paperwork. Often, lying only in my underwear under a fan, I enjoyed the contrast of the words and theories I was reading and writing about with the physical freedoms of feeling a cool breeze on warm skin.

Here in Chicago, the afternoons vary so much through the year. In the middle of winter it can be dark and grey not long after four o'clock. But in the summer the heat and humidity can rival any country I lived in in the tropics. When Shayla was a baby, early afternoon was the time for her main nap. That was when I caught up on my own sleep in the early days, and later, when

I managed to catch up on the most pressing household chores or work commitments. Now Shayla no longer has a nap, but, on the days I am home with her, I still enforce a quiet time. She will sit in the living room on the sofa, a colouring book in front of her, her pens scattered around her. Or she will pluck ineffectually at a jigsaw puzzle. Often, after twenty minutes of activity, her thumb goes into her mouth, and she will remain still, watching me with hooded eyes, twisting a finger in the hair around her ears.

She is unbearably adorable at these times, and my heart aches with the heaviness of my love for her. I move around her, tidying up the living room, which is invariably her chosen playroom for the day, and at times, sit on the floor below her, sorting out my papers. Sometimes she leans forward from her seat on the sofa and plays with the necklace and earrings that I am wearing; often she is a quiet presence behind me, her breathing stertorous, punctuated with occasional sucking sounds.

The living room has large windows which let in sunlight all day. I'm so pleased with how it looks: I wanted it to be an oasis of peace in the evenings but a warm and welcoming room during the day. It is spacious, with a rug we brought back from India on the floor, and brightly-coloured, mirrored cushions on the sofas. I suppose I didn't want it to look American, but it does speak of a comfortable Western life: the bookshelves, the coffee table, the polished floorboards, the cabinets filled with ceramics and photographs. There is a bank of photo albums in a shelf under the window sill. In this digital age, I insist that we print off photos regularly: I love the tactile pleasure received from turning the pages of an album and looking at days gone by.

I never used to take photographs. All through my travels I collected, instead, tickets and fliers, posters – objects I believed to be more potent reminders of the places I lived in. Most of these I have had blown up and framed, and they pattern the walls of my study. They look beautiful and arty, but I have come to appreciate the simplicity of a memory strengthened by a photo. While the family's relief when I got married had been annoying — I was finally becoming a real person — I realise that my own behaviour has given their views some credence. It is only since my marriage that I have started collecting photos, my life now warranting cataloguing and recording.

There is a photo album for nearly every half-year of my life since Sebe and I were married. Since Shayla was born I must have taken hundreds of shots, marking every milestone, every precious moment. My favourite at the moment is of her in her sand-pit, studiously filling a bucket, head bent, hair shining in the sun. And Sebe seems to find me photogenic: it is he who is more often behind the camera. In his study in the house he has, in a frame on his desk, a photo that he took a few days after I had arrived in Chicago. When I saw it I felt immensely touched. Not only because he had chosen to frame it and display it in his private space, but because the photo was not of me laughing alluringly into the camera, a confident, satisfied wife. I am leaning against the railings, looking at the lake, the sun setting behind me. I have turned my body away from him, the cameraman, and only one half of my face is shown. I remember that moment well; I had spent a few minutes enjoying the evening calm, wondering at how I had never imagined I would be living in a big American city, and wondering about how this new chapter in my life would unfold. When I asked Sebe why he had chosen that photo in particular to frame, he had answered that he felt it truly captured my essence. Those words floored me.

Among the photo albums that we keep in the living room we have two labelled 'Wedding'. Privately, we call them 'Wedding I', and 'Wedding II: The One We Enjoyed'. While officially we have only been married once, at the church in Alleppey, on joining Sebe in Chicago we had another church service followed by a reception involving all the members of our families who had not managed to make our last-minute marriage in India. They included Sebe's mother, who had been reluctant to travel at such short notice, his brothers and families, and my brothers too. The two ceremonies were completely different, not least because our relationship had developed in the interim months.

Fortunately for me, Sebe's uncle, who was hosting the first wedding, lived only a few miles away, on the other side of Alleppey. So I did not have to endure a long car-ride, on winding narrow roads, in the heat, decked out in all my finery, only to arrive at the groom's place sweating and dishevelled. Both sides had agreed that the wedding should take place in the largest church in Alleppey, which happened to be a short walk from my grandfather's house. The party after would be held in its large hall. And so my cousin drove my mother and I the short distance, in his new Indica, to the church. He had insisted that I did not walk on such a special day. Leaving the house, I had been called back by my mother into the living-room. Inside, she had laid her hands on my shoulders briefly, then on my head. On the wall beside us was a portrait of my grandfather, who had died a peaceful death two years ago. Next to it, one of my father, taken the year before he died. She was struggling with her emotions, I could see, blinking back tears. "He would be very happy, *mol*," she whispered. By now I was also struggling and opened my mouth. I was not sure what to say, and was spared that difficulty: my cousin called gaily from outside that we should be going.

Climbing out of the car in front of the church, I was momentarily blinded by the bright sunshine. When my eyes adjusted to the light, I saw the imposing entrance, now crowded with a multi-coloured mass of sari and kurtas. Nearly all of my mother's friends, acquaintances and remaining relatives were attending. Very few of my own friends were able to come: we had not given anyone much advance notice and a lot of the girls I knew from school lived in other parts of India or abroad. For Sebe, it was even more bizarre. Only his uncle and aunt would have been known to him, and his American cousin who had surprised us all by turning up. He had grown up in the States, hence had no school or childhood friends in Kerala, and had visited India only a handful of times. His mother was absent, and his brothers were unable to get the time off. For him, the service in Alleppey must have felt like a formality in preparation for the family get-together that was already being planned in Chicago.

He was standing to one side of the entrance, dressed in a dark suit and tie. He must have been feeling hot and nervous, but he managed a small smile when I looked up at him. I just ducked my head in what I hoped was a pleasant-enough fashion. I had been heartened by his smile. We had hardly spoken after our morning together in Ernakulam, and I had been worried that I had asked too much of him. "You look very nice," were his only words for the next few hours. I whispered my thanks before the two of us were ushered into our positions in front of the altar. The guests all settled into comfortable positions behind us, and a respectful silence descended. When Father Anthony arrived, resplendent in his robes, everyone started singing and the mass began.

As the service progressed, standing at the front of the church, Sebe a presence at my side, I felt strangely tranquil. The church was quiet, cool, occasional coughs and splutters coming from the congregation behind us. Father spoke in lyrical, elegant Malayalam, and then repeated everything in English. Although he had the best intentions, it was an unnecessary process and managed to extend what was a plodding service to a near-unbearable length. In the course of time, too, the atmosphere changed. The Hindu temple a few hundred metres away started testing out its loudspeakers, in preparation for an upcoming festival. Bhajans were trialled; in mid-flow they would be changed or another would begin. The sounds were disturbingly erratic, unbelievably loud, and I was no longer listening to Father. And then a few minutes later further competition arrived: the melancholic notes of the muezzin, somehow being carried all the way from the mosque near the train station on a mischievous wind. Several babies started crying, and at one point, there was a chorus of hungry voices drowning out the words of the homily.

Soon after, we exchanged rings. I looked up and saw Sebe smiling slightly. So I smiled back and then nearly giggled with relief. I felt ridiculous: I was wearing far too much heavy, ornate jewellery for my liking, and I could feel my hair slipping down from its clips. This wedding had been long-awaited and was in many ways momentous. But the casual noises from the congregation behind us, the cacophony outside, sounds of daily life in Alleppey carrying on regardless, the occasional church attendant traipsing in and out carrying a bucket, Father and his inaccurate translations, all lent a degree of comedy I had not expected. Sebe looked remarkably composed, and his hand when he held mine felt cool. I think he comported himself admirably, especially as for him these were fairly unfamiliar happenings.

The photograph of us standing outside the church, vows exchanged and newly-wed, shows a nice-looking couple. In the background is the white stone of the church, the steps leading down to its sandy forecourt. The bride is swathed in silk, the groom looks dashing. Several small children scattered at our feet, elders by our side. Everyone is smiling, the sky is blue behind us and it is clearly a happy event. We look like thousands of couples before and after us.

The party that followed was a boisterous affair. My mother, looking relaxed and radiant, traversed the hall, catching up with cousins and friends whom she had not seen for many years. Sebe and I were stationed at the front of the room, on a stage, behind a table covered with a heavy white cloth. Other than a quick, "Are you OK?" as we took our seats, he did not say much more to me. The music that was playing was very loud, old devotional favourites, and later, when my cousin took charge, the latest film songs. I was similarly taciturn, my eyes fixed in front of me. I was wearing the manthrakodi he had given me. It was a luxurious red, stiff with embroidery, and scratchy against the skin of my shoulders and neck.

Well-wishers lined up to shake hands and give kisses, most commenting on how they still pictured me as a schoolgirl in plaits, and how Sebe's father, a local Alleppey lad made very good, was remembered with much affection. How sad it was that both our fathers had passed on and could not see this happy day. Many quizzed Sebe about his job and home in Chicago. He answered every question patiently, sometimes asking them to repeat it, often responding with a promise to relay their good wishes to his mother. He said some phrases occasionally in Malayalam, and was always rewarded with loud laughs and playful punches. No question fazed him, and even when I had tired of the seemingly limitless interest in his salary and the size of his apartment he was replying patiently, "No, it's not very big. But it's near the city."

When the food was being served, Sebe's aunt appeared with a large coconut, carved hollow inside and then re-filled with its own water. Two straws, and two garlands. We had to first put the garland over each other's heads, and then drink from the same coconut. We did so conscientiously, studiously avoiding each other's eyes. When we had nearly drained the coconut, Sebe removed his straw and said to me "You finish it." Loud guffaws, whistles and claps, erupted from the audience, who had been watching in silence, expectantly. The women shouted in English, "Nice man!"; the men responded, "Watch out!". I couldn't help laughing, and I turned to see Sebe grinning back at me. It remains my favourite memory from the day, and luckily, my cousin managed to capture it in a photo, now framed and standing on our cabinet.

Later, in Chicago, although we wore the same clothes, the photos tell a different story. The church blessing and reception had been booked for a date several weeks after the wedding in Alleppey, just in case my papers were delayed. In the pictures, taken by a professional photographer who snapped and snapped ceaselessly, there is more collusion between us, more touching, our bodies more at ease with each other. In one, taken as we entered the hotel room that had been booked for the party, Sebe is removing some confetti from my hair with his right hand, his left hand gripping my elbow. Our hips are near-touching, my hand reaching up to my own hair, I am smiling, saying something looking up at his face. By then we had made love and were learning about each other. We had moved into our new house and were making ordinary, mundane decisions about fridges and sofas and curtains. I had been welcomed into his family by his brothers and mother. I felt like a wife. And it shows: in that photo, we look like a couple.

The guests at this second reception had been limited to family and close Malayalee friends: inviting the whole community in Chicago, or Sebe's non-Malayalee friends would have made the party immense and much less intimate than the family desired. Once again, Sebe and I were greeted by well-wishers, but this time we mingled freely with everyone. We walked around the tables, occasionally sat with the guests. We held hands as we moved around, and Sebe always pulled me forward to introduce me. I tried to appear as relaxed as he was, but I was very nervous. His marriage had been just as long-awaited as mine, and I knew that inevitably comments would be made later, when people returned to their houses and digested the evening, about whether they thought he had fared well or not. But over the evening I began to feel less tense, less on show. Everyone seemed pleased to meet me, and Sebe never left my side. With each conversation I watched as Sebe exchanged reminisces and shared anecdotes with old friends. My brothers were also there with my sister-in-law and my small nephew and niece. Years had passed since we siblings had all been together. After being close allies in childhood, we had embarked on adulthood alone. But I could see ahead to a revisiting of our old camaraderies; Sebe and I had already planned to go and stay with my older brother in Houston for Thanksgiving.

"So, welcome to Chicago," Sebe's older brother said, after most of the guests had left, and we were all gathering our things to leave.

"Thanks for organising this", I said. "I really enjoyed it."

"Our pleasure, of course." He helped me put a shawl around my shoulders. "How's the house?"

"Really lovely. We'll have a house-warming when we get the carpets upstairs sorted."

"No hurry. Settle in first."

Everyone was attentive, accommodating. Pleased at the union. It looked like it would work well.

*

A few days ago, making sure that I had the right paperwork, sorting out my passport and travel documents, I came across my old Indian passport. On seeing the well-used blue cover I was filled with an urge to see what I looked like in my mid-twenties. I have a few photos from my temp days in London, and then after that, for nearly a six-year period I have only two. Neither of them shows me with any clarity, and so I looked inside my old Indian passport, a relic from that time of my life. A tiny photograph showing a stranger's face looked back at me. I looked neither like myself nor unlike myself. The hair and shape of the eyes were familiar but I seemed devoid of expression. With its blank white background, I could have been anywhere, at any time of the day. My lips were pressed together, whether in a suppressed smile or in impatience I could not tell.

But as I looked more closely, small fragments of memories began to fit together like a jigsaw. The t-shirt I was wearing that day was red, with a v-shaped neckline. I remembered it well; it was short-sleeved and made of a thin material that suited the climate. In my ears were small silver earrings shaped like elephants. They had been a stalwart when I could not be bothered to spend more than ten minutes getting ready. My hair was pulled back in a tortoise-shell clamp that I could remember was particularly efficient in holding my hair up off my neck, perfect for the heat. I checked the date: I would have been about twenty-five years old in the photo. I stared at the small square, quietly looking at my younger self. And my younger self — wide-eyed, intent— looked back at me.

6

The students have all finished their exams and are lounging around on the grass in the sun. Through my office window I can hear snatches of shrieks, laughter and music. I love this time of the year, even though everyone complains of the heat. We have a fan in our office which blows continuously from May onwards. Our room catches the sun in the afternoon and can heat up during the day. While I find the warmth liberating, and love the chance of wearing sleeveless tops, light skirts, after wrapping up judiciously over the winter, my office-mates find it unbearably stuffy. I share the office with Rob and Joanne, both part-timers like myself. They are so nice, the two of them. Rather than showing any professional jealousy, they have been utterly supportive and encouraging of my project. After all my years observing educational systems in villages and communities, I have a chance of setting up a pedagogical exchange. When I first talked to the college about it, about how I envisaged the research could be conducted, as well as what partnerships could be set up, it was Joanne in particular who advised me on how to transform an idea into a funded project.

Joanne is from a small town in New York State but has lived in the Chicago area for about twenty years;

Rob is a native of the city. Perhaps because they, like me, have travelled, I feel an affinity with them that I don't with most of Sebe's friends. Perhaps, with them I am just me, whereas in Sebe's circle I am the product of his unexpected, hastily-arranged marriage. Joanne is completely irreverent when she talks about our nuptials. And yet, her easy description of it being a slightly mad but perfectly workable method is refreshing. She adores Sebe. When she first met him – he had come unannounced to take me out for lunch in my second week at the college – she had pronounced him, on my return, 'delectable'. I had not seen my husband in that light, and I have to admit that her comments did make me look more carefully at Sebe that evening.

"So, how did you guys meet?" she had asked while I settled back into my desk. I hesitated, contemplating how much to reveal, but then gave her an abridged version of the events as they had happened.

"So you've known each other for a grand total of about ten weeks?" she calculated. I nodded, wondering whether to start feeling irritated.

"Cool," she said. "How romantic. Wish that could happen to me."

"I'm sure I could arrange something," I joked, in relief at her reaction.

"Difference being you are a stunner, and I am just, well, me."

Joanne is the most interesting person I have met so far in my new life in America. She lived in Turkey for about ten years after graduating from Harvard, and her side of the office is covered with souvenirs from her days in Istanbul. But with her crazy, frizzy orange hair, penchant for purple cheesecloth, her very leggy tallness, and her very loud and confident voice, I think she is intimidating to most people. And men in particular seem to give her a wide berth.

Through Joanne I have a group of girl-friends, of varying ethnic origins – Japanese, Bermudan, Italian – who organise get-togethers at least once a month. I have slowed down on those monthly nights out since having Shayla, but Michaela, my Italian-American friend, has a little boy, a few months older than Shayla, and so we get to see each other on our days off. And since I moved to Chicago, Cecily, my longest, oldest friend, and I have kept in closer touch.

I think when I saw her in Delhi I sparked off, for both of us a revisiting of our old closeness. I decided to look her up the first full day I had in Delhi, when I arrived in India for our wedding, and when I embarked on, as Sebe playfully refers to, my personal take on Gulliver's Travels. Cecily and I had kept in touch when I first left India for boarding school; she had written faithfully, and the sight of a blue aerogramme in my pigeon-hole later at university had been uplifting. Then, even though I had continued to write regularly, her letters had tailed off. I suppose it was inevitable, our lives at that point couldn't have been more different. There I was, total freedom at my fingertips, going to lectures and seminars dressed in thick jumpers and jeans, mixing, albeit stiffly, with men, and people from different cultures. Cecily had to wear shalwar kameez or sari to lectures, lived with her aunt who made sure she was back home at 5pm every day. She hung around in huge gaggles of girls, not a male in sight.

I had tried to make my letters as understated as possible. I had tried not to sound too gleeful about my new experiences, never mentioning my philosopher boyfriend. But that had probably made my letters dull. Thinking back, I wonder if Cecily had wanted to hear every single detail instead of my sanitised, sensitively-edited extracts. Anyway, by the time I had finished university, we were still keeping in touch, but infrequently. And then later, we started getting each other's news from our families.

I heard about her marriage through my mother. Her husband, Joseph, was a Keralite who had been brought up mostly abroad, mostly in the Gulf states. When they were introduced, he had an excellent job in Dallas, and Cecily's family were delighted when the match was a success. She had lived with him in a fully-furnished, fully-paid-for apartment overlooking the city for three years, until his company offered him the chance to go back to India to start up a project in Delhi.

When I phoned her that morning in Delhi the call was answered by her maid, and a few moments later, "My God, tell me this is a joke."

I had laughed.

"No, it's really me."

"And are you calling from Outer Mongolia?"

"No, from right here. Delhi."

She had shrieked.

"My God, I can't believe it. I'll send a car, you must come here right away."

She had sent her driver to pick me up from my flea-ridden guesthouse, and he had driven me, in my faded jeans and crumpled red kurta, dusty sandals, clutching a bag of grapes in the back seat. She had become plump, but was as chic as ever. Her curly unruly hair was still long, pulled back into a chignon at the top of her head.

She was grinning from ear to ear and actually hopped with delight when she saw me. She ran to my side of the car and opened the door.

"Let me see you," she said and pulled me out of my seat. By then I was laughing and trying to gather my bag and the grapes from the car.

"You look fantastic," I said as she hugged me.

"You look skinny," she said. "How do you do it? Worms?"

She lived in a long bungalow with a big screened verandah, and a roof terrace, in one of the more desirable colonies of New Delhi. Inside was dark and cool, with Rajasthani prints on the walls, and rugs covering the wooden floors. We walked through some rooms, Cecily explaining what each of them were, but I was not really listening. It was all beautiful and homey and a very old friend was holding onto my arm. It was quite a lot to take in.

"*Ividde irrikke kunye. Ellaam parrayanum.* I know why you are in India but why on earth are you here in Delhi?"

"I thought I would spend some time seeing more of our great nation."

"You mean the great nation behind the dirt and noise and the pollution?"

"That's the one."

We laughed. It was so easy to fall back into the banter.

"But the wedding isn't far off. Shouldn't you be back home getting ready?"

"I won't need much time to get ready. I just need to throw on a sari and turn up."

She had laughed again, but I could see that she was concerned. She had reached forward and took my hand.

"Have you spoken to him at all?"

"A few times on the phone. He seems nice enough."

"I'm sorry we can't make it. We're going to Singapore day after tomorrow."

"Of course. I understand. We didn't give anyone much notice."

There was a pause, and I saw that Cecily was still looking at me. She must have found it strange, my nonchalance. Perhaps she had even found the news of my marriage strange. As teenagers we had both been romantics: Cecily overtly, I, secretly. But we had never shared thoughts about boyfriends – we had not had any — and now, here we were, launching straight into a future where we would share experiences again. We would both have husbands and all the accompanying accoutrements.

"He seems nice," I said again.

"No, wait. I must hear everything but we must have tea. And it looks like you need some food. I have iddiuppum in the kitchen. We can have that. Joseph likes to have Kerala food in the house all the time."

"Is he here?"

"No, at work, not back until six this evening. Wait, I'll just get our tea ready."

She had gone out of the room with a swing of her hips and I had looked around. Huge cream-coloured sofas, heavy deep-crimson curtains. The formal reception room. I had thought: so this is the life I can look forward to. A nice living room, comfortable sofas, a husband arriving back from earning a good living in a few hours. Time to make something tasty for dinner, to dress nicely, to arrange my hair. Conversation about the day's events and then perhaps some time spent listening to music before going to bed. Crisp sheets on the bed, a heavy coverlet. A routine of cleaning teeth and brushing hair. Bedside tables with lamps. Who will fall asleep first, I had wondered. Him or me? I remember feeling not displeasure at these thoughts, but a relenting, a slight disappointment in myself. I was, I admitted, ready to have such material comforts.

We had spent the morning exchanging news of old classmates, and reminiscing over old adventures. She had insisted that I stayed for lunch, and as we were eating had told me that she and Joseph had been trying for a baby for three years and she was beginning to reconcile herself to the idea that it wasn't going to happen. And I was filled with sadness for my dear friend, and for myself, too, and the darkness inside me, and I began to notice how behind the robust exteriors, we had both become fragile. I think we have sensed this in each other, and, after a long intermission, we have renewed a regular contact. I'm hoping she and Joseph will visit us next year.

*

While I value my ties with my old school friend, with my girl-friends here in Chicago I find another perspective. We are all itinerants. We were all born somewhere else, and have married men who are more entwined with Chicago and its establishment than we are. We are all hyphenated Americans, although I have yet to think of myself as an American of any kind. Our kids will very likely not suffer the adjustments we have made in our new lives. It is Tomoko, my Japanese-American friend who returns most often to see her family, who live, not in Japan but Hawaii. She bemoans the fact that her parents have relocated, denying her a reason to shell out on a long-haul flight to Tokyo. I am lucky in that respect. While I trotted around the globe, my mother was static, offering me an ever-lasting connection with the shambolic and eccentric life of my youth.

When Sebe and I went back to India a year and half after our marriage, my mother wanted to know how I had settled in to life in the States, and I told her about my new friends. As most of Sebe's family are in Chicago, we spent most of the two weeks we had in Kerala at my mother's house in Alleppey. She had a satisfied, relieved air: I was married, settled, no longer a black sheep.

"So things have worked out?"

It was a question. We were in the dining room, drinking tea while Sebe had an afternoon nap. Afternoons always have a particular feel, probably because the whole town agrees that it is time to take things easy. Fewer cars drive down the street which runs by the side of the house, there is the occasional tinkle of a bicycle bell, but generally there is a quiet that is unlike the quiet at any other time of day. It is why I grew to love that time of day, and it was often, in my childhood, the time for confidences, shared with friends, usually Cecily, who would come to visit. We would lie on my bed, in a bedroom darkened by closing curtains to keep it cool, and as teenagers do all over the world, listen to music, and talk about films and dreams and futures.

"Yes," I said.

"You are happy?"

"Yes, Ma."

We slurped our tea.

"And he is a good man, isn't he?"

I briefly reflected on her words. A 'good man' could mean different things to different people but decided to nod my head.

"He's very sweet."

"Yes," she smiled, "he is." And she picked up another biscuit. "I felt the same about your father when I married him."

I was surprised. Obviously being a respectable woman now, I was going to be allowed into my mother's treasure chest of memories of her marriage. I waited for her to continue.

"I can say this to you now, but love was not enough for your father and I."

I had never heard her talk about love before. In fact I had always assumed that love had never featured in their relationship. Now, sitting in that same house, facing each other not as adversaries but as companions, my mother was opening up and I needed her to continue.

"Compatible as we were in many ways," my mother carried on, "there were other compatibilities that were needed." She sighed. "Sometimes his lack of... sophistication irritated me. But that was not so important. In those days a girl really married into another family, not like for you." Her mouth turned down at the sides.

"His family were always a nuisance. Except Francis, of course."

She glanced at me.

"But you probably found out a lot about Francisuncle when you stayed with him."

I nodded again.

"I have to admit that I was jealous of him." She smiled at my face. "Yes, I was!"

I put my cup down and waited for her to continue. The fan above us stirred ineffectually.

"I suppose, like I was jealous of your father. He always had an easy way with you. A way that I couldn't ever manage. You always talked to him, laughed with him. I seemed to scare you." She sighed again, and fingered the bangles on her hand. "I was always so worried about you. Worried that you would suffer the same fate as all the girls in his family. But you were never going to. I should have trusted your father more."

We were silent.

"Do you miss him, Ma?" My voice sounded small, anxious. A physically older and frail mother I could handle. But this heart-to-heart was different. I was suddenly terrified that she was lonely.

She sighed again. "No, not really. It's been too long. And I keep myself busy. I think I like being my own agent, actually. As a widow I was relieved of a lot of burdens other married woman need to bear."

She rose to her feet, taking her cup with her to the kitchen. I followed her.

"But," she continued, "I do miss you, *mol*. I've missed you for a very long time."

I knew what she meant. I turned my mother to me and I hugged her close. We stood like this for some time, cheek to cheek. The skin on her face was impossibly soft, like that of a baby. Her body was light in my arms, her hair, still thick but grey, smelled pleasantly of the coconut oil she used.

"I worry about you," she whispered.

"Don't worry about me."

"I worry that I did not prepare you for all this..."

"Shhhh". I was comforting her, rocking her. "I'm fine Ma. I'm happy."

A few days later Sebe and I told her that I was pregnant. I had taken a test the day before we had flown out of Chicago. Sitting on the toilet, the blue line that had told countless would-be parents the same news, sang out to me. I burst out with the news as soon as Sebe came home and he had wrapped me tightly in his arms and lifted me off my feet. That night Sebe had made love to me with the utmost care.

"It's OK," I had whispered, pushing my hips against his, "we won't break the baby." But later, as he slept beside me I was wide awake. How could I have said that?

Fear gripped me, and my hands gripped the sheet. Sebe and I had never sat down and decided: it's time to start a family. We were both amenable and our marriage was a testament to our agreement. We would cherish a child, that was understood. He was breathing deeply, one arm flung over his head, unknowing, I felt, of the woman who lay beside him. He seemed exposed, vulnerable. We were both still naked under our sheets, and his other hand was curved around my thigh. I gently removed it and turned away from him, my hands moving over where his mouth had so recently been, my breasts, my stomach. The same body, or had it changed? My eyes would not close, I was afraid of what I would see if they did. I had let my thoughts run free. I hope you understand, I hope you know how much I loved you. I hope you know that my heart broke, that it is still broken. That you will always be inside me, my little soul. I was, by then, the pillow below me damp with my tears, acutely aware of the fragility of happiness. You can love, you can lose. I slept fitfully. But nothing happened that night. And in the morning I felt a relief, as if I had passed a test. My body had survived. Survived and I was whole and I had made a new life.

We had decided to tell my mother our news only towards the end of our stay to avoid all her anxieties about me travelling around in the early stages. But our conversation that afternoon had made me want to reassure her more. It was working. My new life was working and we had a baby on the way to prove it. We chattered excitedly about upcoming milestones, planned for her to come and visit not long after the baby was born. Sebe took us all for an ice-cream in the evening, where we bumped into some friends of my mother's. I can still remember her voice, brightly, proudly, telling them about her daughter, standing next to her, expecting.

My mother suggested that we go and stay a few nights somewhere, and we persuaded her to join us. I didn't want to leave her alone when journeys back to see her were rare. We decided to travel to the hills and stay in one of the old tea-plantation cottages that were now available for rent. We hired a driver and set off after breakfast for a two-night stay. The ascent began not long after we had passed the new airport that now served Kochi. We climbed and climbed up twisting roads, narrow and surrounded by trees. No longer coconut trees, but with thick branches, clusters of leaves. I felt very ill half-way, and we had to stop the car so that I could get out and retch by the side of the road. My mother patted my back, and told me it was a good sign, and Sebe hovered in the background. We finally reached our destination, a red-roofed bungalow, overlooking rows and rows of tea-plants, mountains in the background, an evening chill in the air. The bungalow had other guests: three thirty-something Keralite women, all friends, visiting from Mumbai. They were long and glossy, dressed in tight jeans, and cashmere jumpers, sunglasses in their hair. They talked at the same time, laughed a lot, and were happy to have more company for the evenings. It turned out that they knew my mother's brother and questions and answers about other possible connections ensued.

Sebe drew me outside, and we walked around the garden of the bungalow.

"Last time we were in India, I was a lot more nervous," he laughed.

"Was there ever a time when you thought you would just pull out, just change your mind?" I asked out of genuine curiosity.

He took my hand as we negotiated the rocky path that led further down the hill.

"Well, I guess yes, when I was in Chicago, before flying out. And those days when we were waiting for you to stop gallivanting around wherever you were gallivanting..."

"I needed time..."

"To think, yeah, I remember." He grinned and pinched my cheek affectionately. I smiled back.

We walked on in silence until we reached a natural viewing platform.

"But when we met," he continued suddenly, "after that first morning, I was OK. I mean, I was nervous about other things, but not about marrying you."

"What other things?"

"Oh just what you would think of me. That kind of stuff. You were a bit...intimidating."

"Intimidating?" I was incredulous.

"Yeah, believe it or not. With your pensiveness, and those huge eyes, just watching me. Not to mention I found you really quite ..."

"Oh stop," I said, embarrassed. Took his arm, and we turned to walk back up.

"Now you know it's all a façade," I said, "I'm just a myopic old bore." And we laughed.

But that evening as we sat at a large dining table with the other and were served the meal cooked by the kitchen staff of the bungalow, I mulled over what he had said. I looked over at where he was sitting, between my mother and the youngest lady from Mumbai. She was looking up at him while he was talking, captivated by his charming American accent and flashing white teeth. When she laughed at something he said she touched his arm very briefly. The other ladies were sitting on either side of me, and with my hand resting on my suddenly slightly rounding belly, I listened quietly to their voices.

7

I've made a list of things that Sebe needs to remember while I am away. He is perfectly capable, I am sure, of managing without me, but I want to avoid a calamity caused by the few gaps in his knowledge of our household. We have assumed the expected gender roles in many ways. I keep the house ticking along, he looks after the car and payments. I deal mostly with ferrying Shayla to kindergarten and her activities, he contributes more at weekends. I am in charge of our weekly menu, he takes care of any repairs that are needed to the house. But I have to admit, that more than I imagined, it is Sebe who, with his native's knowledge of the city, is willing to shoulder the responsibility for everyday decisions. He knows the city and its ways much better than I, and so I nearly always defer to his judgements. When we had our housewarming, about three months after we had moved into our house, it was Sebe who fixed the date and sent out invites. I hardly knew anyone who was being invited, anyway, except for Harvey, Theo and their wives; Sebe's family were only dropping in much later. I had thought to make an Indian feast, but it was Sebe who suggested that we keep it simple and just have a barbecue. It was he who went and bought the drinks and found the cuts of meat and fish.

By then our house looked a bit more complete, but still had that fresh, expectant feel. We had chosen the furniture together, discussed colours and fabrics. So, in effect, the decoration had been a joint effort. Since those first months, though, we have gradually acquired our niches of expertise. I recently bought some new rugs for some of the bare floors in our studies and in the dining area; a decision that Sebe showed no interest in. We have some new crockery that I bought on a whim, knowing that he would be happy with it if I were. He chose our new television in the living room, and sorted out a speaker system for the whole house so we can listen to music in nearly every room. But without a doubt, it is the garden where I have had complete control. It definitely has my stamp on it.

The night of the housewarming I fretted over what to wear. The party was also an occasion for Sebe to introduce me to yet more people he knew: old friends from school, football buddies, more work colleagues. I was only too aware that I would be under scrutiny, and I suppose I wanted to impress. He found me in front of the mirror in our bedroom, trying to decide between the light-green and the dark-blue dress; both new, both unworn.

"You'll look good in either," was his answer when I asked for his opinion.

"No, decide. You have to help me."

He smiled, came up behind me and put his arms around my waist.

"Relax. Try and enjoy the evening."

I groaned. "I hate being on show."

"You won't be. Everyone just wants to see the house and meet you and will then move on to having a drink and enjoying themselves."

I didn't believe him.

After much agonising, I settled for the light-green dress. On the beautiful late-spring evening that we had been lucky enough to choose as our date, I hid in the kitchen busying myself with unwrapping the salads I had made and cutting slices of bread, feeling even more nervous as the first guests arrived. But Harvey found me there before long and dragged me by the hand into the living-room, then the garden where Sebe was starting up the barbecue. It was Harvey who led me around the gathering crowd, introducing me as if he had known me his whole life. In fact, I had only met him twice before. But he threw his arm around my shoulders in familiar fashion, and I was grateful when he gave each new cluster of guests a quick, complimentary biopic, as well as the good news that I had found a job at the college. After ensuring that I had met everyone, he got me a drink and then stayed behind the makeshift bar, handing out drinks and re-stocking the ice.

And Sebe hardly left the barbecue. He was joined, later, by two of his friends from school, and they cooked up the food in between drinking their beers. He occasionally caught my eye and we would exchange a smile, but this was mostly from across the garden. I was not sure if it was a conscious decision on his part, but I greatly appreciated it. Without Sebe at my side, I was less the curiosity: the house took centre-stage. The party became just another party; not yet another showcase of our marriage. It was the garden that provoked most conversation: I had sectioned areas off and had started planting a few vegetables. I had also cleared a small area where I was hoping to grow bushes that would attract butterflies. Everyone asked me after my plans. They laughed with delight when I admitted that I had inherited peasant genes from my father's side, and described the joy I received from tilling the soil. I began to relax and passed the evening in a blur of food and wine and names. The party was proclaimed later as a resounding success, a great bash, and I know that it was mostly Sebe's doing.

*

Even though I know he will be absolutely fine when I am away, I have written down certain things just to reassure me that he will not forget. The days that Shayla needs to take a packed lunch to kindergarten because they have outings, the type of cereal she likes having at the weekend, the juices that she tends to spit up in disgust. Where I have found the best deals on basmati rice if we run out, which of my pot plants will need watering more than once a week. I've also listed the phone numbers that are already in our black notebook, but that I think he will need to have to hand in case of emergencies. The doctor, the kindergarten, my mother. I know I should not worry, but I do. The first time that Sebe went away on business, he was similarly concerned.

"Don't forget that you can call my mom whenever or for whatever reason. And of course that goes for Thomas. He'll come round in minutes if you need him." We were in our bedroom. I was lying on the bed, watching as Sebe packed a small suitcase. His suit, shirts and ties were arrayed before him and he was choosing a set for each day that he would be away. I watched as he meticulously folded them before putting them in neat sections in the case. He was not so fastidious with the t-shirts and jeans he wore at home.

"I know," I said. In fact, I was still a bit shy with Sebe's oldest brother, the patriarch now of the family. He was a consultant surgeon at a large Jewish hospital in the city, very successful in his career. His wife, an American Malayalee from Detroit, ran her own design company from an office in their beautiful, sprawling house. "Are you sure you don't want to go and stay with them?" Sebe asked, as he chose three ties, and tucked them carefully into a stretchy pocket in the box.

They lived in a suburb not far from us, but also had an apartment overlooking the lake right in the heart of the city. We had been for dinners at their house, but I had never spent any time alone with any of them. I did not feel sure enough to do so for the first time while Sebe was away.

I shook my head. "There's really no need," I said.

He straightened up, came round the bed and sat beside me. He laid his hand gently on my stomach, caressed it with small circular movements.

By then my belly was large and round, a mound even when I was lying down. My bump was 'neat' as the gynaecologists described it, but it was still noticeable. I revelled in the extraordinary femininity it bestowed me with and I luxuriated in my new, full, six-months-pregnant, curvy shape. We had both marvelled at the changes in my body, marvelled at the kicks and movements, communications from the tiny individual growing inside me. The baby showed personality, becoming more active when I was resting, as if an indolent mother would be reprimanded, and growing quiet in the middle of the morning, a time for a nap.

"I'm sorry I have to go," he said.

"But you shouldn't be," I said. "You should enjoy it. And I'll be fine."

In fact, when he left early the next morning for the week-long conference in Miami, I realised that evening that I missed him more than I thought I would. Coming home from the college, I turned the key and opened the door to complete silence. I had expected to feel a sense of some liberation when he left for the airport. I had the house to myself, and a relaxing few evenings ahead. No need to coordinate schedules, no need to let anyone know where I was. I could eat when I wanted, read in bed for hours at night. I was putting the final touches to the thesis that had been part of my life for many years, and I thought I would value the absolute concentration I could enjoy, focusing solely on my papers without needing to be civil to anyone. But I had grown out of touch with living on my own. I found I wanted to talk to someone that evening, and reading in bed, in total silence without Sebe tapping on his laptop, or watching the football on its small screen, I was aware how loudly our bedside clock ticked.

After the first day, however, it seemed that others, too, did not think that I should be alone. Joanne came round one evening with a bottle of wine for her, and a bottle of sparkling fruit juice for me. Sebe's brother invited me the next night for a family dinner, where I was plied with my favourite curries, and then cajoled into sleeping over rather than driving back on my own. I returned home the following morning determined to attack the last vestiges of my thesis that remained for me to complete. And then met up with my girlfriends, to celebrate my achievements, the following night. I was out so much that I barely noticed that Sebe was not around.

It was different being in Chicago without him. Suddenly, I realised that it was where *I* lived, not just where *we* lived. I had made connections, friends, I had a phone book full of numbers I could call. I knew the best way into the city in rush-hour, where to get the best bread in our area at the weekend. I woke up in a familiar room, and pottered around a house that was filled with things I had placed or hung up or made, and then watered the plants I had planted in my garden. I was settling in.

Sebe called me every day, and was miffed when I often said that I was on my way out.

"You sound like you're doing fine," he said the night I was meeting my girlfriends in town. He sounded put out.

"No," I laughed. "Pining."

"Well, I miss you," he said.

"You can't have time to miss me. With your palm trees and swimming pools and wining and dining."

"But I do."

And when he returned, creeping under the bedcovers – it was 5am and he had insisted that he get a taxi from the airport – he had woken me up, his hands encircling me from behind. He pulled me to him. I murmured my hellos and he had kissed me and repeated, "I missed you. Both of you." When the sun had properly risen, I padded downstairs and made two cups of tea that we sipped together from a tray in bed. He told me about Miami. The hotel had been comfortable but bland; the conference had been interesting but very intensive. As he described the seminars and workshops he had attended I could picture him and the others well.

I had once visited him in his offices downtown, a few weeks into arriving in Chicago. He had said to meet him from work and that we would go to the cinema in the city before heading back out together to the suburbs. I was still getting accustomed to finding my way around the city and had over-estimated how long my journey would take. I was early when I arrived in the foyer of his firm. A tall blonde woman who looked the quintessential city law-firm receptionist, smiled tightly when I gave my name and asked me to take a seat while she buzzed Sebe.

He arrived a few minutes later, took my hand and kissed me. "Come to my office," he said. "I'm just tying something up." And so I had sat in his office, and looked through its glass windows into the impressive board room where the meeting was taking place. I recognised Harvey and Theo, but did not know the other be-suited, groomed men and women. I watched as I saw his lips move, without hearing the words. He looked exactly as he should: a confident professional participating in a productive late-afternoon meeting with similarly confident and efficient colleagues. But I had felt slightly alarmed. I was not known to many of the others behind the window. I was now a wife to this successful man, but other than that description, I did not have an identity. I lived in a house that he had bought, wore clothes for my new life and the new climate that I had paid for with his card, carried his name. All of this had been my choosing, but I felt queasy, like I had swallowed, whole, myself. My whole life had been a series of journeys. Even, I knew with hindsight, my days in Maputo – those days when I had felt, unaware of their fallacy, as if I had belonged – had been, in effect, a long journey leading to my departure. Chicago was my terminus. It was here where I would live with my husband, without a next stage, the next set of goodbyes. When we walked home from the cinema later that evening, Sebe had asked me gently if there was something bothering me. I had not talked much and would not join in a dissection of the mediocre film we had watched. "I just need to settle in a bit," I said, when he pressed me. He had squeezed my hand, concerned. I had given him a weak smile in response, but had said no more.

*

So it was with some smugness that I told him, that morning in bed, how well I had coped without him. And Sebe was gracious, not wounded by my playful assertion of my independence, but happy that I had managed. Lying close together, his one arm around my shoulder, the other laying protectively on my bump, I felt a contentment, a peace, that was foreign.

Later that day I submitted my thesis, proudly bringing home my own bound copy. We had a mini-celebration that evening, with sparkling grape juice, deciding to save the champagne for after the baby was born. But after eating dinner, my heartburn returned and my feet began to ache. The baby was kicking furiously, and I felt extraordinarily tired: I had overdone my nights out while he had been away. We had hoped to go for a drive and dessert somewhere, but I said that I wanted to have a bath and then read in bed. As we cleared the table, Sebe picked up my thesis.

"I've never read any of this. Would you mind if I looked at it?"

It was true. While I tapped away in my study at home, and my office at work, Sebe would either be at work, or sorting out his own paperwork. While Joanne and Rob had both read and advised me on various sections, commented on drafts and re-drafts, Sebe had not seen a thing. It was not that he had not shown any interest, but it seemed that learning about each other, as we had been doing over the last year and a half, had precluded any further discoveries. He knew, now, that I liked my coffee black in the mornings. He did not know my views on the hegemony of Western culture.

I was pleased he had asked, and he followed me up the stairs to our bedroom. I went into our bathroom and started running the bath. When I came out I saw him lying on the bed, leaning against the pillow, the bedside lamp turned on. My thesis was in his hands. He looked extremely competent, suddenly, and I was reminded that he was a lawyer, used to poring over things with care, scrutinising details. I felt awkward all of a sudden and hurried into the bathroom, closed the door. I spent a while soaking, until the water had grown quite cool, wondering what he would think and whether he would find it well-written.

When I came back into the bedroom, Sebe was still there, but lying back, his arms behind his head. My thesis lay face down, next to him: he had read, or skipped through, about a third already. I didn't say anything, moved to the dressing table and sat down. When I looked at him in the mirror, I caught his eye.

"It's very good," he said. "Really interesting stuff."

"Thanks."

I stayed at the dressing table, watching his reflection in the mirror.

He sighed, and brought his hands from behind his head, crossed them over his chest.

"You've been so many places," he said.

I was quiet.

"God, I've hardly left Chicago. Typical American."

"That's not true," I said turning around on the stool to face him. "You've been to India."

He raised his eyebrows, made a face.

When he remained silent, I stood up, started putting my clothes away in the wardrobe.

"Do you feel that this is home now?" he asked suddenly.

I looked at him.

"Why do you ask?" I said.

He shook his head.

"Well, I don't know. You've been all over."

I was thrown by his question; it was not something I had ever given myself a chance to think about. True, while he had been away I had noticed a 'settled' feeling. I had realised that I had my favourite haunts in our side of the city, that people called me up, visited me, knew where they could find me. I had started friendships I could see becoming long-term. In twenty years' time I would be able to talk about how things had changed in the area, how we had never had to deal with this, I pity the young couples who have just moved here. I imagined myself as a variation on Ammachi: she had long put her Thekkaddy days, being surrounded by the hills and trees and tea-plantations that made it so winsome, behind her. But as I watched Sebe, who was now staring at the ceiling, I knew he was asking me something else.

He was wearing an old grey t-shirt, with the faded emblem of the University of Chicago Law School. I knew that he had loved his time there, had even contributed to its Law Review. He still kept in touch with his roommates and the following year he had a reunion to attend.

I walked over to our bed, lay down beside him. He didn't turn to look at me. His face was impassive, but his fingers were tapping his chest in an impatient rhythm.

"I'm carrying your child," I said. I had not prepared the words, they just came to me. I reached out and touched his cheek, and to my relief, he caught my hand and turned to me. Smiled, and nodded. As if to say, yes, that's right. That's where we are now.

8

When I was chosen to lead the fieldwork, I sat at my desk in my study at home and stared out of the window. Outside it was mid-summer. The air was humid, the temperature high. Chicago swelters in the summer, something I still cannot believe after the long, freezing winters we endure. I have a view of the back-yard from my desk, and can see the bird-box that I have put out next to Shayla's swing-set. I always hope that a bird will come and feed while she is swinging; she would be enchanted. But of course she makes so much noise, kicking her little legs in the air, and scares them away. My thoughts were on the logistics of the trip ahead: how to get visas, arrange the meetings on the other end. How to present the project in a non-patronising way to a foreign audience. How to gather a small team together to advise us. Most issues I could resolve beforehand by email. I had already started setting up a website to gather respondents for the project that could be accessed by anyone, anywhere, anytime. How easy.

All of this would have been unheard of a few years ago. Letters would have had to have been written, posted, flown in aircraft thousands of miles away, sorted, delivered, read, considered. I still find it hard to believe that I arranged my postgraduate studies, not that long ago, using snail-mail. I have only dabbled, but if I chose to apply myself, I could use the internet to reconnect with many of my old classmates from Alleppey, now transplanted to the US. Sebe is even less immune from discovery: I have seen pictures posted of nearly all his close friends from the age of five to their spiky-haired teenage days and beyond. You would think that everyone can find everyone on a social media site. A few years ago, to celebrate their twentieth anniversary Sebe's law form used their site to invite anyone who had ever worked for them to attend a dinner and dance at a hotel in the city. I had met people there who had known Sebe as a fresh recruit from law school. I even met Angie.

I had been unsure of leaving Shayla, then a ten-month-old, with Ammachi that evening as she had been out of sorts all day. I had rung Sebe at work and told him that he would probably have to go without me. He had said that we could wait until the evening to decide; Shayla could be better by then. I was still not convinced by the evening, and it was only at Ammachi's insistence that I went upstairs to get changed. I put on my old faithful dangly earrings and when I kissed Shayla goodbye, she briefly grabbed one of them in her little fist. Ammachi and Sebe both had to make me leave the house with assurances that we would be called back if Shayla appeared to take a turn for the worse.

So, with my feet-dragging, by the time we arrived in the city, the dinner had already started. Appetisers were being served, and we hastily found our name places. I sat down, but Sebe went off to see if Harvey was all right about the speech he was to make later that evening.

On my left was a tall, dark-haired woman, a few years older than me, dressed in a clinging pink dress. She watched Sebe move away, and then turned to me.

"I can't believe that we've been seated next to each other," she said. "I'm Angie."

Before I could say anything, she continued, "I'm an old friend of Seb's."

She picked up her fork and poked at the crayfish salad.

"You must be his new wife."

I murmured my responses, and looked at the mound of crayfish, smothered in a creamy sauce, on a bed of lettuce.

"This is my boyfriend, Greg," she continued, motioning to the man sitting next to her, a strong-looking redhead, with a neat beard. He nodded his hellos, a forkful of salad going into his mouth.

"Seb's new wife," she explained again.

By now I was beginning to feel uncertain about how the evening would play out, but Greg reached over and shook hands. "Hey there," he said in a deep, baritone. "So nice to meet you. I was beginning to think that Ange had made it all up so that I'd be extra nice to her."

Angie slapped his arm playfully. "No, I suffered just as I said I had. And now fate has it that I'm sitting next to my successor!" She rolled her eyes at me.

I smiled in some relief, and we introduced ourselves properly. I knew that her break-up with Sebe had been a bit messy. They had agreed to separate, but she wanted to stay in touch as friends, and as they were still working together – she was a paralegal assistant – Sebe had demurred. They took to meeting every Thursday evening after work, to have a drink and share their news. But, inevitably, those chats turned into recriminations and revisits to painful events. Sebe had told me that he began to feel that they were an opportunity to catch him off guard to explain why he had behaved, as she accused him, like a cad. When he told her one Thursday that he thought it should be the last, she hadn't taken it well. But she had conceded eventually, and when she left the company to join another law firm, they had dropped out of touch.

While we finished our salads, I watched her surreptitiously. So this was Sebe's old flame. She was funny, attractive and relaxed in this awkward situation. She had known Sebe when he had been younger, more ambitious. More self-centred? More selfish? More ardent?

My thoughts were interrupted by Sebe's return. At first he stared open-mouthed, "Angie. Have you met...?"

"Hi Seb." She threw down her napkin, got up and gave him a hug, her arms around his neck. His hands stayed by his side for a moment before clasping her briefly.

"I've met your charming wife," she said breaking away. "And you can meet my charming man, Greg."

Greg stood up, shook Sebe's hand. Sebe glanced at me, his face slightly red.

"How funny we should be sitting next to you..."

"It's great," Angie laughed. "It's been a long time."

I got to my feet, put my hand on Sebe's arm. "Why don't you sit here for a bit?" I gestured to my empty chair. "You can catch up a little."

He looked at my face, slightly worried.

I smiled. "I'm going to call Ammachi. You've got to eat your salad before they clear it away. I'll be back soon."

I walked out of the dining area and into the hall. I phoned Ammachi, who answered a little sleepily. Shayla was fine. Yes, she was sleeping, and Ammachi could hear her breathing on the baby-monitor. I ended the call, but hung back a bit from returning to the table. I stood at the doorway, and looked around the room.

It was a handsome dinner. White table-cloths, sparkling glasses, a jazz band playing in the corner. We had been promised dancing later. The waiters and waitresses were smart, black-clad, fast on their feet. Everyone seemed to be laughing, the ladies throwing back their heads to reveal long white throats, the men all displaying admirable teeth, feasting on the sight of faces and throats and cleavage. I saw Angie talking animatedly to Sebe turning her head to Greg, and then back to Sebe. Back and forth, back and forth.

"Don't you want a drink?" a voice said behind me. Theo.

He leaned forward and kissed my cheek.

"No, I've got one on the table. I'm just having a break."

He caught sight of the phone in my hand.

"Shayla at home?"

"With her grandmother."

We looked together at the crowds. He glanced over at our table.

"Is that..?"

"Yes, it is."

"How did that happen?"

I shrugged.

He put his hand on my forearm.

"Are you OK about it?"

I looked at him. Theo has nice green eyes, long brown lashes.

"Absolutely fine."

He nodded, his eyes darting over my face, and then dropping to my arms.

"Great bangles."

"Thanks."

"Nice dress."

"Thanks."

"You look great."

I burst out laughing. "Thanks. Are you trying to butter me up or something?"

"No, just telling a beautiful woman that she is beautiful."

"I'm just fine with it. It's nice to meet her. And she's really lovely. I just needed to check on Shayla."

We hung back from the party a while longer quietly watching Angie, Greg and Sebe, a trio now on the table.

"I know you're not worried," Theo broke in, "but Seb was never like he is with you when he was with Angie."

I crossed my arms over my chest. Perhaps because I didn't say anything, Theo continued.

"You must know that he is crazy about you."

"I'm not worried about it Theo." And perhaps because my voice was brittle, he put his hand again on my forearm.

"Yeah, I know, I didn't mean..."

"I'm just thinking of a younger version of Sebe and a younger version of Angie."

"Yeah, I know."

He was slightly flustered and started telling me about an upcoming holiday that both Beth and he had been planning for months. As our conversation waned we stepped back into the room. Theo walked back to the table with me, greeted Angie who gave him a big hug as well, and introduced Greg. Sebe stood up to let me sit down back in my chair, and moved over to his. The main course arrived, then dessert, and dancing.

When we got back home, it was after midnight. I crept upstairs and looked down at the small body encased in her yellow sleeping-bag, her arms bent, her fists against her ears. I had decorated her room with outlines of animals – kangaroos, elephants, fish – and even in the dark of the room I could still make out the shapes, watching over her. I leant forward and kissed her gently. When I straightened up I saw that Sebe was standing beside me.

"She looks fine," he said.

I nodded. He put his arm around my waist and we stood there a moment, looking down at Shayla.

"Did you have a nice evening?" he asked, sounding a little tentative.

I nodded. "And it was nice to meet her."

We didn't talk much more, just got into bed. I turned on my side and watched the patterns of lights on our blinds.

I recalled Angie's head moving from Greg to Sebe, back and forth from new to old, old to new. She had sat between them, telling one that she was happy and one that she was healed. I hadn't known that she had been so cut up about their break-up and when she said she had 'suffered', even in jest, the word had given me a small jolt. I had had a glimpse of an earlier chapter in

Sebe's life. A chapter he had lived before we met. To me he was solicitous, caring, unselfish. Perhaps he had not always been so. I realised that while everyone was expecting me to feel disconcerted, perhaps even jealous, what I actually felt was envy. Sebe had met Angie, and they had both moved on and it was all so terribly civilised.

In the morning Sebe mentioned again how strange it was to bump into Angie like that. While he squeezed some oranges for juice, and I helped Shayla with her spoon and cereal, he talked on about how she had not changed much in the last years, how she seemed very happy with her new life. As he calculated the odds against such a reunion occurring, I listened with only half an ear. The meeting did not strike me as unlikely. They both lived in Chicago, worked in the same field. It was almost inevitable that at some stage their paths would cross. In modern life it was not impossible to get together with your old flame, and wish each other the best for the future.

And yet, as I was thinking but did not put into words, even in this hyper-connected world that we live in, not everyone is within reach. Sometimes you can love someone, feel one with them, and then never see them again, never hear from them again. They might one day walk out the door, walk out of your life, and you are left alone, holding an unsatisfactory photograph, a dark knot inside you and untrustworthy memories.

That summer afternoon, when the project was finally confirmed and the fieldwork mapped out, I sat at my desk, my laptop open in front of me. While the city and its suburbs sweltered in the heat, while my husband was a few blocks away with my three-year-old daughter at a birthday party, while the house was still and quiet with only the hum of the fridge and ticking of the dining-room clock to be heard, my heart thumping, and my hands trembling, I let my fingers dance over the keyboard and I googled his name.

No returns. I waited a few minutes before I googled Chimoio. The town was doing well for itself; there was even an airport now nearby. When I saw the hyperlinks advertising charter flights from Tel Aviv (Tel Aviv!) to Chimoio, I could not help but think back to the long car journey we made from Chimoio to Beira, in order to fly down to Maputo. Now, we could have flown direct. I wondered what other changes had happened in the country that I had grown to love, and then hate. I wondered how he had changed, if at all. And I knew that I would have the chance to find out.

*

I cried at the airport. I couldn't help myself. Shayla looked quizzically at me. We had told her that I would be away for a few days. For a child that age time is immaterial. She talks about 'yesterday' all the time, even when she is referring to a year back. We took her on holiday to the coast last year, to show her the sea. She was absolutely enthralled by the sand on the beach, the waves, the salty smell of the sea air, the shells that we picked. She spent hours in the sun transferring a bucket of sand into another bucket and then back again. She loved the sand. That's why we got the sand-pit for her in the back-yard. That was close to eleven months ago, but she still talks about when we went to the beach 'yesterday'. I don't have the heart to correct her. She'll learn the vagaries of time soon enough, and I am content to hear her happy memories of those days in the sun. While she had been saying that she didn't want her Mama to 'go', I'm not sure that she even understood what that meant. Because at the airport, she didn't cry, while I held her too tightly, as I sobbed silently.

"Hey, hey," said Sebe, holding both of us, his girls, his arms around my shoulder and hers. "We'll be OK. You'll be OK. You'll be back before you know it."

Ammachi took Shayla away to buy me a chocolate bar for the journey, and Sebe led me to a seat.

"You'd better go through soon," he said, "But we have some time."

I nodded, leaned my head against his shoulder.

When I looked up, I saw he was watching me. He had that same searching look that he had for the first few years of our marriage. Who is this woman, I could imagine him thinking. Who is she?

Last week, after putting Shayla to bed, we had both had showers to cool down after the hot day, then lay on our bed with just a sheet over our naked bodies. Sebe had moved a fan into the room which lifted the sheet lightly, before letting it fall gently. He had run his hands up and down my legs, then over my breasts, and then his mouth had done the same. I know that my husband still desires me even though we have settled into a routine dictated by our jobs and young child. That night, after he rolled onto his side, he pulled me towards him again. I usually turned to my right after, and he would lie against my back. But this evening we lay face-to-face, our breath mingling.

"Is there anything I should know?" he asked.

"About what?"

"About this trip?"

I looked into his eyes, brushed his hair from his forehead.

"No," I lied. "Why do you ask?"

"All those secrets you have inside you. Any secrets about this trip?"

It pained me to hear him, then, talk about secrets. It was a long-standing joke between us. I had much earlier on claimed that some experiences I had were too difficult to explain to someone who had spent all of his life in Chicago. I had teased him about his conservative, sanitised American ways and told him about the women I had met in Africa and South East Asia, all of whom would have gobbled him up. He teased me back about my 'quaint British expressions' and my seemingly never-to-be-rectified inability to understand American Football. That night, I was not sure he was joking.

He never delved. The closest he had reached to a prurient interest in my previous life had been in the Indian Coffee House in Ernakulam, a few days before we got married. I appreciated this, as I saw it, magnanimity that Sebe showed. Perhaps for him it was enough that I had accepted his proposal. Perhaps he knew that there may be things in my past he would find hard to accept if he knew about them.

I laid my forehead against his.

"I love you," he said. His voice was urgent, pleading.

Of course, by then, Sebe and I had talked about love. He had said the words to me first, and I had responded not long after. I did love him. I knew he loved me. But I still had that ache inside me, a yearning, that after so many years had not abated.

"I love you too," I replied. It was not a lie, but it was not the full story.

How to explain? I found it impossible, and I knew that he would find it difficult to comprehend.

In my bedside cabinet, to my right as we lay together on our bed, sandwiched between the pages of a book, is a letter. It is dated from two years ago and is from my friend Anne. I met her while I was studying in London, and we hit it off. It was with Anne that I spent evenings drinking wine, kicking myself over my foolish affair with my equally-foolish lecturer. She is a few years older than me, strawberry-blonde hair, bespectacled, completely self-sufficient. She amazes me with this self-sufficiency, her calmness, and her fierce independence. I left later to start my fieldwork in Indonesia, and she remained in London. We have maintained irregular contact via emails, and whereas soon after we had studied together I settled down and married, Anne has continued travelling the world.

A few years ago she joined VSO and got a placement in Beira. She was there for two years. After spending the first six months settling into her job and the new lifestyle, she started spending weekends and holidays travelling around the country. She drove with a colleague to Chimoio, and she found Jafar's flat easily enough from my directions. She left a note through his door that she was a friend of mine and that she would like to meet him for a drink, if he was free in the afternoon. She suggested a cafe on the main square.

He arrived a few minutes after the time she had suggested, and they talked for about half an hour. When he stood up to go she told him that I was married, living in Chicago, with a year-old baby. She wrote to me later that he had laughed; told her that he had thought once that he and I would have that same life. He told her that he hoped I was happy.

"I think he still looks the same," she had written, "From how you described him. And he wanted to hear about you. When he said goodbye I get the impression that he would rather have stayed, because I reckon he wanted to ask a lot more about you. He did ask if I had a picture of you. I didn't I'm afraid. You wanted to know if he was well and happy, and he looked well, and I think he looked happy."

If I close my eyes I can picture the scene well. My friend Anne, dressed in sandals and dress, sitting at a white plastic table in a white plastic chair. There was a café just off the main square in Chimoio, and it was probably there that they had met. It would have been hot, at that time of the year in the afternoon, and there would not be many people walking around. The café would have a radio tuned into a station playing zouk music. In the glass-fronted table-top fridge at the front of the café would be lines of *bolos de nata* and biscuits. Anne would have ordered a coffee with milk, and would be stirring some sugar into her cup, waiting.

I could imagine Jafar finding the note under his door when he had returned. Was Naman still living there or had he returned to Maputo? Did Carlos still work for him? Anyway, Jafar must have stared at the note for a time. It would have been written in English, unless Anne had learned enough Portuguese by then. How had he felt? He must have felt some curiosity to go out to meet her. Had he expected more? Had he expected me to have written him a long letter, sent a parcel, sent photos? I regretted that I hadn't planned much better. It had been on an impulse that I had told Anne about Jafar when I heard she was travelling to Mozambique. I had said that he was 'an old boyfriend', a description that he would have abhorred. She hadn't asked many questions, but she may have decided on a certain amount of tact. I was, after all, a married woman with a baby.

Part of me never expected anything to come of it. Anne could have easily found herself wrapped in her teaching, could have spent a long time adjusting to her new life. It would have taken her some organising to get a lift or a bus from Beira to Chimoio. I wondered why she had made so much of an effort. I had not talked about Jafar in the context of my disastrous campus romance: perhaps therein lay the reason. She may have intuited that the sudden mention of an 'old boyfriend' in Mozambique belied a deeper description.

What had she thought of him? I can imagine Jafar speaking to her. He would greet her with a customary kiss on the cheek, order her another coffee. If he still smoked, he would pull a cigarette from his breast pocket and light it up in front of her. He must have wondered why I would ask her to try and get in touch. Maybe he would have understood that it was one way for me to find out if he was still alive.

He will have known that I had long left Mozambique; Rassul or Eduardo would have told him. He had never tried to say goodbye. But he had left his flat, walked down the stairs, crossed the road, and spoken to an unknown Englishwoman bearing news of me. Again, an unravelling began, made stronger by the knowledge that he was there, still there. My heart raced, thudded wildly in my chest. Perhaps, in some way, he yearned. Just as — I could in my thoughts freely admit — I still yearned.

When I had finally fallen asleep that night, I had dreamed my dream again. I am in the back of a taxi. It is hot, dusty, the landscape is faded, bleached. The driver is talking, complaining of the heat. We are driving fast, we reach the city, then I see him. He looks up, our eyes lock. I open my mouth, he turns away. The taxi speeds away, I lose sight of him.

*

I hugged Sebe, gave Shayla another kiss and held her small form against mine for another delicious minute, kissed Ammachi, then left them waving goodbye. As I turned and waved again I noticed how they seemed to have assumed a form of their own. Sebe's arm was around his mother's shoulder; Shayla was on her grandmother's hip. They were, I felt with a stab of pain, complete. They would manage without me. I turned away, and with that movement I realised I was looking forward.

I was looking ahead of me to a life without them. I was leaving them and my existence of the last years. Feelings surged through me: excitement, apprehension, and then disdain at my own fickle self. I shivered involuntarily, and pulled the light cotton jacket I was wearing closer. I willed myself not to turn around again and run back to the departure hall. My feet would clatter on the shiny floor. My bag would be banging against my rib-cage. I would round the corner and they would not be there. They were a figment of my imagination. They were not real, and this truth had been revealed that day. For five years I had been living a virtual existence in an alien city, unknown, untouched.

Someone bumped into me and I was shaken out of my thoughts. A hand gripped my elbow to steady me.

"Sorry 'bout that".

He moved on. I pushed my hair out of my eyes, tucked it behind my ear. Carrying my holdall through security and into the departure lounge I tried to still my unsettling thoughts. The bright lights and familiar noises of long-distance travel, the chattering hum of passengers, the occasional squawk of a tired child were reassuring. I met Rob and Joanne in the departure lounge, next to the coffee bar as we had arranged.

"Goodbyes all done?" Rob asked. I nodded, knowing that my eyes would be red and swollen. He gave my arm a squeeze. "They'll be fine," he said, and Joanne gave me a hug.

It was going to be a long flight.

9

Avenida Patrice Lumumba, named after the much-loved, but short-lived Congolese hero, was, when I lived in Maputo, one of my favourite roads. At the lower end of the road, before it snaked uphill towards the cliffs and the handsome hotels of that side of town, there was a big white house, shaded with trees, and nestled between two other grand houses. From the second floor of the house, VSO ran a library for the use of anyone who wanted to read books in English. The library was manned by an old man who determined whether you could enter or not by whether or not you looked foreign enough. Only a foreigner would be gauged competent enough in English to be allowed entry. I had first been told about this library by a colleague at work, and when I had gone to find out if it was indeed true – that in the middle of Maputo, there was, amazingly, a library of anglophone fiction – I had been wearing denim cut-offs, flip flops and a sleeveless t-shirt. I obviously looked scruffy enough not to be mistaken for a Moçambicana, all of whom dressed with great care and attention. I was buzzed directly in.

A large, high-ceilinged room, light pouring in from three sides, branches of the trees along the road scraping the windows. And rows and rows of bookshelves, all filled with books. There was a small section of books in German and in French, but the rest were all in English. I was in heaven. I had no television in my flat, and as I spent lot of time on my own, waiting for Jafar to appear, I read voraciously. I had already finished all the books that I had come with, all the books in the university library, which at the time were a paltry selection. This library offered me hours and hours of entertainment. I browsed through the titles. They were all donations from former visitors and NGO-workers to Maputo, and the eclectic nature of the choices offered were a delight. *A Rector's Wife* sat next to *A Farewell to Arms*. Nothing was alphabetised, and so the unexpected pleasure was in finding a book that you really wanted to read by chance. I was not discerning. I went every weekend, and took out five or six books each time. I added authors to my reading repertoire that I would never have chosen had they not been in that light, bright room, above a shady, quiet, street.

As I pick my way over the roots of the trees that have broken through the tarmac of the road and the concrete of the very narrow pavement, I try to locate the library-house. I am not sure if the one that I am looking up at is actually the correct one. I have been surprised at how much I have forgotten about the city. While I have been confident enough of its layout to take charge of the day-to-day meetings and appointments, there are still times when I have to think: do we turn right here, or left? Was that café a bit further along or was it the other way? Not least because the city has changed. The one city shopping mall, with a supermarket inside, had been forlorn. Shelves were half-empty, and shop-units half-full. Now it is a glittering, busy mall, boasting South African high-street shops and a revamped, well-stocked supermarket. There are new supermarkets outside the centre, more shops in the Baixa. Maputo is on the up.

But much of the city I remember remains the same. There is still an air of world-weariness, a shabby glamour that lends to it an allure to which Rob and Joanne have succumbed.

"God, I can see why you loved it here," were Joanne's words when we had a tour with our university guide, Manuel. And I could see, as they did, how beguiling it was. The sun was languid as we had travelled in the southern hemisphere's winter. The sky was a brilliant blue, cloudless, and the handsomest buildings had been renovated and re-painted. Joanne, with her orange hair and short dresses and her long legs, has been attracting much attention as we walk around. She is loving it, and I have to stop myself from giggling at Rob's aghast expressions when she flirts with Manuel.

Manuel had greeted me in Portuguese when we arrived. He said he could remember me from when I used to work there, even though he had never been my student. I replied in Portuguese, re-discovering words I had not used for years, and we tried to establish mutual friends. Simon was still heading up the department, but was on leave, and had left his regrets that he would miss my visit.

"Dona Clara, your friend, you know she has left and is now back in Australia," he told me. "And Maurice also left the same year that you did."

I had kept in touch with my colleagues from those days for the first years after leaving Mozambique, but then over time we had stopped writing to each other.

"The *profesora* still looks the same", Manuel said gallantly, smiling at me. "I would have recognised you easily. But you look better."

"I was very thin those days."

"You are still slim, but you look better. When you left you were looking tired."

I wonder how Manuel can remember so much of me, and I wonder if it could be too egoistic to imagine that my story had been retold many times over. "There was this girl who used to teach here, *uma indiana...*" With the passing days my Portuguese has become more confident, but the certainty of my desires has lessened.

*

I find a low wall outside one of the houses and I sit down. There is a beautiful frangipani tree just behind and I stretch my hand to pick a flower. I love the scent. I used to put these flowers in my hair when I lived here and I do the same now, tucking the flower into the hair behind my ear. I glance down at my feet, covered by the thin film of dust that I remember well. Some things don't change, and Maputo's dust is one. And yet, I know that I have changed.

I have been enchanted as before by the sensual Latin sounds, by the warmth of the weather, the beauty of the people. But I see now, with older eyes, the ill-dressed children selling peanuts and sweets from trays on the roadside, the chapas filled to bursting on their way out of the centre, carrying hard-working people back to the outer suburbs, the dignity of the guards standing at the entrance of each building, entrusted with the unenviable task of ensuring security – there would be many occasions for them to intervene – but supporting a large family with a meagre salary. I am aware that while I felt I knew the country enough to declare love for it, and then hate, I was not privy to its every mood and nuance. I had lived a self-contained life, far from the myriad of complexities it held. I knew nothing of the villages up north, of the malaria programmes still needed across the countryside, of the orphans left behind by AIDS or landmines. I had lived here with the self-centredness of youth, entranced by my perceptions, and then shrouded by my sadness.

When Shayla was born I was instantly besotted. A small, warm being, mine to treasure and cherish. And as she grew, as she started smiling, started sitting up, started crawling, my mind would wander. I would fly over the oceans and imagine another Shayla. A darker child with corkscrew curls, clinging to my legs in shyness, looking up at me for approval, slipping a small hand into mine. She would grow into a long-limbed and beautiful girl, with braids in her hair, and I would remember Matilda and how she sat on Jafar's lap while he repaired her tape-player that evening, years ago in his uncle's house in Chimoio. I wondered what kind of life the little girl would have had, growing up in Maputo, vulnerable to all its potentials, good and bad. These thoughts were impossible to banish, and I let them play in my head. And with them were entwined thoughts of Jafar. Always Jafar.

I trace a shape with my foot in the dust. The light is still bright but from the shadows that are growing around me I can see that I will soon need to head back to the hotel. We leave tomorrow, and I have not yet packed. Ten days was just enough to set up the links we needed to set up, but not enough for me to take a few days off to fly to Chimoio. I had warned Joanne and Rob that I may try and catch up with some old colleagues without them towards the latter end of our stay. They had been compliant and uncomplaining when I had pushed them through a gruelling schedule in order to leave me some free time. But papers were delayed, project proposals needed to be amended, and without warning we were each asked to deliver a lecture to the faculty. I had asked Manuel to look into flights to Chimoio for me, and he had said that he would assist me and even accompany me whenever I chose to go. This hasn't happened, and as I sit on the low wall I cannot help but feel deflated: my romantic idea, my flirtation with infidelity. How ridiculously hopeful, how ridiculously executed.

This morning, our first morning without appointments and engagements, the first full day completely free ahead of us, I left Rob and Joanne having breakfast, and went down to the reception. I asked the clerk, a young woman with small pearl earrings in her shell-shaped ears, braids in her hair and beautiful ochre-coloured skin, to order me a taxi.

"*Onde vai a senhora?*" was her question, as she held the phone to her ear.

I gave her Rassul's address, and she tried to hide her surprise. It was a street in a very ordinary neighbourhood, possibly not far from where she herself lived. When she had hung up, I decided to elaborate.

"To visit an old friend from when I lived here in the city."

She was intrigued but good training prevented her from asking many questions.

The taxi pulled up into the small cul-de-sac where Rassul and Linio had lived with their three children in a second-floor-flat in a yellow building. The road was shaded by trees, and as before, a group of children played with a football which they kicked to each other, and then at a target made of a pile of empty cans. When I looked up at the second floor window, I knew that they were not there. The windows no longer held the gaily coloured curtains that Rassul had made, but were bare. I waited on the street, unsure what to do as the children played around me. Finally I turned to one small boy and asked him if he could call his mother. He stared open-mouthed as I spoke, let his eyes travel up and down the black, sleeveless summer dress I am wearing today, my silver bangles and silver earrings. I could only be a foreigner and what would a foreign lady want with his mother? Slowly he walked to the door of the building opposite and buzzed the intercom. A few minutes later a youngish, pale yellow woman came out of the building, wearing a flowery housecoat, curlers in her hair.

I asked her whether she knew Rassul and Linio. She looked at me curiously but remained silent. I continued that I had known them a few years ago, and that I had been a friend of Linio's cousin, Jafar. This information must have sealed my credentials because she relaxed, and asked if I would like to come into her house for a drink. I politely declined, and then waited for her to speak.

"They left for South Africa," she said, "about three years ago. The little boy became very ill, and they needed a good doctor. Rassul's elder sister lives in Nelspruit, and arranged for them to go to the hospital there."

Rassul's youngest: a cheeky scamp unlike his two older, more moderate siblings.

"And Ruhi?"

"He was fine after the treatment, but he will need to be checked every year. So Linio decided to take a job in Johannesburg with Rassul's brother-in-law so the family could move to Nelspruit."

"Do you hear from them?"

"They come back every Christmas. Rassul's mother is still alive, living in Matola."

I nodded, and thanked the woman. As she turned to go, my voice a small echo in my head, I asked. "And have you seen Jafar?"

As she spoke, I saw her lips moving and realised that I could not hear what she was saying, the blood was pounding hard in my ears. I clenched my hand into a fist, and steeled myself.

"...and came back to say goodbye to them. That was, like I said, three years ago."

"But not again?"

She shook her head. "He went back to Chimoio after they left. I have not seen him again." Her son crept up and took her hand, stared wordlessly at me. Took her hand and thanked her again.

"*Nada, nada*," she murmured, picking up her boy and placing him on her hip. I walked down to main road and decided not to hail a taxi, but walk back to the hotel. My feet found their way to Avenida Patrice Lumumba.

*

And so. The frangipani in my hair tickles my cheek gently. I smooth my dress down and stamp my feet to rid them somewhat of the dust. He is alive, as I had already ascertained from Anne — or at least he was two years ago. And now I know that he has maintained his close relationship with Rassul. She will have undoubtedly told him everything about what she knew of my last months in Mozambique. A wasted journey and a wasted few years clinging onto an episode, a mere episode in a long life. A blink in the eye, immaterial to everyone else involved but me. Whether he knows or doesn't know, what does it actually change?

I stand up and breathe the air in deeply. I have tears somewhere inside me, but for now anger at my own foolishness suffices.

I have phoned Sebe every other day and last night he sounded tired.

"Got everything done?" he had asked.

"Are you OK?"

"Just tired. And a bit sick of having my mom around so much."

I chuckled.

"Can't wait until day after tomorrow," he said.

"Give Shayla a kiss from me."

She had come on the phone a few times, but had bored of speaking to a disjointed, delayed, tinny voice that she found hard to recognise.

"Love you," I said.

I start walking up Patrice Lumumba, keeping my thoughts blank, letting my ears distinguish between the various noises around me: the bird in the tree, the faint sound of the sea in the distance, the hooting of the chapas, voices calling to each other from windows on opposite sides of the street. Some may think that engineering a whole project in a far-flung country in order to have a conversation with someone is excessive. Today I agree with them. I will write a long letter, I decide, and leave it with Manuel. I will make sure that I say everything I need to say. I will give him my very best wishes for the rest of his life.

The concourse in front of the hotel is made of a mosaic of black and white stones which gently massage my feet through my thin sandals. I look up at the sky. It is a clear light blue: cheerful, brazen in its dismissal of my regrets. As I walk through the revolving door of the hotel, the receptionist who earlier in the day helped me find a taxi, calls out to me. "You have a visitor, *Senhora*". And turning to where she is pointing, I see rising to his feet then circling past a South African tour group waiting with their guide, their luggage a large mound in front of them, Jafar.

10

Autumn is coming to an end, and the trees on our road are now bare, spare. The colours of the leaves, the huge piles gathered for collection or for burning, still fill me with awe. I never ever get used to the changes that happen through a year; I suppose I have spent too much of my life in the tropics to take them for granted. A few weeks ago I took out our winter clothes, realised that I need to buy Shayla new boots and a coat as she is on a growth spurt at the moment. I bought Sebe a new cashmere scarf for his birthday, in golds and greens, that I think really suits him. The academic year started a month ago, and I have the first pile of assignments to mark in front of me, on my desk in my study. I have my pen in my hand but I am reluctant to start. I stare out of the window, my elbow propped on my desk, my chin in my hand.

When I arrived back in Chicago, those months ago, tired and achy after the long flight, the air, even at two in the morning, had still held the mugginess of summer. Sebe was waiting for me, bleary-eyed, unshaven. We had been delayed from Johannesburg, and while I had hoped to see Shayla at the airport if we had arrived on time, I knew that now she would be in bed, Ammachi sleeping in the guest room. As always, Sebe looked pleased to see me, his face lighting up when I came through the arrivals gate. He grabbed my bag off my shoulder and wrapped me in a long hug. "Missed you," his voice whispered in my ear. His chin was pleasantly scratchy, and I inhaled his familiar soapy smell. We stood like that for a while before moving towards the exit. In the car on the drive to the city and then beyond he told me about how his ten days had been.

Shayla had been fine the first few days but then had started giving Ammachi a hard time. She has learned the word "no" and the phrase "not yet", which while it has been in common currency with her parents, had yet to surface with her grandmother. In my absence these responses had become favourites, resulting in an exhausted and over-indulgent grandmother. Sebe suggested that we take Ammachi away for a weekend to thank her, and leaning back on my seat, watching the street-lights flashing by, I had agreed.

Sebe has been embroiled in a particularly complex tax case for the last six months, and as luck would have it, things reached a head while I was away.

"I needed to spend longer at work just to get things done, then my mom would ring, 'Is Shayla allowed a chocolate before bed. She tells me she gets one every night?'"

I laughed.

"Some ironing out to do," I said.

"Definitely."

I laid my hand on his arm, and he momentarily took one hand off the steering wheel to squeeze mine.

"Thanks," I whispered.

He nodded his head, smiled at me. He looked tired, and for the first time I noticed a few flecks of grey in his hair. "I'm proud of you," he said, "but you have a lot of making up to do."

I laughed again and squeezed his hand back.

I spent the following few months in a daze, falling back into my life with ease. There was so much to do to catch up around the house, little jobs that I had been putting off; and of course, looming over us, the report that Rob, Joanne and I had to submit on our project. They both came over a few evenings every week to spend time in my office at home, so that we could write it up together while Shayla slept upstairs. We would finish the evening off with a glass of wine around our kitchen table, reminiscing about the extraordinary ten days we had had, the sights we had seen, the sounds we had heard: the sensuous and heart-breaking country we had briefly encountered. Joanne has decided to take leave of absence for six months in order to go back and spend a little more time travelling around, and she can simultaneously check on how our partnership ideas are running. I am sure that Manuel will be thrilled.

Sebe worked long hours soon after I returned to put his case to bed. He finished three weeks later, with a successful conclusion, and we went out for dinner to celebrate, to the same seafood restaurant that he had taken me the very first time I had met with Harvey, Theo and their wives. I wore the same dress that I had worn that night, my red halter-neck, and Sebe kissed my neck when he saw me. "You look great." He touched my forearms and back, "You still have a bit of tan. It really suits you."

"Thanks." I leaned against him briefly, and then we got into the car and drove to the city. We sat next to the window and looked at the city sky-line around us.

"Well," Sebe said, clinking his glass of wine against mine, "you made it. And I made it."

We ordered and waited for the food to arrive. He reached across the table, and took my hand.

"I have to say that I was worried," he said.

"Worried?"

"You were really strange before you left."

"I was worried about leaving you two..."

"No," he shook his head, his eyes not leaving my face. "It was something else."

I didn't reply. I looked down at the gleaming cutlery in front of us, and picked up a fork. The prongs were long and straight, and I thought actually how clever an instrument it was. How creative human beings were. We had solved nearly all our niggling problems through ingenuity.

"I'm sorry," I said finally.

He was still looking at me.

"What for?" He looked, suddenly, uncertain.

I reached out with my other hand and took his other hand so that our bodies and arms made a circle.

"For being how I am."

"I love the way you are."

"Thank you," I said and lifted his right hand, and kissed his fingers. "Thank you, Sebe."

The season slipped into autumn, and I decided on a new project for our garden. With Shayla's help I have cleared a large section in the north-west corner. I have bought an assemble-yourself greenhouse and have set it up. It may be ambitious but I am going to test those peasant genes I have joked that I inherited from my father: I am going to try and grow some of the plants and herbs from my childhood: paavake which I hated as a child but for which I developed a craving for when pregnant with Shayla, fresh chillies, and curry leaves. My uncle sent some advice via the email and my mother has said she is really looking forward to seeing the results and using them when she visits us next year. Shayla has been a steady helper, patiently handing me the small plastic bags that I had to tie over each bitter-gourd bud before winter sets in, using her trowel to mix in the compost, sometimes so enthusiastically I fear she has caused havoc with the seedlings. My neighbour has started talking over the fence, asking me about the greenhouse: I think I have started a trend for our road.

Cecily and Joseph paid us a surprise visit in early autumn. They have moved back to Dallas for a couple of years, and flew to Chicago on one of their first free weekends. Holding Shayla in a tight embrace, Cecily had exclaimed at how like me she was. Pleasure surged through me at those words. But my dear friend was hiding unhappiness. She and Joseph are still trying for a baby. The two of us went for a walk after dinner, leaving the men to do the dishes.

An evening walk is a habit I still enjoy, even though most people are indoors by then, television or computers on, behind closed curtains. We wore coats and boots, and I lent Cecily a warmer hat.

"I was worried about you when you came to see me in Delhi," Cecily said, taking my arm and squeezing it. "You seemed so distracted. But I had nothing to worry about."

Our feet crunched through piles of leaves.

"And you?" I asked, squeezing her arm back.

"Well you know that Joseph and I are very well-suited. I couldn't ask for much more. Just one thing."

I nodded in understanding.

"But you can never know, can you," she continued. "Our parents want the best for us, they choose the best man for us, but they can't cure us of everything in life. You won't be able to do that for Shayla either."

And I was quiet, hoping that my little girl would in some ways be as different from her mother as I have found I am from mine. This was something I could not tell my dear old friend as we strolled along the pavements that cool autumn night.

*

The last day I spent in Mozambique is indelibly sketched in my mind. We both decided, without speaking, to go for a walk on the promenade behind the hotel, the Marginal. The sea was a glittering deep blue to our right, and as we walked we passed the wrought-iron old-fashioned street lamps that harked back to Maputo's more glamorous past, and a few vendors selling brightly-coloured cloths, reminders of its pride in being, now, a more shambolic but warmer old lady.

He was older, like I was, a little heavier, but had the same litheness, the same stride. He was wearing a long-sleeved shirt in a light-green colour over dark blue jeans. He still wore his hair short, and his face with the high cheekbones and planes was still unchanged. We walked silently for a while, and then I asked him how he had known where I was.

"You must remember that this is a small town in a city," he said and smiled. I had forgotten how that smile made me feel. He looked down at my face, his eyes crinkling at the sides, and then slowly surveyed me, taking in my whole person; my face, my limbs, my dress, my sandals.

"You look beautiful," he said, with a sweep of his hand gesturing at my hair, to my feet. "Really beautiful."

"And you," I said quietly.

He grinned his wide grin. "As always." *Como sempre.*

We walked a little more, then stood at the low wall overlooking the ocean, and I recalled standing on the other side, years ago and thousands of miles away, standing by the sea with Sebe that day in Ernakulam.

"I've never stopped thinking about you," I said and with those words I felt such an ache, and such a sadness, that tears filled my eyes.

He glanced at me and put his hand under my chin.

"But you have a husband and a baby now," he said, his voice light.

I wiped my eyes with the back of my hand. I nodded.

"And you?"

He looked back at the sea.

"I have a wife, although we will never marry. And she has two children. Two teenagers. And so now I am their father."

The sea lapped against the wall; the tide was returning.

"I'm glad," I said finally, "I'm glad that you are happy."

He shrugged his shoulders.

"When did you come back to Maputo?" I asked.

He had stayed in Chimoio for years after leaving the city. There was a new impetus to improve the town;

it was the capital of Manica province, and it was near a Zimbabwe that had a vibrant economy. And with Zimbabwe's subsequent decline, Chimoio rose. It remained a small, sleepy town, but a popular venue for provincial and regional conferences, a centre from which aid work could feed into the surrounding lands and further north. Jafar had become involved in a large project to improve the sanitation and water supply in the town, and then the region. While it was not at the same level as his work in previous years with the NGOs, it had impact and he had been employed on good conditions. It was only after that project ended, two years ago, that he had decided to return to his birthplace in the south. By then his mother had died, and he being the eldest remaining son had been in charge of arranging her effects, and organising his sisters' chaotic lives. When things had settled he had started looking for work, but to date he had not found anything long-term.

"I'm at the Ministry of Agriculture, at the moment," he continued, "but I will need to find something else in three months." He reached into the front pocket of his jeans and pulled out a cigarette packet. "I will find something."

He lit his cigarette and caught my eye. "Yes, I still smoke, but you will see, much less." He took a few drags and then carefully stubbed the cigarette out against the wall, and returned it to the packet.

"My strategy."

"It's a strategy, at least."

"*Sim.*"

A couple in dark sunglasses and matching white sports-clothes power-walked behind us, their small dog panting behind them on a leash. A trio of teenage girls, one black, two *mulattas*, swayed hand-in-hand in skin-tight jeans and high heels, laughing and flashing interested looks as they passed us.

"And your husband..." Jafar began.

I turned to him. My chance to explain. The script had been rehearsed, what I would say had been memorised. But we had started at a different place from how I had always imagined: the cues had altered and I could no longer recall the phrases I had chosen.

"It's true you saw his photo," I said, "But will you believe that I did not know him and that I hadn't decided to marry him when you found it?"

As I said the words, I also thought what use was this conversation? We had hurt each other years ago and survived. We had found our happinesses with other people and we had created new lives, new identities in separate worlds.

He shrugged again as if he knew what I was thinking. Perhaps he was also thinking that we had always been doomed, that our narrative was too daring and had always been under threat. I remembered the play that we had seen, and how the audience had been in stitches. Laughing at the actors. Laughing at us. I thought about the mission that had brought me here, to this side of the Indian Ocean, and I felt despondent. I realised that I had never spoken to anyone about the tiny lost life, never talked of our little tragedy. As such, it had not existed in the world of words, only in my thoughts. Only as a cloud in my heart.

"I know what happened," he said, still looking at the sea.

I think we stood there, not talking, for many minutes, perhaps even an hour. Eventually, he turned his head, then his body to me, put a hand against my face, and with his thumb wiped my tears away. I cried without making any sound, the tears flowing easily, and I imagined them dribbling off my chin, splashing onto the low wall, into the sea. He took my hand, led me to one of the black-iron benches that were dotted so picturesquely on the promenade and we sat side-by-side. By now the air had cooled and the few people who remained on the Marginal were walking up and down, taking in the extraordinary blue of the ocean.

He was quiet, and when I glanced at him I saw that his hands were tucked into his armpits, his legs stretched out in front of him. We looked together at the waves and heard the seagulls. A large white boat in the distance was making its way north, to Mombasa, perhaps, and then beyond.

"Can I touch you?" he asked.

And closing my eyes, I nodded. He ran his hand up and down my arms, then down the length of my thigh to my knees and up again. He traced the outline of my face, my cheekbones, by cheek, my chin. His hand dropped to my neck, and he stroked my collar-bones, fleetingly the tips of my breasts. He wiped the tear from my cheek, and then put his fingers on my lips. We sat like that for a long time. I'm not sure what passers-by must have thought, but with my eyes closed I was unaware of anyone watching. At one point he kissed me on the lips, I remember, and I opened my mouth to him. He had his hand on the back of my neck in a half-clasp and we listened to the swell of the waves.

*

Outside my window it is starting to snow. Shayla's tomato plants didn't do very well this year, but she didn't want to throw them away. The snow dusts their withered stalks with a white powder, covers the blemishes and decay. Her sand-pit has been covered up and dragged into the garage for the winter. My bushes have lost their leaves, and the grass on the lawn is fast-disappearing under the soft white flakes. The wisteria over our front door is a spray of tough brown twigs. Ahead of us we have weeks of cold, white snow.

Sebe comes into the study and puts his hands on my shoulders. With the gathering dark outside, I see our reflection in the window become sharper and clearer. My hand rests lightly on my belly, feels the soft flutters from within.

"What are you thinking?" he asks.

I don't speak, but later I will. The leaves will return, as will the warmth. Rain will fall and spring will come.

Acknowledgements

I owe Alan Paton much gratitude for inspiring and moving me immensely as an adolescent, with his novel, *Cry, The Beloved Country*, the title of which I have half-borrowed for mine.

My deepest thanks must go to Kerry Glencorse for reading more than a few drafts of my novel and helping me find my voice.

My daughters, my two precious cubs: for their love, encouragement and their heart-warming, and at times misplaced, confidence in my abilities.

And James: for everything he is to me, for always thinking the best of me.

Lightning Source UK Ltd.
Milton Keynes UK
UKOW04f0018100415

249375UK00002B/11/P

9 781781 483619